THE DARCY DILEMMA

A WITTY ROMANTIC COMEDY

Hazel Hatman

THE DARCY DILEMMA

ISBN: 978-1-7392875-1-1

Editorial Assessment: Eleanor Leese

Copyeditor: Claire Strombeck

Cover design: Fully Booked Design

First edition

To Ma and Pa

Who have always supported me

Contents

Lord of All I Survey

When the sun shines, the cuckoos call, and the green wheat shimmers in the fields, it is easy to believe England is God's own country.

Perched between the pillars of the square, copper-roofed cupola which tops the Italianate Hall, is the diminutive figure of the Honourable Eleanor Mortimer. Contemplating the vista of bountiful fields alternating with flourishing woodlands, Eleanor feels this particular corner of the shires is certainly blessed. She sighs and lets peace sink into her soul as the sun seeps into her skin, for she knows this is but a brief period of respite before the tidal wave hits.

The eldest daughter of Peregrine Mortimer, twenty-third Baron of Larkford, Eleanor is heir apparent to the Larkford Estate. Up here, she can feel her connection to every part of it – each rundown building, each gnarled trunk, each blade of grass. If she reaches out with her hand, it seems as though she might touch the lead roof of the old folly, marooned on its island and left to rot, yet she knows it is a mile distant. Here, there is no expectation as to how she should walk or talk or behave; there is only the land, the same earth trodden by countless Mortimers before her. It is theirs to do with as they will – albeit within the constraints of planning controls, environmental laws, and the depressingly omnipotent banks.

But Eleanor is not here to gloat over her precarious empire; she is here to keep watch. Earlier in the year, she had been working quietly at her desk in the Estate offices when a call was put through.

"Frankie Wordsworth," a cultured voice had introduced themselves, "Locations R Us. Silly name and so embarrassing to have to announce it to the world, but we are what we are."

Eleanor waited. Despite strict instructions to her assistant, some sales calls always seeped through. If this was another company selling digital media services or home styling, she would give short but polite shrift and disconnect the call.

"We are under contract to a UK-based production company, and we are very interested in visiting Larkford to discuss the possibility of using it as a film location."

That was unexpected. Eleanor's first instinct had been to issue a refusal, but Frankie had used the short pause as she'd collected her thoughts to sneak in a ball-park figure for daily hire.

Eleanor had swallowed her words. "And how long might the hire run?"

"A two-week set-up period, probably four weeks of filming – but that would have to be confirmed when they finalise the production schedule – and a few days to close down. We could be done and dusted before the peak season summer holiday."

A quick mental calculation and the positions had pivoted: Eleanor, no longer reticent; Frankie retreating.

"You understand that we cannot commit to anything until we have made a site visit to check suitability. And I must warn you, there are other locations being considered."

"Obviously," Eleanor had said, maintaining an air of professional detachment even as she'd allocated the money to projects long-postponed but badly needed.

A date was set, and Frankie visited one miserable January day, with Eleanor as her guide. Contrary to her expectation, Frankie had no interest in the grand Italianate façade of the north wing on which the nineteenth Baron of Larkford had lavished so much money and attention. Instead concentrating on the older, smaller south wing which overlooked the gardens and the lake, Frankie paced and photographed and exclaimed.

"Oh!" the location manager said. "Look how each of those panes reflects the myriad facets of sunlight."

“It’s the original handblown glass,” Eleanor explained, pleased with the evident appreciation of her home.

“You can’t fake it. Float glass just doesn’t have the same richness of character.” Frankie sighed. “And you’ve got a ha-ha! Those clever Georgians. Such a simple idea, using a ditch to keep the livestock out of the flowerbeds.”

“Well, a fence would have spoilt the view.” Eleanor’s tone was a little smug.

Frankie’s eyes lifted across the garden to the water and the gothic woods beyond. “And what a view! What lovers spurned and troths plighted against this backdrop, eh?”

Together they explored the Estate, from staircase to stable, meadow to graveyard. As they stood on the bridge, built shortly after the English Civil War, admiring the sparkle of the sun on the lake, a question occurred to Eleanor.

“How did you even know Larkford existed?” she asked.

“Serena.” The answer was given swiftly, a confidential whisper in her ear and a hand laid on Eleanor’s arm. And Eleanor understood at once. Serena was Eleanor’s cousin and best friend, and had been single-handedly responsible for all the colour in Eleanor’s teenage life. As the eldest child, Eleanor had always been inclined to responsibility and dutiful obedience. As an only child, Serena was anything but.

A short prompt from Eleanor was all it took to uncover the story. Frankie and Serena had been lovers but both working in the same industry as location managers had proved impossible to meld with a relationship, each of them away on site for most of the year. Both had chosen work over love, but they still retained an affection for each other and met up whenever their London stays happened to coincide. At the last rendezvous, Frankie, pulling hair out over finding Regency locations that had never appeared in film before, had spilled the problem to Serena. Eleanor found it typical of her cousin that, without so much as a courtesy call or a request for consent, Serena had disclosed full contact details for the Mortimer family. But that was Serena’s life motto: better to ask forgiveness than permission.

It was only after the fees were agreed and the contracts were signed, together with a draconian non-disclosure agreement, that Eleanor discovered the production was a new eight-part remake of the eternally popular *Pride and Prejudice*. Eleanor doubts the historical accuracy of using a house newly refurbished in 1790 as a backdrop for the penurious Bennet family – surely an old-fashioned Tudor or Jacobean park would have been more appropriate – but she is wise enough to hold her tongue. She is a clever girl and the opportunities to exploit the fictional Longbourn in the Estate's wedding business are not lost on her. After the series is released, what girl would not want to marry her very own Darcy here?

Eleanor shifts her position for her leg is starting to fall asleep. The irony of Larkford standing in for Longbourn is not lost on her. The parallels in a story of a family in constrained financial circumstances, with five girls unmarried, to her own situation is too close for comfort. Although the Mortimer girls are in no danger of eviction should they be afflicted with the untimely demise of their father, parts of the Estate having long ago been put into a trust to avoid annihilation by death duties, they are in rather more danger of it falling down around their ears.

For five centuries, Larkford has passed from father to son, but the current Lord Larkford has no son. When Eleanor inherits, the Estate will come into her control, but the title will pass elsewhere, solely because Eleanor is a woman. Somewhat pre-occupied with the pressing issues of gender pay-gaps, domestic violence, and sexual assaults, the trivialities of the hereditary peerage has failed to ignite the passions of crusading feminists. So, it remains an injustice that goes unrectified, generation after generation. When British law was changed to ensure a firstborn princess would have the same right to the Crown as a firstborn prince, Eleanor had hoped that the wider issue would soon be resolved but a similar act of Parliament that would have extended the same rights across the nobility was rejected by the House of Lords. A defeat, she can't help but think, brought about by an alliance of aristocratic mothers heaving querulous bosoms at the thought of disinheriting their lacklustre sons and crusty noblemen who would rather see a title become extinct than it pass to a woman.

Eleanor is lucky. She will, at least, inherit the land. Although the title and the Estate have by tradition passed together to the eldest son, they are not constrained by contract. While she firmly believes nowhere should a girl be born less than her brother, the reality is, she has little time to dwell on this inequality. In days gone by, her great-grandmother might have lounged on the lawn in the sunshine, drinking gin cocktails served by a liveried footman, while she contemplated a game of tennis before changing for dinner, but Eleanor's existence is rather less languid.

The Mortimers are asset rich but cash poor, although poverty in this instance is a relative term. Eleanor and her sisters were all privately educated, can safely navigate the black slopes at Courchevel, and are proficient in at least one musical instrument a piece. Baroness Larkford has been assiduous in the pursuit of her daughters' acquisitions of accomplishments. Although not one of them can cook, clean, or iron, they can all tell a Vermeer from a Rembrandt, a Meursault from a Montrachet, and know the correct mode of address for the younger son of a viscount.

Although Eleanor has occasionally found this knowledge useful in the past, mercifully for the Estate, her days are spent somewhat more industriously. Eleanor's shoulders are slight, but upon them rests the prosperity of the hundreds of people who derive a living from the estate, not least her own family. Together with her father, Eleanor acts as part curator of historic assets, part farmer, part residential and commercial landlord, and overall, as chief executive officer of Larkford's conglomerate of enterprises. This is a weighty endeavour because, as fast as the Mortimers rake the money in, it flows out again.

It is no accident that Eleanor is sitting in the northwest corner of the cupola. From this position, the deleterious state of the roof on the east wing is to her rear. The roof has now reached critical condition; if it is not repaired soon, damage to the structure will become unavoidable, and that would be even more costly. Each year, for the last few years, maintenance of the Hall and its park has drained over a million pounds from the Estate coffers, and the roof is a massive undertaking. Eleanor trembles every time she considers it. The house that once afforded such a carefree existence to its inhabitants is now a burden. Sitting as she is, above rooflines, above the tree line, her view unimpeded for miles, Eleanor whispers the resonant words, which always come so easily to her, "*Instead of a cross, around my neck, they hung the albatross.*"

Eleanor has been engaged in watching the progress of a little red car, dipping in and out of view, as it navigates through the forest which lies north of the Estate. It takes Rats Hill Corner at a speed even locals, who have driven these roads all their lives, would deem hazardous and then is lost to sight again in another band of woodland. Her eyes drop. Trees, fields, trucks – the circus of lorries and trailers, parked up opposite the old red-brick stables, looks like the fair has come to town.

The roof, the roof, the roof. Or rather the need for money to fix it is responsible for the plethora of wardrobe trucks, production vehicles, and luxury motorhomes stationed outside her office. The redundant stables were long ago converted into commercial space, most of which is rented out to local businesses. Occupying one corner of the U-shaped block, Eleanor and her team spend their days administering the estate businesses and inventing novel ways to turn the enormous liability of a stately home into an asset. Commercial, agricultural, and residential rents form the largest part of Estate income. While they have avoided the full-blown commercialism that has bedevilled other grand houses, they still open their gardens and grounds through the summer, run a wedding hire business, and even a woodland burial ground.

The assumption of easy money did not long survive the contract signature. Eleanor had been presented with a list of demands from the production company, all of which had to be completed at break-neck speed. That list had subsequently been succeeded by spreadsheet after spreadsheet and Eleanor found herself run ragged. She had also begun to wonder whether this was only the tip of the iceberg and whether worse was yet to come once the company had boots on the ground.

The first of the film crew arrived a fortnight ago with their cameras and other paraphernalia, closely followed by lorry loads of hoggin to cover the worn tarmac drives that criss-crossed the park. Their dollies have tracked back and forth in front of the seven-bayed south wing, artfully clipping out the north and east extensions, catching the splendour of the architecture in all sorts of light. The cameramen have ranged around the Estate at all hours, filming sunrises and sunsets, misty mornings and ethereal evenings. Some of the Estate workers have been persuaded into costume as they go about their work to form a rural backdrop of shepherd and dog herding sheep, gardener hand-trimming topiary, and ploughman homeward plodding his weary way.

Today is arrival day for most of the cast, although Mr Darcy himself will be delayed – a filming clash keeping him in murky Manchester. In what Eleanor believes is a deliberate policy, all the main roles are being taken by young, relatively unknown stars or bit-part actors from long-running series: crime, sci-fi, soaps, hospital dramas. The producers want fresh faces, fresh places for a re-telling of a story already told many times before.

Eleanor's attention is drawn to the forecourt below as the little red sportscar, top down to enjoy the summer sun, screeches to a halt. The driver was obviously travelling too fast to read the small sign directing film crew and cast to the north drive which would lead them to the old stables.

Eleanor stands as the driver looks up. She recognises his face and makes haste to descend. It has begun. It seems Mr Wickham has arrived.

Enter Mr Wickham

Sunday afternoons are quiet on the Estate with few staff around. Aware her parents are out and her twin sisters are unlikely to bestir themselves, Eleanor hurries down one of the side staircases to intercept the visitor. She makes it out onto the tarmac in minutes, although not without sustaining some damage; she is slightly sweaty and dishevelled when she greets the newcomer.

She walks towards him, smile fixed, her hand outstretched. "Hello," she says, her voice warm in welcome. "I'm Eleanor. I work for the Estate. May I help you?"

Eleanor always struggles with self-introductions. She does not own Larkford, so cannot make that claim, but to introduce oneself as heir sounds so presumptuous. If she had been a boy, she would have been entitled as a courtesy to call herself "Lord", but that last bastion of male chauvinism that is the British peerage deems the eldest daughter of a baron a commoner. She could, of course, introduce herself as the daughter of Baron Mortimer, but that would reduce her status to that of a child, and Eleanor has more regard for herself than to draw her identity only from her father. So she contents herself with the innocuous "work for" and leaves others to draw their own conclusions.

"Oh, hi!" The young man turns towards her and takes her hand in greeting. "Jamie Smythe. I'm looking for the film crew's quarters."

There are some men – Eleanor has only met a couple in her life – who are so captivating, it appears as if the Lord has granted them their very own rays of sunlight to spotlight their magnificence. They do not have to be handsome, but that isn't a problem for Jamie Smythe, for he is truly beautiful. With his tousled locks and sculpted bone structure, he is breath-taking.

She notices when his eyes flick over her, taking in the dusty jeans and baggy T-shirt, and she sees the exact second she is relegated from person of interest to person of no interest. Eleanor is no stranger to this type of reaction and she keeps her smile.

"I know who you are," she says agreeably. She has watched his progress in an alternative teen show where he started as a minor vampire and progressed to a regular. He is pleased at the recognition, one tiny compliment to feed an actor's vanity. "You've missed the turn," she continues, then looks at the low-slung sports car, considers for a second the pot-holed drive, and adds, "Unfortunately, you risk scraping your lovely car if you take the North Drive. You're better off going back the way you came."

Eleanor is now close enough to read the number plate: SX1 4NML. *Sexy animal. Oh good Lord!* She reflects wryly that the Universe has balance – Jamie might have been granted beauty and charisma, but modesty and good taste were clearly omitted.

She can see the bags piled on the passenger seat of his vehicle but she makes the offer anyway, expecting it to be refused. "I can go with you, if you like, and show you. It's easy to walk back from there."

But Jamie nods and starts stuffing his bags somewhat precariously behind the seats. When he opens the door for her to climb in, despite her best intentions, Eleanor is charmed. She directs him away from the grand drive he has entered by and takes him along the service track which heads past the woodland burial ground and back onto the highway. From there, it is less than a mile to the turn-off for the business park in the old stable and carriage house.

Mercifully, Jamie drives at a slower pace than his arrival, probably so he doesn't miss Eleanor's directions, and beyond her clutching her seatbelt to stay upright as he swerves around the corners, the journey is uneventful.

Eleanor would expect someone accepting help might make conversation with an opening remark as to the weather or maybe an enquiry as to whether she comes here often, but Jamie does none of that. Instead, after a silence Eleanor dubs awkward but which Jamie does not seem to mind, she opens with: "Have you come a long way today?"

"Nah! Just from London."

Eleanor, who would deem a trip to London as a major outing, can find nothing to say in return, but Jamie seems prompted into dialogue.

"Bit remote here, innit? Bet there's not much night life round here."

"There's foxes and badgers."

"Is that a nightclub?"

She smiles at the town-dweller's assumption, but Eleanor is kind – while she may mock his ignorance in her own mind, aloud and rather more charitably she says, "No, they're nocturnal animals." And then – because no one likes to appear foolish – she continues, "There's usually a lock-in after quiz night in the Blue Lion and a couple of pubs in Bridgetown feature local bands on a Saturday. But the nearest nightclub is in the county town about a forty-five-minute drive away." Although, having seen the way he drives, Eleanor privately revises the estimate down to thirty nail-biting minutes.

"Who owns the big house?" Jamie asks as they turn off the road.

He slows to navigate the track which leads to the business park. While in better repair than most of the Estate's roads, it isn't without its dangers.

"The Hall?" Eleanor considers for a moment the complex web of tenures and trusts but goes with the simplest answer: "Lord and Lady Larkford. You'll get to meet them. I think they are intending to invite the main actors to dinner." When he brightens at the prospect, she realises he has rather more regard for the aristocracy than she does.

With its blocky Tudor styling, the old stable block and carriage house clings to the sides of a large courtyard, now a carpark. It is one of the few buildings on the Estate to escape the modernising efforts of Eleanor's forebears; in a Georgian version of value engineering, it was allowed to retain its old-fashioned red-brick façade when the Hall was re-modelled, despite being within view. It is from here Eleanor and her team run the Estate, and it is here that the circus has come to town.

Eleanor directs Jamie where to park his car and helps him with his bags. She has no idea which of the trailers is earmarked for him, so she leads him to the office temporarily assigned to Frankie and leaves them together to work it out. She stifles a little laugh, perversely pleased, to see him light up at the sight of Frankie's voluptuous figure and pre-Raphaelite curls. Eleanor skips off with a wicked delight that having made his lack of interest in her plain, he is about to receive his own rebuff.

She has almost made it through the pointed arch of the carriage-house, when Jamie catches up with her, his hand closing around her arm to arrest her progress.

"I'm sorry," she says. "Did you need something else?"

He shakes his head. "Nah, I wanted to thank you. I hope I've not put you out, like."

"Not at all," Eleanor demurs. "I live at the Hall." She nods towards the imposing façade less than half a mile in the distance, then bids him "Good luck!" and walks off, thinking.

Just when she believes she has him neatly pegged, he surprises her. At least there is nothing wrong with his manners.

As she reaches the tarmac apron in front of the big Hall, her father's four-wheel drive roars up the main entrance road. Whilst the estate vehicles are always bought and then kept until they have given decades of service, refunding their purchase price many times over, the family's cars are leased –the illusion of wealth for modest outlay. She waits for the big, shiny car to come to a stop because she knows what is inside; one more errant daughter is home, to further add to the family madness.

Eleanor, who has missed the acerbic wit of her sister for months, wraps Anna in her arms and whispers, "You'll never guess who I just met?"

"The President of the United States? The Dalai Lama? Who else could get you so excited?"

"Jamie Smythe!" And Eleanor regrets her proximity to her sister as Anna emits a squeal with ear-piercing high notes, in mockery of a fan girl.

"I am overcome." Anna flaps her hand as if cooling her overheated face. "And?"

"And nothing." Eleanor steps back and gives a small shrug. Then she drops her bombshell. "He gave me a ride in his car."

"And did you steam up his windows? Make out on the back seat? Come and tell me all you got up to. I suspect it is pitifully little, which is a shame – that man could give me a ride anytime. *I* wouldn't waste an opportunity of that kind." Anna pants like a desperate groupie before reverting to her usual cool, professional demeanour. She slings her arm around Eleanor, and the two of them head inside to await the approach of chaos in the form of the twins.

We Are Family

Half a millennium ago, Eleanor's wily ancestor had purchased Larkford Park from the Crown after the estimable King Henry had set out to plunder the treasure accumulated by the monastic traditions of poverty and piety. His portrait hangs above the grand fireplace in the Great Hall and Eleanor had seen it almost every day of her life growing up. Nothing records how the ancient Mortimer came by the purchase monies for these fertile fields and forests, once owned by the great abbey in Bridgetown but Eleanor has always thought he has the look of a rascal. Sometimes she wonders quite how disreputable her forebear might have been to obtain dispensation to purchase the Park. What service did he provide the venal King Henry? Did he sell his daughter's virtue? Or was the explanation more mundane? Was he merely the acknowledged by-blow of a powerful man? Many noble families, so proud of their bloodlines, were started thus.

No matter – as soon as William Mortimer had taken ownership, he erected a tidy, little mansion, built of brick, to house his thriving family. It served the Mortimers well for the next couple of centuries until Nathaniel Mortimer, Eleanor's many-greats grandfather, disgusted with his forebear's modest taste and, rich from judicious investments in sugar plantations worked by enslaved people, had substantially enlarged the house adding the east wing and hiding the dated brick walls, cladding them in white stone. He at least had enough familial pride to leave William's portrait in place but when he plopped a dome over the old building's courtyard, and added a magnificent staircase, he made sure it was dominated by a gigantic depiction of himself, like a general on horseback although he was careful to avoid battlefields like the plague.

By the time Queen Victoria died, the industrious Mortimers had constructed the grandiose north wing, an entire fifteen bays and three storeys, complete with must-have cupola and a large portico, enabling their noble guests to dismount from their carriages in the dry, built with impeccable timing just before the arrival of the motorcar.

This was the heyday of the family, and the original five-hundred-acre park enlarged by shrewd acquisitions of land locally left them controlling several tens of thousands of acres, together with a house in London's fashionable Chelsea for when one wearied of country life.

But the twentieth century was less kind to their fortunes. In a corner in the library is Eleanor's favourite painting – it is also probably the most valuable in the collection as it was painted by a notable artist of the day, but it is also the only treasure the family will never sell. It depicts Lord Larkord's grandfather as a child, together with his older brothers a few years before the outbreak of the First World War. The family was nearly wiped out as, one by one, the pride of Mortimer blood was blown apart by German artillery. Percival, tall and strong with an unruly mop of dark hair and a captivating grin that could charm the knickers off any under-housemaid, died at the Somme. Thomas, the younger brother, captain of the first eleven cricket team and a talented sportsman, was killed within two weeks of his brother. The family reeled. When the news came a year later that Edward had been blasted out of the sky over Verdun, Lady Larkford took to her bed for a month. The lineage was hanging by a thread, with Peregrine Mortimer thirteen years old at the start of the war. When the Armistice was signed two days before his eighteenth birthday, his parents breathed a quiet sigh of relief.

Over another hundred years passed to bring us to the present. The boundaries of the original park itself remain intact, and a patchwork of fields and buildings are still under the family's control, but the vast acreage of the past is gone. While their fortunes have declined, the Mortimers have not been without good luck and the Second World War left them largely unscathed. With the advent of improved healthcare, the Mortimers have proved to be long-lived, giving them ample time to plan for the impact of death duties – the financial beartrap which led to the grisly fate of demolition for a thousand other stately houses. Eleanor and her father cling on. Larkford is still theirs – both a blessing and a curse.

Peregrine Mortimer, the current baron, in an understandable reaction to his own dour upbringing, had married an effervescent beauty, whose ability to convert even the humdrum to fun he had found irresistible. It remains her chief attraction today, now that age has lined the smooth skin of her face and weight has reduced the sharpness of her cheekbones. It is her good fortune. For many of her friends, once-radiant beauties but lacking a Pillar of Fire and thus forced to endure the attrition of time, have found themselves divorced, replaced by younger look-a-likes. "Character lasts, beauty doesn't," as Eleanor's Aunt Mary is fond of saying. "If his greatest compliment is how pretty you are, make certain there is a marriage and no prenup." It is a truth Aunt Mary herself discovered through unfortunate experience.

For all that, Lady Larkford is still a fine woman, aided by a careful application of expensive cosmetics each morning, a cultured voice, and graceful manners. Although, after four full-term pregnancies, it would take a miracle or an obsession for any woman to retain the shapely figure of their youth, and Sarah Mortimer is flighty by nature. The kindest description of her now would be matronly, but Lady Larkford has always understood the importance of clothes in disguising one's shortcomings. Dresses in fine fabrics that fit well take years off a woman. Early on in her marriage, lacking the budget for haute couture, she had identified a decent dressmaker in the local town and has had her outfits made for her at the fraction of the cost of a named designer.

Lady Sarah Cavendish was twenty-two when she had met her future husband at Ascot. Those were the last of the days where you didn't have to pretend you worked, and you could merely exist, frittering your days away in idleness and pleasure. The youngest daughter of an earl, Lady Sarah had a traditional outlook on life: she wanted to marry an aristocrat; she did not want to work beyond instructing staff in their daily, mostly unvarying duties; and she wanted to produce a male heir.

Two out of three wasn't bad. Each pregnancy raised new hopes and each time they were disappointed. After three girls, she and her husband had discussed whether to risk a fourth attempt. They'd rolled the dice and fate had answered with twin girls. Lord Larkford had drawn the line. No more. Even though she knows the sex of a child is determined by the sperm donated by the father, Sarah feels that in this, the most important duty of a Lady, she has failed – a fact that is often stressed by her mother-in-law.

But it is not in Lady Larkford's nature to dwell on misfortunes, and she moves through her assigned life with a cheerful optimism that, somehow, all will work out because, in her personal experience, it always has.

After an abundance of aperitifs, she has been known to confide her hopes in her sister-in-law, Mary. "Eleanor is still young; Kate was a Middleton at her age."

Mary wisely forebears to mention the long-term romance that preceded Kate Middleton's nuptials and makes a vague noise of encouragement.

"A Duke would be perfect, but there aren't many of them under sixty," Lady Larkford moans.

"Nor unmarried," Mary reminds her.

"Pish! Divorces are so common nowadays. It's just a shame she is not prettier. Still, she is clever."

Eleanor, whose attention had flittered away from her book as soon as her mind had registered her name being spoken, feels she should remind her relatives of her presence.

"I am here, you know?"

Her mother ignores her. "Perhaps a politician would do – one destined for the highest office, of course."

"Same problems there," Mary commiserates. "And do any of them have money?"

"One or two of them must, surely." Lady Larkford takes another sip of her sherry as she considers. "They do tend to drone on, though. Imagine having to eat your crème brûlée with someone waffling on about Environmental Land Management."

"What's that?"

"No idea. Something I heard Peregrine mention yesterday. I wasn't really listening. But you are exactly right, Mary. They could be sixty and boring, but if they had money ..." Eleanor's mother shrugs almost spilling her re-filled glass.

"An entitled, rich politician then, Sarah?" her sister-in-law summarises, her head to one side.

"Never," says Eleanor.

"The thought makes me quite giddy," says Lady Larkford, lost in a dream of a grand cathedral wedding, attended by the great and the good – perhaps even a President.

Sarah's matrimonial fantasies are doomed. Eleanor has always known her life will be dedicated to the preservation of her family's heritage, and the protection of those who live and work in it. She long ago accepted the responsibility and reckons she has been adequately compensated by the understanding her life has purpose, something that she has watched her friends struggle to find. Affluence can produce meaningless lives wasted in drink and drugs. And she knows that in the mammoth undertaking that awaits her, navigating her little corner of England through the choppy waters of the future, she will need the support of a partner with whom she has the deepest understanding, the strongest of connections, and the greatest respect. Eleanor will not marry for rank or money. Eleanor will marry for love.

When Eleanor looks in a mirror, she has yet to identify her mother's contribution. Logically, those twenty-four thousand genes must be there, but to all intents and purposes, Eleanor is her father's clone. She thinks like him, and she looks like him – she has none of the delicate beauty of her mother's youth. Eleanor herself is aware of this – how can she not be? The mirror shows nothing remarkable, certainly nothing to rival the charms of some of her younger sisters, and she is not incorrect in her assessment. Her face is plain without a single striking feature; neither is it thus marred. Her eyes are too far apart and her cheekbones more solid than sculpted. But Anna has often told Eleanor that what Eleanor sees is her features at rest; it is the animation of Eleanor's face, Anna says, that gives it its charm, the genuineness of her smile, the sparkle in her eyes when she contemplates mischief. And apart from lazy Sunday afternoons, Eleanor dresses well. She has followed her mother's lead in having her working wardrobe made, not bought, and while she will never be a fashion influencer, she also manages to avoid most trend traps. Despite Eleanor's own opinion of her ordinariness, even she would admit she has had enough admirers to gratify any woman's vanity.

Still, Eleanor knows her tally of admirers is far outweighed by her younger sister's. Her mother's genes might have got lost in her, but they are evident in Anna, the second child. She has been blessed with her mother's beauty, combined with her father's sharp mind. She watched the burden of expectation her sister shouldered and is sincerely grateful she was not born two years earlier. Indeed, she lives with the nagging concern something might happen to Eleanor and she'll become the next sacrifice – an event which could only result in a disagreement of such magnitude, it would end in a rift in the family that would never be repaired. Anna gloried in her independence throughout her teenage years and departed for medical school in London with no backwards glance of longing for Larkford, returning only for high days and holidays, and sometimes not even then – shift work providing the perfect excuse to evade her mother's plans for family celebrations.

Anna lives in the Chelsea house; it was converted to five flats in the eighties and now, with the London property market, has proved a star performer in the estate's rental portfolio. Newly renovated, the best flats in the block bring in ten thousand a month. The family retains the attic flat for their own personal use. Un-refurbished, it is inclined to overheat in summer and is chilly in winter, but Anna doesn't complain. She keeps a low and distant profile in case her mother turns her attentions towards London.

Occasionally, when she is particularly jaded, Anna misses the camaraderie of her clan, and at these rare times she makes a flying visit to the family bosom. A day, two at the most, is enough, and Anna can return to the long hours and stress of life as a junior doctor, appreciation of her chosen profession restored. Most of her colleagues have no concept of her background; many of them are solidly middle-class, often the offspring of medics themselves, a few pioneers in social mobility from their working-class roots. They provide an adequate hunting ground for lovers, but she avoids anything serious because that would entail taking them home to Mummy.

Anna's intention is to become an anaesthetist. She jokes, "I prefer my patients asleep or dead, and I don't have the stomach for pathology." While Anna isn't cruel, she does tend to be careless of other people's feelings which can have the same effect. Those lucky enough to be cherished by her are blessed with a charming, witty, loyal friend for life, because while Anna does not make friends often, neither does she throw them away.

Whenever her schedule allows a Wednesday evening off, she sees her younger sister, Jasmine. If Anna had to rank her sisters in order of favourites, Eleanor would undoubtedly be at the top and Jasmine would undoubtedly be at the bottom, but she knows Jasmine's list would put her at the top. Out of love, that curious affection that springs from shared experiences in your formative years, Anna makes time to keep track of Jasmine, to curb some of her more excessive impulses and maintain a bridge between her and the rest of the family, for Jasmine despises them all.

A political activist and card-carrying member of the Labour Party, Jasmine abhors her feckless younger sisters but applauds the humanitarianism of Anna's vocation. They meet for dinner, usually in a vegan restaurant close to Anna's hospital, where Jasmine holds forth earnestly on the latest global issue to attract her notice. She could live in the Chelsea flat with Anna, but to Anna's relief, Jasmine prefers to share a house with like-minded radicals. If Jasmine could ever bring all her fierceness to bear on just one issue, Anna is sure she could change the world. She does not sell her sister short, for all that Jasmine failed to follow Eleanor to Oxford – a fact that has rankled Jasmine for years – she is as clever as her older sisters.

The same cannot be said of the twins. They both have their mother's beauty and their mother's brains – lots of the first and little of the last. Phoebe and Lily will need to marry well because neither of them is capable of earning an income adequate for her spending habits. Fortunately for them, there are enough rich men in the world stupid enough to value attractiveness over ability. They are young, yet, both nominally attending university, revelling in being irresponsible and dedicating every minute of time to having fun.

For them, term ended days ago, but no one expected them to abandon the joys of the London scene for some weeks; they were wrong. A whisper of a hint that a swarm of film stars had descended on Larkford found the twins on the first train home. Eleanor is waiting to see if they spontaneously combust when they discover one of the stars is the exquisite Jamie Smythe.

For all that she tries to maintain an air of calm detachment, Eleanor is excited. The film studio is hosting an on-site pre-filming party. Many of the cast will be present, most of the producers, technicians and support staff and invitations have been specifically extended to the noble family. There is an air of anticipation threading through the ancient Hall, reminiscent of bygone balls filled with long-forgotten beaux.

As of old, Eleanor thinks as she heads to her room to get ready, a concentration of new young blood cannot surely be gathered in one place with no consequences?

The Party on the Parterre

Larkford Park consists of five hundred rolling acres of fields and woods bisected by a river running south-east to north-west. Some three centuries ago, the river was dammed to form a long lake, a broad head at the top by the dam and a long tail tapering into the original river, shaped much like a tadpole. The grand Hall backs onto the tail, the formal gardens, the topiary walk, and the parterre running down to the water from the tall French doors.

To one side of the gardens, close to the edge of the tennis court, a large marquee has been erected at sufficient distance to be outside of camera shot. The tent will provide the canteen throughout the filming, but for tonight it is the bar.

Eleanor is feeling pretty. Anna came to her room and spent some time carefully twisting her hair into a low, classic chignon and she has also applied cosmetics with more than usual care. It has been nearly a year since Eleanor attended any type of celebration where she was not personally responsible for its success, and she is determined to indulge some high spirits. Well, as much as allowed by a single glass of white wine spritzer …

Eleanor and Anna descend the stairs to the party together, arm-in-arm and giggling like affected schoolgirls. The twins, still arguing over which one will wear the strappy sandals both consider essential, will follow on later, although it appears one of them will have to go barefoot because neither of them has anything else that will do.

The evening sun is still strong with hours to go before it sets, so neither Eleanor nor Anna misses the elegant figure of Jamie Smythe lounging on the low garden wall. Indeed, it would have required great effort to avoid him, situated as he is in the direct path from the great porched entrance door to the catering pavilion. He stands at their approach, a smile further enhancing his handsome features, his toned torso leaning forwards in happy anticipation.

"Well, hello again," he greets them, his Essex accent decidedly less marked than earlier, and although his words are addressed to Eleanor, his attention is all on Anna. "We meet once more."

There is nothing like growing up plain in a household of beauties to keep you humble, and what has made Jasmine bitter has made Eleanor modest. She notes Jamie's lack of use of her name, the way his eyes fix on her sister, and she makes the introduction without rancour, although a small obstinate part of her refuses to help him out with recalling who she is.

"Anna, Jamie Smythe," Eleanor gestures between the two of them. "Jamie will be playing Mr Wickham."

Jamie steps forwards and, taking Anna's hand, raises it to his lips. In his posh film voice, he says, "Charmed, I'm sure."

His salutation produces two very different reactions in the two very different sisters. One shudders at the corniness and the other giggles – ironically the reverse of their usual responses.

Anna bats her eyelashes. "So tell me, Jamie, are you so very wicked as your character?"

"I try never to disappoint a beautiful woman's expectations, whether they want me to be very, very good, or very, very wicked."

The suggestive comment is also received with great appreciation by one of the sisters, and it isn't Eleanor. With the same good manners he displayed earlier, Jamie offers to fetch them each a drink and disappears into the bar tent.

Anna turns to Eleanor with a gasp. "Oh my God! He's even better looking in real life than he is on film! How is that even possible?"

She goes on to rhapsodise about how he fills out his designer jeans and the clear line of his pectorals under his tight black T-shirt, and Eleanor indulges her sister for a few minutes. Anna's admiration of his physique is cut short by the arrival of the man under discussion, three drinks held in his large, capable hands. Eleanor retrieves hers and makes her excuses. She has no wish to play gooseberry, and it is clear both of her companions are intent on each other, although who is in greater danger is open to speculation.

Eleanor wanders off but, spotting a young man fiddling with his phone and looking rather dejected, she settles herself on the bench beside him. The cottage garden beds stretch out on either side and the air is full of the scent of stocks and pinks, sweet alyssum and honeysuckle.

Shying away from an overly curious bee, she opens with, "Hi, I'm Eleanor. Are you one of the crew?"

"No." His reply is morose. "I'm Tom, I'm one of the cast. I'm playing Bingley." He retreats back into himself the moment his words are done and checks his phone again.

"I hope you don't mind my asking," Eleanor perseveres, "but are you all right?"

A half-hour later and Eleanor would have taken back the question if she could. It is like pricking a balloon full of water.

"Sorry, no!" His eyes redden and he sniffs. "My girlfriend's just found out she's pregnant and she's not best pleased I'm here. She won't answer my calls or texts. I'm scared she's going to break up with me, but what can I do? I'm under contract; I can't leave here. She doesn't understand how tight filming schedules are."

Eleanor is caught by her own kindness and by Tom's evident distress. As the sun sinks towards the horizon, more people roam between the flowerbeds, the sounds of their merriment a counterpoint to the misery before her. She intersperses murmurs of sympathy with words of advice, but she well knows in moments like these that no one welcomes sense. Her job is to listen, to reassure, but after a considerable passage of time, never has she found the bluff tones of her father's voice quite so welcome.

"There you are, Eleanor. You'll never guess!" Her father is chuckling. "I've just stumbled over your sister in the arms of a very pretty boy indeed. I didn't know whether I should fetch my shotgun or give the lad a medal for courage!" Lord Larkford glances down at the wretched lad beside her and says, "And whom do we have here?"

Tom, faced with the robust male presence of Eleanor's father, pulls himself together enough to offer his hand and his name. He is an actor, after all. If he can't manage the semblance of self-possession, he's in the wrong career.

"I'm Tom. I'm playing Bingley."

Eleanor finds the need for two appellations curious; name and role. She's noticed it seems to be common tonight: Sam, first assistant camera; Amelia, Lydia. She wonders what hers would be. Eleanor, daughter of the Baron? Or Eleanor, general dogsbody? Her father, master conversationalist that he is, has engaged Tom in a discussion of his previous roles. Five minutes with Lord Larkford and Tom has cheered up more than the hour she wasted.

She takes the opportunity to escape. A quick kiss to her daddy's cheek, a nod to Tom, and the excuse she needs to refill her glass, and she is away. Turning from the bar with a glass full of fizzy elderflower, a soft drink that has the singular advantage of looking remarkably like sparkling wine, Eleanor hears her name called and is inordinately pleased to see Frankie waving from a table in the corner.

Frankie's denotation of Eleanor is "Eleanor, Serena's cousin", and that seems sufficient for everyone at the table. Three women are sitting with Frankie: Chloe, make-up; Claire, Charlotte Lucas; and, older than the others, Mia, standby art director. Three empty wine bottles attest to their presence since the bar opened and Eleanor is quickly drawn into their current obsession – the one missing star, Mr Darcy.

"Ptolemy Hyde's a right grumpy sod," Claire announces, for while the cast have already met for read-throughs and dancing lessons, they remain strangers to the crew.

Chloe is rather more sympathetic. "People say that all the time about the lead actors. I think it is only that they are more demanding and, let's face it, quite a few of the junior cast are workshy, talentless hacks … Present company excluded, of course."

"She's right. He *is* a right grumpy sod," Eleanor says, and four pairs of eyes swivel in her direction. "He was in my college at Oxford," she offers by way of explanation, "but he's also an excellent actor."

Chloe nods at her to continue.

"He's in that crime drama set in Manchester. Do you know the one I mean – all rain-swept vistas and disused Victorian factories? He plays that shifty detective from Moss Side who you're never quite sure whether he is bent or not?" Eleanor takes a sip of her drink, enjoying the rapt audience. "But Tolly's as posh as they come. He's a trust fund boy, doesn't have to work a day in his life if he wants. It's all acting. He's very good."

A fire of interest appears to have been kindled in the women. Her scant knowledge of Ptolemy is turned inside out, but her own interest in him – the subject he studied, the friends they have in common, their family connections – is inadequate to answer the women's queries. While she can reassure them of his preference for women, she has no idea as to his current relationship status, his favourite colour, or ideal meal. Nor does she have any clue as to his star sign.

One of the bar staff comes to collect glasses and the women lean back. Eleanor recognises the barmaid as one of their housemaids, not long employed, and, giving her a friendly smile, Eleanor says, "Oh hi, Annabelle. Have you been here all the time?"

Annabelle flinches and her face falls into a fearful frown, as if she's been caught red-handed. Eleanor has no objection to the Estate's employees generating extra income so long as it doesn't impact on their main jobs. Why should her family be the only ones to benefit from the windfall of the filming? But she guesses Annabelle is unaware of this.

The young maid mutters something which sounds like, "Yes, Miss Mortimer", under her breath and escapes back to the bar, fully laden with glasses, while Eleanor's companions return to their examination of the cast.

"Anyone seen Jamie Smythe yet?" Chloe asks and Eleanor nods.

"Beautiful but knows it."

"Tom Davey?"

"Taken."

"Is there anyone you haven't met?" Chloe demands and Eleanor has to laugh.

"Loads. You've picked the only three I've spoken to."

"They're the only three who matter. It's not like anyone's going to go gaga for John Twelvetree now, is it?" says Chloe, naming the actor playing the elderly Mr Bennet. "Although, come to think of it, he might do for Mia here!" She giggles at her own wit and nudges her friend.

But Mia isn't laughing. "That's not funny. Do you know how many times I've been hit on by guys who are twenty years older than me? What makes them think I want to be changing their incontinence pads? And why does society think it's okay for these men to be dating their daughters' age group while vilifying women who like younger men?"

Frankie moves to distract with a change of subject: "What about Lizzy and Jane?"

"Both straight," Chloe replies with a challenge, "and anyway, what about Serena?"

"Serena and I are complicated, but I wasn't asking because I was *interested*; I was asking because I was interested in what they're like. Are we going to have drama off-screen as well as on?"

Eleanor is grateful someone else has raised the issue of Serena because, while she quite likes Frankie and has to work with her, Eleanor loves her cousin. She has no wish, though, to alienate Frankie this early into filming.

"They're both married," volunteers Mia, "but what does that matter? You all know what it's like. When you're working long hours with someone, and they are there and you are lonely … And every touch, every breath starts to assume significance. You're on location and the world is someplace else. Before you know it, you're either divorced or visiting the STI clinic, or both." Chloe puts her hand on Mia's and gives it a squeeze.

The discussion moves on to other people and other films, and Eleanor makes little contribution, but she stays with them. The women are entertaining, their wit flowing as freely as the wine. An hour before midnight, sense prevails and Eleanor makes her excuses to retire.

The paths are lit by solar lights, but Eleanor ignores them and takes the most direct route home. Cutting across the grass proves to be a bad idea when her feet tangle with a pair of long legs and she lands directly on top of the muscular form of a prone man.

An explosion of profanities is cut short by Eleanor's cleanly enunciated apologies, and she realises in short order that she has tripped over Jamie Smythe. Despite the man's initial diatribe, he gets to his feet quickly and appears to be eager to accompany Eleanor the short walk to her door.

"You weren't quite straight with me this afternoon," he says in a playful tone, which holds only the slightest indication of how much he has drunk. "Should I be calling you my Lady?"

"No," Eleanor sighs. "That's my mother. I'm just plain old Miss. Like any normal person."

"But you *are* the Baron's daughter? The eldest, yes?"

"Yes," she says.

"And you do run the Estate?"

"Yes." Eleanor is grateful to reach the safety of her front door. "Well, this is me. Good night. Your trailers are that way." She helpfully points north, where a string of lights illuminates the track towards the campground.

For one awful moment, Eleanor fears Jamie is going to lean in for a kiss, but at the last he shrugs and turns back towards the party.

Eleanor climbs the grand staircase to her room, the portraits of her ancestors frowning down on her from age-darkened canvas. While the evening has been enjoyable, she cannot shift the feeling the stage is being set for Act I Scene I.

The sense of portent stays with her even as she enters the familiar environs of her own bedroom. Her harp sits in its corner, seldom played these days. The furniture is all old – heavy, unfashionable, dark hardwoods. But Eleanor loves it, the thought that her fingers trail over the same chiffonier as countless Mortimer girls before her, that feeling of connection between past and present captured in the carved wood.

Despite the warm, balmy evening, Eleanor crosses the room to close the window, shutting out the noise of the party which seems set to continue into the early hours. She pulls the thick damask curtains across before she kicks off her shoes and starts to prepare for bed. She has just dropped a nightdress over her head when there is a tap on her door and Anna walks in without waiting for an invitation.

She clambers onto Eleanor's bed and lies back as if exhausted.

Eleanor's curiosity is aroused. "I didn't expect to see you tonight. Last I heard, you were getting down and dirty with cutie-pie. Although, you might have mislaid him because I tripped over him on my way home."

"Discarded, rather than mislaid."

"Oh?" Eleanor prompts. "Aren't you going to see him again?"

She joins her sister on the big, wooden bed and links their fingers.

"No." Anna sighs. "It really is a mystery as to how the good Lord created so much beauty and so few brains in one body. I tried really, really hard to ignore it. But when I asked if he liked Jane Austen and he said he'd never met her, I sort of lost the vibe."

"He asked me if I was the Baron's daughter."

"Yeah, sorry about that. I didn't realise you were incognito." Anna is quiet for a moment, then continues. "He seems a little fascinated by our father. Took a selfie with him. Imagine if Daddy starts trending on social media?"

Both girls smile at the ceiling, then Eleanor says, her voice softer now, "Do you think we'll ever find anyone as good as Daddy? I love it here, I really do, but I have to admit, sometimes I get lonely."

"Don't let Mummy hear you. To paraphrase the immortal Jane, our mother feels the approach of your years of danger and would rejoice to be certain of you being properly solicited by baronet-blood within the next twelvemonth or two! Give her the word and she'll have a shrewdness of suitors here before you've finished your sentence. And there won't be a chin among them."

"You joke, but it's easy for you."

And Anna stays quiet because she knows the truth of it. While she hasn't chosen the easiest path through life, she feels it much preferable to Eleanor's.

"It's not like I can sign up on a dating app."

Anna laughs. "I can see your bio: *Eleanor, twenty-seven. Lives with Mummy and Daddy. Works for the family firm and likes old stuff. Looking for someone who loves big, draughty houses. Catfishers need not apply.*"

"Yes. Just every conman north of the Thames!"

"Or worse – some guy who's not averse to cutting your finger off and sending it to Daddy in a padded envelope."

"Thanks for that," says Eleanor, wrinkling her nose. "That's exactly what I want to be thinking of as I drift off to sleep tonight."

"There are always those apps for the elite?"

Eleanor snorts. "Rich people who only want to date rich people? No, thanks!"

"Yeah. Probably all a bunch of entitled arseholes. It's not like we don't know any of those already." Anna turns on her side to nudge her sister.

"Well, if I get desperate, at least I know I've got Mummy and her friends as a last resort. But, Anna, the truth is I do want someone. I never thought I would still be single. But there are so few eligible men around here."

"Perhaps you are being too choosy? After all, what is a chin among friends?"

With a laugh, Eleanor replies, "I don't believe I am. To continue with the sayings of the mighty Jane, all I want is '*a man of sense and education who has lived in the world*'."

"I hear Ptolemy Hyde is playing the erstwhile Mr Darcy. He would fit the bill creditably." Eleanor scoffs at Anna's sly remark.

In the years since Oxford, Eleanor has spent the majority of her time at home, learning the business of running the estate. When she does get away for the odd party in London or weekend with friends, she has barely registered Ptolemy's brooding absence. From time to time, there is the shimmer of illusory contact; she was almost certain she had heard his refined bass voice on commercials for high-end luxury products, including one make of car. And while neither she nor Ptolemy are active posters on social media – something she has always thought a mistake for a person in his profession – the rumour mill being as it is, she has generally been kept apprised of his affairs.

She knows when he records roles for games and graphic novels, and she heard within minutes when he landed a part in that edgy new crime series set in the darkest depths of Manchester. Eleanor finds it amusingly ironic: the epitome of the English upper-classes, the cricket-playing, morally upright, polished Ptolemy, has made his name playing an evil Mancunian cop. On the other hand, if anyone were born for the role of Mr Darcy, Eleanor is convinced it was him. Ptolemy will have no need to act: the arrogance, the conceit, and the disdain for others are the embodiment of his character. Ptolemy will have an easy time of it; he will, after all, be playing himself.

Still, there had been a time when Eleanor had thought that Ptolemy *would* fit the bill creditably and the excuse that she does not see Ptolemy as a potential partner is unlikely to convince Anna.

Embarrassed to divulge all her previous history with him to her sister, she goes with the easier, "I'm not pretty enough for Tolly."

Anna, who lacks the talent for insincere reassurances, merely says, "Perhaps." Then she squeezes their conjoined hands. "Come and see me in London. I'll do my best."

"When are you leaving?"

"Tomorrow morning. I'm starting a week of nights."

"Then you probably won't be up by the time I've left for work." Eleanor gives her sister a hug. "I'll miss you."

Eleanor slides under the thin summer quilt and Anna, with one last wink of suggestive naughtiness, slips off the bed and goes in search of entertainment.

Real Life

When Eleanor was fourteen years old, she had a seizure – a full-blown, falling on the ground, twitching seizure. She and Anna were on the West Drive down by the lake, on their way to buy sweets from the post office in the next village, with nothing more distressing on their minds than the choice between strawberry laces or marshmallow fluffs. Then Eleanor stopped. She looked vague for some seconds, and while Anna was calling her to get going, she dropped.

Anna had no idea what was happening, but she knew they needed help. Mobile reception at that time being patchy on the Estate, she made the brave decision to leave her sister in order to fetch it. The nearest house was the Winters'; they lived in one of the two West Lodge gatehouses, which stood either side of the drive. Anna ran faster than any sports day race, and the sprint took her less than a minute. Mrs Winter, who had just sat down to rest her eyes, was startled into wakefulness by Anna banging on her door. She responded to Anna's urgency with her own. A Teaching Assistant at a Bridgetown primary, Mrs Winter could recognise a tonic-clonic seizure when she saw one, and sent Anna back to her house to phone for an ambulance.

Two futures were decided that day. Anna became fascinated by the human body and its frailties, and Eleanor discovered loving parents and ample fortune cannot prevent disability. Follow-up investigations revealed Eleanor's well-known moments of absence were not just daydreams; they were more significant. For the first time the word "epilepsy" was used.

In retrospect, Eleanor realises her parents had been almost cavalier about her safety growing up. That she had survived to adulthood had been by good fortune rather than intent. As an adult now, she permits herself none of the risks her parents had blithely allowed. She is grateful for her juvenile freedom – a childhood full of activity rather than restriction, boating on the lake, scampering up trees, and cycling around the neighbouring villages.

For many years Eleanor's medication has been effective, especially when combined with a self-care package which prioritises sleep and reduced stress. Her parents feared university might destroy her delicately balanced health, but Eleanor had no wish to become a freak to her friends by having a fit in front of them, and she was careful to manage her days. In reality for Eleanor, Oxford University was all fun and little stress. She knew this would be the last time in her life when she would be free to do whatever she wanted, to study whatever she loved. She was also aware that it mattered not a whit to her future whether she came out with a first, a pass, or a fail – her path in life, post-graduation, was already laid out before her.

Eleanor went to Oxford to enjoy herself, and that is what she did, within bounds. With her medication, she was abstemious in her attitude to alcohol. She learnt early how to make a white wine spritzer last all night, and avoided partying when she had commitments the following day. In the end, she spent three whole years at Oxford without a single fellow student guessing she was a person who lived with epilepsy.

When Eleanor returned home from university, keen to demonstrate she was deserving of her position in the Estate's management, she had put together a project that had the potential to vastly improve the Mortimer income.

Among the parcels of land her family still control is one hundred acres of very poor agricultural land, the soils too sandy to support cultivation. One of the reasons they still own it is because it was never of sufficient value to warrant its sale. It does, however, lie close to a main road which eventually runs into the motorway to London. For the last five years, Eleanor has been building a consortium of local landowners and they are attempting to establish an entire new village, with over a thousand houses, a school, a health centre, parks and an industrial estate bringing much-needed jobs.

None of the land is fertile, there are no serious environmental concerns, and the local council is desperately short of its housing allocation. With a strong local-homes-are-badly-needed-but-not-in-my-back-yard population, the council, finely balanced between two political parties, has found it impossible to agree on which towns and villages should be desecrated by mass construction.

Eleanor's proposed site has no major existing settlements to blight. There is one small hamlet, but they can be screened from the new development by a convenient strip of woodland, and no matter how loud they shout, the impact of a few dozen homeowners will always be limited. With all these points in favour, her proposal should be a done deal. Sadly, not. Eleanor has nursed her project along, but the amount of work it has taken is increasing. The addition of the requirements from the production company is enough to destroy Eleanor's equilibrium.

She has yet to find a balance – to care deeply but to be able to walk away at the end of the day; to acknowledge the pressure but to remain positive. About two weeks ago, on the very day the film crew were due to arrive, she had had her first seizure in six years.

Now, she must be more careful. Keeping herself safe needs to climb her priority list and increased caution is mandatory. Eleanor knows her escapes to the cupola are a risk, but even that is calculated. It is surrounded by a three-foot-high stone balustrade, and Eleanor is careful to stay away from the edge. The chances of her falling off the roof, while not zero, are not high. During the summer, the possibility she may die of exposure if she slips into unconsciousness are remote. The cupola's ability to calm her troubled mind is beneficial, and so she permits herself this rare indulgence.

Eleanor was previously seizure free and is confident she will be again. The rest is to be endured. The biggest inconvenience, as those who live in the countryside with sporadic public transport will understand, is the suspension of her permission to drive until twelve months has passed without a seizure. Local taxi companies, prioritising the regular income of school runs and lucrative airport pick-ups, are often unable to help.

Lord Larkford saw a coincidence of events and grasped an opportunity. When Eleanor first heard her father's proposal that he employ Jacob Winter as a driver until her suspension ended, she was not pleased. She ranted and protested and expostulated fulsomely.

She made the economic case, "The Estate can't afford it."

Lord Larkford looked over his newspaper and calmly remarked, "I think you will find the investment would be offset by an increase in productivity. A driver frees one up to work on a journey."

Slightly nettled at the thought her efficiency might be in question, Eleanor responded, "But the expense is unnecessary. The twins are home – neither of them are working and both can drive. And Mummy can help out occasionally."

But Lady Larkford was not at all on her side. "I think a driver is a wonderful idea. He could pick up your father when he goes drinking with his golf buddies instead of dragging me out at all hours. And, to be honest, it *is* getting rather difficult to keep ferrying you around. Your Aunt Mary was quite put out last week when I cancelled on her at short notice to help you."

Eleanor changed tack. "But Jacob?" she said, blushing slightly. "I mean, is he fit to work?"

"Robert tells me the boy is mending well. A little light duty will be fine."

"He was badly injured, Daddy," Eleanor ventured. "Can he even drive a car?"

"He can manage a standard automatic perfectly well."

Noting the irritation in her father's voice, Eleanor had let the matter drop.

When she heard nothing further, she thought maybe she had carried the day. But the next time she asked her family if anyone could give her a lift to the council offices for a meeting at nine the next day, her father had put down his book, looked over his glasses and said, "Jacob will be here at eight tomorrow."

When Eleanor leaves the house in the morning, a couple of days after the party, she knows she has lost another bit of her privacy. Eleanor has grown up with housekeepers all her life and is well-aware you can have few secrets from the person who changes your bedsheets and empties your bins. But a driver is another level of interference – he will know where she goes, whom she is with, and what she is doing. She knows it is necessary, but that does not mean it is welcome. She cannot help but resent the intrusion and the loss of her independence, for all it is not the driver's fault.

As she walks out of the front door, Jacob is waiting for her at the bottom of the steps, standing with legs apart and arms clasped behind his back. He is freshly shaved and pristine, wearing a chauffeur's cap, a charcoal suit, and a tie in the Mortimer colours of azure striped with gold, a tiny coat of arms embroidered at the tip. It is a uniform worn by all the Estate staff who don't wear logoed polo shirts.

She walks up to him, her resentment with her father and her own fallibility, expressed in a childish desire to aggravate.

"Lose the cap," she commands, "we're not Royalty."

She does not wait for him to obey; she raises her hand, lifts the peaked hat from his head and presses it to his chest.

Jacob, cap tucked under his arm, merely steps forwards and opens the rear door for her. Eleanor walks around the vehicle, opens her own door, and clambers into the front passenger seat.

He settles beside her, and with an insolent grin says, "Good morning, Miss Mortimer."

"Good morning, Jacob. You may call me Eleanor," she replies with her best attempt at civility.

If there is one thing about this arrangement which is going to irritate her more than it already does, it is if Jacob treats her like an ancient spinster.

"My friends call me Jake."

"We're due at the council offices in Norton at ten, Jacob."

"Aye-aye, Nora," he answers impertinently.

And Eleanor can't help it – she starts to smile. Then, before Jacob gets the wrong idea and thinks she is mollified, she opens her laptop case, extracts a report, and starts to read.

Eleanor's pet project is stalled. A crucial issue has been identified in the access to the main road. It currently opens on to one carriageway of the highway only and will require major work to bring it up to the standard required. Despite the enormous funds which will be brought in from the community infrastructure levy – a tax on each square metre of accommodation – the council are arguing about the solution. The access must be improved but the council are resisting a simple roundabout and are instead insisting on a hideously expensive major junction with multiple roundabouts and slip roads.

Today is a key day. Eleanor, together with representatives from the two other large landowners, the consortium's highways consultants, and the intransigent local authority highways engineer, are due to convene for a difficult meeting. Eleanor has been preparing for this for weeks, and the landowners have agreed a unified front. It will be to no avail.

When she climbs back into the car following the meeting, scarcely noticing Jacob holding the door open for her, Eleanor is desolate. The meeting, full of what one could only call robust argument, has left her drained, and her headache is dangerously close to a migraine. She feels sick and she looks it. She recognises the need to de-stress before it escalates to a seizure.

The first thing Eleanor does is call her father. She tells him of the participants and the problems; she describes in excruciating detail the minutiae of the meeting, and when she is finished, she collapses back into her seat and closes her eyes. Lord Larkford has been wise enough to listen, venturing little opinion and much encouragement. Jacob drives in silence until, as the country around them becomes more familiar, Eleanor rouses herself enough to say, "Let's stop at the Jolly Farmer for lunch. I can't face going straight back into the office yet."

Without quibble, Jacob pulls up at the pub, still some miles away from the office. It's not one either of them frequents, and that is just as well, as Eleanor is not in the mood for small talk with locals. It's a lovely day, so they sit outside. Jacob takes his cue from Eleanor, and they order a burger and a fizzy drink apiece.

"Why did you take this job, Jacob?" Eleanor asks as they wait for their food. "You'll be at my beck and call at all hours of the day."

"I believe your father phrased it more kindly." Jacob catches her eye and looks directly at her, an unforgivable level of impertinence if he were truly at her beck and call. "He made it sound like I would be helping you at a time in your life when you could do with a little support. I remember when you were a little kid, Nora. I was fond of you then."

Until he'd left for secondary school, it had been Jacob's job to escort Eleanor and Anna home from the local village primary every afternoon, the pick-up being too much for their mother to cope with – having to manage the younger three with only the help of a housekeeper, a handful of housemaids, and a nanny.

"Ah yes, my silvery-tongued father. Well, we both know you aren't here just as my driver, are you? You're my babysitter, so that much at least hasn't changed."

"If you don't want me as your babysitter, I hear Jonas Brown was keen for the job."

When you live in the country and most of your neighbours are your tenants, you know a deal more about their lives than most would wish. Jonas Brown lives at 1 Forge End Cottages, a terrace built in the time of Queen Victoria by Eleanor's ancestor and still owned by the estate. Jonas has a reputation for drinking too much on a Saturday night and picking fights, especially when his football team loses. It doesn't happen regularly, for the landlord at the Blue Lion, well aware of the village gossip, makes sure to limit Jonas's intake but he can't control what Jonas drinks at home. Eleanor and her father have discussed terminating his tenancy but that would leave his wife and children homeless. So, as long as his wife chooses to remain with him and Jonas pays his rent, he stays put.

Eleanor, feeling less combative now she has lost this round, says in a milder tone, "I heard you left the Army." It is as close as Eleanor dares go. "You could have gone anywhere – why come back to Larkford?"

"It's a good place to heal." Jacob's answer is more honest than she finds comfortable, and she looks away, reluctant to meet his eyes.

Food arrives, giving both an opportunity for silence and a chance to reflect. When they finish, Eleanor pays and they return to the car with no further exchanges other than those required by courtesy.

The peace holds until they are pulling up to the Estate Offices. As Jacob guides the car into Eleanor's reserved parking place, he says, "I've been thinking …"

"Is that a rarity?"

"About your access road problem. The junction before is the intersection with the B-road and that's already a roundabout. That road swings southwest. It can't pass far from the bottom end of your site. What if you brought traffic in there? You may have to re-design your layout, but it's worth investigating, isn't it?"

Eleanor considers the solution Jacob is describing while she gathers up her things and exits the car. He is right – it's not without its drawbacks but it is feasible. And may be valuable, if only as a bargaining chip.

Her tone softens for the first time that day when she says, "That's not a bad idea at all. You should think more often."

Then she closes the car door and heads towards the office to deal with the latest crop of emergencies. She also makes a mental note to pull Jacob's personnel folder and review it thoroughly. If he is to know the particulars of her life, she will know the detail of his.

At the Sign of the Blue Lion

While the noble family at the Hall has experienced hard times, modern economic reality has not been avoided by the village either. The village school, housed for generations in a Victorian villa, windows set high so wayward pupils would not be distracted by the whimsies of nature, closed its doors in the last decade. Infants and juniors are now bussed to the large primary in Great Barrow, although the family's influence is still manifest in its seat on the board of governors. The redundant building, where once rote-learning chants echoed, has been re-purposed as a community centre and now resounds to the rhythms of yoga classes, rumbustious Scout meetings, and the rather less well-tempered parish council planning meetings.

For three hundred years, the village pub had brewed its own ale, the brewhouse tacked on to the rear of the common room, belching its vapours to the skies. But for the last fifty years, it has succumbed to the economies of scale and the Blue Lion now buys its beer from the big brewery based in Bridgetown. The landlord, who succeeded his father and his grandfather before that, mourns the death of the old ales and regularly threatens to revive the tradition. Under his steady stewardship, the inn does a vigorous trade. The food is good enough to satisfy the undemanding, the portions sizes ample, the prices reasonable. Wednesday night is quiz night, drawing in most of the village regulars and the occasional team from Bridgetown. After the winning team is declared, most stay to while away the evening hours over another pint or two. As one might expect, given many derive their living directly or indirectly from the Estate, pontification on the noble family's affairs is not uncommon.

While it has been more than half a century since anyone has felt the need to tug their forelock in the Lord's presence, he is still regarded with respect by most. His solid management of the Estate and generally beneficent attitude towards his tenants are widely appreciated, especially when contrasted with the horror stories of brash new landlords, whose money has been made in the cut-throat world of commerce and who are wholly focussed on profit. The Baron and his daughter remitted rents during the pandemic for those in the direst of need, but this act of charity brought them as much condemnation as praise from the drinkers in the local pub. Chief among the detractors is one Jonas Brown, not at all happy he had to work and continue to pay his rent while his neighbour sat out in the sunshine, rent-free.

Lord Larkford, though, has many supporters, not least of which is Jacob's father, Robert Winter, who has worked for the Estate since he left school at sixteen. For the last decade, he has headed up the team of gardeners and groundsmen who attempt to keep the five-hundred-acre park in some order, despite the chaotic essence of Nature.

On this sunny evening, the quiz yet to start, the residents of Larkford have turned their attention to the spectacle that has appropriated the park. Although the production company has taken the precaution of applying for the temporary closures of the public footpaths and bridleways which criss-cross the grounds, more than one local has found time for a rare constitutional which just happens to pass by the cameras and stars. Robert, a gossip of no little talent, is leading the discussion over which of the film stars might be good enough for the ladies currently residing at the Hall – especially for his favourite, Eleanor. Through some torturous grapevine, he has gained knowledge that Ptolemy Hyde, the actor scheduled to play Mr Darcy, was at Oxford University at the same time as Eleanor. The fact Ptolemy was but one of twelve thousand undergraduates has passed him by. Robert is offering good odds on a match between the two, but Jamie Smythe is also a contender, his appearance at the pub the previous night markedly enhancing his status.

With a filming schedule that is both tight and tiring, few of the cast and crew have made their way to the Blue Lion. Jamie, though, had come in search of convivial company, and that he had been generous with buying rounds was sufficient to ensure he is described as a very good lad by the patrons of the local pub. The reverend, the aptly named Aaron Parrish, who had stopped in for a pie and a pudding, and is staying for the quiz (being university-educated he is generally regarded as an asset), finds his opinion being solicited. He chortles good-naturedly and says instead, with a nod to the buxom barmaid, "I think it more likely Jamie marries our Kylie here, given the attention he was paying her last night." His comment provokes a ribald laugh; no one had missed Jamie's fascination with Kylie's breasts – it was lucky that for once the barmaid's hulking husband had been absent.

Although it might surprise Eleanor to find herself the subject of such a debate, she would understand their interest. Putting aside the natural inclination to gossip and nosiness as to a neighbour's doings, the villagers have a genuine concern over the succession. Tenants and employees alike worry she will choose someone flighty or profligate, as if a sensible woman in this day and age cannot run her own business separate to the influence of her husband. Still, while there is general agreement that Eleanor has inherited her father's sense of responsibility and a large dose of his shrewd acumen, her marriage remains the subject of some speculation.

The punters at the pub would be heartened if they knew Eleanor herself has no intention of choosing an unreliable spendthrift for a partner. And in one respect they are correct: Eleanor has had her fill of lovers. Her father and mother met at twenty and she had always expected she would meet her life partner at university but that turned out badly. She has never taken pleasure in playing the field; she is looking for a husband. And it seems more than one eye is turned towards the cast of players assembled for her choice.

Further speculation on the subject is ended by a sight never previously recorded in the history of the Blue Lion – the advent of four beautiful women and Eleanor entering the establishment *en masse*. The Mortimer girls had been so strung out in age by the time the youngest had found their way into underage drinking, the eldest two had moved on. The landlord knew better than to provoke the ire of the Lord's daughters by refusing to serve them, but he also knew better than to provoke the Lord's temper by sending his girls home drunk and incapable. A happy equilibrium was achieved: the girls could drink until they had achieved a pleasantly tipsy sensation; the landlord could continue to ply his trade; and Lord Larkford knew the wildest excesses of his errant offspring would be safely curbed.

Nowadays, Eleanor tends to avoid the Blue Lion, reasoning her tenants and employees would much rather she not oversee their inebriated misadventures. Her father does his drinking at the golf club, but Eleanor just avoids drink – alcohol being a common trigger for epilepsy. She may stop in for a Ploughman's at lunch from time to time, purely to support the innkeeper's business, but otherwise she leaves the villagers in peace.

But it is not the sight of Eleanor that brings a hush to the assembly; it is the spectacle of her companions, immaculately coiffed, daringly dressed, and impeccably made-up. The loudest team, a bevy of young farmers, becomes the quietest, seemingly mesmerised as the quartet sways through the pub towards an empty table.

Eleanor, who has hospitably offered to buy the first round and pay the quiz dues, turns to carry her tray of drinks to her new friends. She greets those she recognises, and as she passes the vicar, she offers a friendly smile and nod. The Reverend Parrish is about to answer, but his attention is called away by his neighbour and he merely waves vaguely in her direction. Eleanor does not recognise the vicar's companion, but the quiz brings in many participants from the surrounding villages and even some from Bridgetown. There is also a cohort of retirees who supplement their meagre pensions with paltry pub quiz jackpots from around the county, all while enjoying a pleasant evening in a country pub.

While Chloe, Claire, Mia, and Frankie flick through the answer sheet, divvying up the categories between themselves and predicting victory in the Film and TV round, Eleanor finds her eyes drawn once more towards the vicar and his friend, only to find the stranger looking at her. Caught, he offers a slight quirk of his lips in apology but continues to watch her, and she is puzzled.

He cannot be a sensible man, for who would look at her, surrounded as she is by birds of much prettier plumage? His motives must be suspect, but whether mercenary or madness, she is undecided. She studies him back. He is handsome enough, more man than boy. He is clean, and despite his height – he sits taller than his holy friend and the vicar is no small man – his clothes fit well, although nothing about him screams affluence. He is tanned, which suggests he is often outdoors, but when she passed by him, she did not notice the hand holding his pint being a labourer's hand. In short, he is not exceptional, except his unwavering gaze speaks of brazen confidence, a quality Eleanor has always found remarkably attractive.

Her friends, meanwhile, have been arguing about their quiz team title.

"'Lady Eleanor and the Dancing Dead'?" Mia's suggestion is met with blank looks all around. "Like in the song?"

"I think your age is showing," sniffs Claire. "I've never heard of it."

"It's not my age; it's my knowledge. I wasn't even born when it was in the charts."

"I think laying claim to a title to which I have no right might be misconstrued." Eleanor's mild words are designed to head off a squabble before it can become entrenched.

"I know! What about 'The Vice Girls'? We've already got our Posh and Scary!" cries Chloe, pointing to Eleanor and Mia in turn.

"'Vice Girls'? That makes us sound like a parcel of prostitutes!" Mia says with a look of distaste. "No, thanks."

"No! But what about 'A Pride of Prejudices'?" Frankie's eyes are alight with mischief. "We've got an ageist, a blondist, a snob, and I'll happily put my hand up to misandrist. I think it's particularly apt!" Even though Frankie has carefully not ascribed roles to any in the group, Eleanor is sure the designation of snob has been laid at her feet, but she has no better suggestion. It is certainly better than being Lady Eleanor or a Vice Girl, and it is a witty play on the words that have brought them all together.

A comment from Frankie brings her mind back to her companions shortly before a hush descends and the quiz begins with the picture round. It is a while before the break between rounds allows Eleanor to drift back to her contemplation of the stranger, and then she finds him moving through the crowd towards the Gents, which is enough only to ascertain his walk is neither shamble nor strut.

"Who is he?" Frankie's words are a whisper in her ear.

"I don't know," Eleanor shrugs. "No one."

She puts the man from her mind and concentrates on her new friends as the quiz resumes. When the halfway point comes, Eleanor is prevented from discovering more about the vicar's companion as their table is besieged by eager lads generously offering to purchase drinks for pretty women who likely earn twice their wage. It's fortunate the break is not over-long, or Chloe and Claire would be too drunk to continue, let alone walk back.

Eleanor and her friends come in second, the top spot going to a team of retired teachers from Bridgetown. It's a diplomatic position: high enough to maintain honour, low enough to avoid ruffling local feathers. As soon as the results are announced, Mia, who has been trying to avoid the overly persistent attentions of a divorced builder with a sweat-marked shirt straining over his beer belly and only one tooth missing, is quick to remind them of her early start in the morning. While Mia is keen to depart, Chloe and Claire seem more reluctant to leave hearts unconquered, and Eleanor surprises even herself with her own unwillingness as she trails out after her companions.

The group slip out, leaving behind a host of disappointed young men, including one handsome fellow who reckons his quiet holiday with his pious friend from college just got far more interesting.

Breakfast at Larkford

Had Eleanor's opinion of conjugal felicity been drawn solely from her own family, she could be forgiven for the belief that marriage is a state of mutual affection. Fortunately, Eleanor had friends enough whose families were the very model of dysfunction, to present her with a more realistic view. Although Eleanor herself has struggled to comprehend how her cultured, intelligent father could love her feckless, frivolous mother, she is forced to admit the truth of it from the evidence of her own eyes. Their fondness for each other has survived the temptations of fit, willing tennis coaches, and simpering, wide-eyed nannies. And if further testament was required, over the years, the impropriety of their behaviour together has troubled Eleanor on more than one occasion.

As Eleanor enters the breakfast room this morning, she considers leaving it immediately, hunger unsated, for her mother is sitting in her father's lap, giggling and wriggling. At Eleanor's hefty sigh, her mother does slip off his knee and take her own seat at the table, and her father resumes his perusal of his pink newspaper. Eleanor is surprised to find her mother at breakfast before her. Lady Larkford is not an early riser by nature. Eleanor and her father usually eat together in contented silence before heading off for work, the rest of the family still slumbering soundly.

The explanation is not long in coming. "I hear Ptolemy is due to arrive this morning," Lady Larkford muses. "His mother and I were very close at one time. Of course, that was when she was still Tissy Latham. We were at finishing school together, in Switzerland."

Eleanor is well aware of this history. Seared on her teenage brain was the humiliation of her mother's shrill cry across the crowded hall of the Parents' Afternoon Tea at Christchurch College as she spotted her old crony. An interval of two decades with no contact had not lessened the effusive delight with which they greeted each other and the entire gathering bore witness. Newly arrived at university, and not yet confident of her friendship circle, Eleanor had pleaded with God to give her a more reserved, or at least quieter, mother, but on this occasion, God declined.

The turn of her mother's mind is not long in becoming evident. "It will be so nice for you to have a friend here. Perhaps we could have him stay here in the Hall with us, not in those awful caravans?"

Eleanor, who has seen inside the luxury motorhomes, is quick to respond. "I think he would much rather stay with his colleagues. It might make it difficult for him if he is singled out for special treatment."

"But think of it," Lady Larkford continues blithely, "the two of you, thrown together. Who knows what will happen? I'm sure I could think of far worse for my daughter's mother-in-law than Tissy Latham."

It has become absolutely imperative to stop her mother now. Eleanor might balk at admitting his humiliation of her to Anna, but nothing but the full truth will stop her mother. "I don't think there is any danger of that, Mummy. Tolly thinks I'm boring."

Ptolemy had, indeed, once called her boring, his words during a drinking game of Date, Love, Hate gleefully later relayed to her by a friend of his. Eleanor had at first smarted under the insult, but there were so many interesting people and events at Oxford, she had soon learned to ignore it. She had thought the interest was mutual; that he too had felt that deep attraction and ease of company. But his words said otherwise, and so she'd forced thoughts of Ptolemy from her mind. In the end, it had affected her behaviour in no way other than an inclination to avoid Ptolemy for the next three years – no mean feat given they were at the same college and moved in the same social circles.

Eleanor's words appear to have been effective. Possibly her mother shares Ptolemy's sentiments, because after the vaguest of expostulations, she turns her attentions back to crumbling her croissant. Eleanor is left to reflect the insults that wound the most are those that hold a grain of truth.

Eleanor is no longer the insecure girl she was when she first went to Oxford, and she is old enough now to realise that the words and actions of a callow teenager do not define the person they grow to be. She finds that, despite her mother's matchmaking, she is looking forward to seeing Ptolemy again. The years Eleanor spent in Oxford were some of the happiest of her life. Sometimes these juvenile bonds, created from shared experiences at a formative age, can deepen and thicken when two fellow alumni are cast together among strangers in the big wide world.

Eleanor's thoughts, in essence, reflect her mother's, but differ in extent. For Eleanor only wishes for Ptolemy's friendship, not his heart. Strong, clever men, brimming with self-confidence, used to be her kryptonite – but no longer, for experience has been a harsh master.

Eleanor has known love, a great draining sort of love, that left her a shadow of herself. A love that nibbled at her soul until it was so full of holes, it was in danger of breaking. At the start of Hilary term in her final year at Oxford, Eleanor had met Sebastien in a coffee shop. He was there with the girl who had lived next door to Eleanor in her first year. The two of them were reading English, Sebastien with the intention of becoming a great writer. Eleanor had stopped at first to greet her old neighbour but had then joined them, and when the friend had left to go to her tutorial, Eleanor had stayed, enthralled by a pair of dark eyes and a strong jawline.

When Sebastien had asked her to stay the night, Eleanor had felt like she had been offered the philosopher's stone. There followed six months where her life was entwined with his, time apart only for their essays and tutorials and lectures. There were occasional evenings out with the girls and his jaunts with the boys. But every night they'd come together in fervent desire, for

Sebastien was a fierce and passionate lover, and Eleanor's heart had been lost, convinced she had found eternal love. She had long accepted her ordinariness, cemented by comments such as Ptolemy's, but Sebastien's unshakeable belief in his own destiny and therefore by extension, her destiny, had given her a confidence she had never known. She admired his ability to dismiss criticism from tutors that would leave her crushed, she was fascinated by the emotional intensity he brought to his work, and she loved the way he revered her. Together, she felt, they would battle the world.

That last summer of freedom before they each had to surrender themselves to earning a living, a group from her college had proposed roaming across France, down through Spain, and then on to Morocco in search of the exotic. Travelling mostly by bus or train, staying in cheap hotels, air-conditioning traded for creaking fans, generating the slightest of breaths in the stifling heat like an old man's sigh, they were determined to gather experiences that would sustain them at dinner parties for years to come. In the end, there were three couples: Phil and Lorna, Sebastien's friends, who had been dating since the first year, Eleanor's friend Charlie Fairfax, and his current fling Trudi (Charlie's girlfriends never lasted long), and Eleanor and Sebastien.

Ten weeks stretched before them. Ten weeks to meander, stopping whenever they were interested. But Sebastien in and out of the colleges at Oxford was not Sebastien confined for hours at a time on a coach or train. While his fellow travellers slept and Eleanor read books on her phone, Sebastien brooded. He was impatient to get places, and easily bored once there. Eleanor began to realise he thought it was her responsibility to amuse him. Each journey, she had to ensure she had activities for Sebastien as well as for herself.

It was not just the journeys where their different characters began to show, but the destinations as well. While Eleanor watched, with tears in her own eyes, an American family huddle around the grave of their father – now also grandfather and great-grandfather – at the D-Day cemetery, Sebastien sat on the grass and threw stones. Climbing the steep lanes of Mont St Michel, Eleanor could picture the awe of the pilgrims and postulants as they neared the abbey, but Sebastien saw only the crowds of tourists and the cheap souvenirs.

As they moved through France, Eleanor found their destinations omitting the fairy-tale chateaux, grand fortresses, and pre-historic cave art she loved in favour of Sebastien's choice of zip-wires and water parks and bars. Sometimes Eleanor wondered why they had left the UK. Not adventurous by nature, Eleanor did not demur, for by now every sigh of resignation prompted an argument out of all proportion to the offence, every frown of a barrage of insults.

The first presaging incident occurred at the Gorges du Verdon in Provence. Phil and Lorna had elected to spend the day at a café, sipping coffee and enjoying the view. The remaining four wanted to travel the breath-taking circular route around the rim of the gorge. Sebastien proposed they cycle it, and Charlie that they hire a car. Eleanor contemplated cycling ninety kilometres in the intense July heat up steep inclines, and sided with Charlie. A car ride also left time to kayak into the gorge. Sebastien sulked the entire journey, refusing to get out of the car at viewpoints. Eleanor realised even Charlie's good nature was strained and she saw his relief when it came to hiring the two-person kayaks. When Eleanor glanced back, wondering why their progress was so slow, she found Sebastien sitting back and glowering, refusing to paddle.

Eleanor learnt that lesson. That he loved her, she did not doubt, but he saw her dissent as personal betrayal. The next time her sense made her doubt his wisdom, she held her tongue. And she almost died.

They had heard about wreck-diving off Cabo de Palos, and although Sebastien had become seized with enthusiasm for the adventure, his friends Phil and Lorna had balked at the cost. Never one to be thwarted, Sebastien had come back one day and announced he had found a couple of guys who were prepared to take them out for a much lower fee. When Eleanor asked why they were so cheap, he merely shrugged and said it was the difference between the tourist market and the local market. His guys spoke only Spanish but Sebastien would act as translator.

That night, Eleanor reminded him of her epilepsy but he dismissed her concerns with the words, "Don't be such a wuss.

You haven't had a seizure in years." And Eleanor thought she would shrivel up at the scorn in his voice. She was becoming used to subjugating her wishes to his, adapting her pleasures to provide for his happiness. And Sebastien had a point; her medication was effective. So, although it was a risk, it was only a small one. She balanced that risk against the immense resentment not doing the dive would invite. Still, she was concerned enough the following morning to ask Sebastien to tell the dive instructors about her epilepsy. After a short exchange, he turned to her and said, "They say it's fine."

It was Charlie who took her to one side and whispered, "Are you sure you really want to do this?" Eleanor could not find the words to lie to her friend, so she just nodded. It was Charlie who stayed by her side, and it was Charlie who brought her to the surface when the inevitable happened. It was also Charlie who shouted at Sebastien, causing him to sulk for days.

The experience underwater had been magical, but in retrospect Eleanor did not believe it was worth the price she paid. Charlie had offered to take her to the nearest airport and to fly home with her, but Eleanor was ashamed of her own stupidity and felt embarrassed enough that she had jeopardised the trip for all of them, so she had refused his offer. Eleanor was furious with herself. She knew her disability was her own responsibility to manage and she had always promised herself she would never bow to peer pressure and jeopardise her health, yet she had done exactly that.

The others in the group were subdued until one day they hit Puerto Banus. As they walked along the marina, Charlie had come to an abrupt stop. "Am I seeing things or is that yacht called *Tedaline*?"

Eleanor had looked over to a sleek motor yacht, all sharp angles of gleaming white and smoked glass with the word "Tedaline" printed on the stern in cursive letters, at odds with its modern sophistication. Charlie already had his phone out and a quick conversation later confirmed, "It's my auntie's. They're in port for the night. They pick up a group tomorrow. She says we can stay overnight."

By the time the group had walked up the gangplank, the skipper was coming to meet them. Their clothes were taken and returned laundered as they lounged on the deck in dressing gowns, drinking Champagne in the sun. Dinner of grilled langoustine and Mediterranean vegetables was served as the sun went down and all slept that night under sheets of the finest cotton.

Recharged, with grateful thanks to the staff, the group left and continued their travels, cheerfulness restored. All except Eleanor. Day after day, Sebastien's intensity began to overwhelm her. She did not question that he loved her. That *she* loved *him* enough, she now began to doubt. That this was justification of his accusations only led to a perplexing mix of emotion where guilt and love and insecurity intermingled, leaving Eleanor directionless.

As they travelled on through Morocco, their differences only multiplied. The snake charmers in the marketplace which Eleanor viewed as a pantomime, he saw as of cultural importance. The monkey perched on Sebastien's shoulder, as fodder for social media, almost made Eleanor cry with the creature's limp lifeless tail and its glassy eyes.

Finally, they reached Essaouira for a beach break before they were due to fly home. The first night they made their way to a restaurant on the beach front for dinner. The slight breeze rolling off the calm sea and the moonlight shining strong had called to Sebastien. For him, nothing could be more magical than swimming under the moon and stars; it spoke to his very soul. But Eleanor took one look at the cold, inky blackness, and nothing on this earth, short of a drowning child, could have persuaded her to enter that mire. The tide was out, and Eleanor's mind saw stingrays and jelly fish and sharks in the deeper ocean. She had no knowledge of this coastline – there could be rocks, vortices, riptides, all sorts of dangers. Above all, in the dark, no one would see her if she slipped under the water; no one would find her; no one would save her. For once, Eleanor's fear was greater than her regard for Sebastien as she faced the horrifying reality that she no longer trusted him to keep her safe.

While Sebastien plunged with wild abandon into the sea, Eleanor sat on the shore. In an attempt at appeasement, the others paddled in the shallows until a fuming Sebastien strode out of the waves like some furious Neptune and disappeared into the warren of unlit streets behind them. Eleanor and her friends waited in embarrassed silence for him to return, but when it got late enough for the restaurant to close, they persuaded her to return to the hotel and wait for him there.

But Sebastien had pre-empted them; he had the room key and he had retired to bed. The door to their room was locked; her gentle taps went unanswered. In despair, she knocked on Charlie and Trudi's door, and spent that night and all the following nights on their floor, knowing how unwelcome she must be. She had no clothes, no money, no toiletries, and felt the ignominy of having to ask her friends for help. Sebastien stayed in their room. Food, left outside his door by an anxious Eleanor, disappeared, but Sebastien remained absent.

Worried her lover was having a breakdown, Eleanor waited. Calls, texts, approaches from all of the group were ignored. On the day they were due to leave, minutes before the taxi arrived for the airport, Sebastien opened the door and asked Eleanor if she was sorry. And Eleanor finally understood – all of this was punishment, long-drawn-out, meditated.

The last of her love for him faded like a ghost exorcised as she collected her passport and bank cards, shoving as many clothes into her rucksack as she could find to fly home. There on the Arrivals concourse at Gatwick, with Sebastien's parents present to control him and her parents at hand to protect her, she told him it was over, forced to humiliate him publicly to ensure her own safety.

Eleanor today knows her own worth. She does not need to see to see admiration in another's eyes to feed her own self-confidence. And Eleanor has had her fill of brooding heroes. No longer does she sigh for a Heathcliff or a Mr Rochester. The arrogance of a Mr Darcy holds no attraction. For it has been many years since she realised that in love, a little lightness goes a long way.

Mr Darcy Makes His Entrance

Filming starts early and goes on into the evening, using all the advantage of natural light. Eleanor heard the crew at an unreasonably early hour this morning as the technicians started the two-hour setup. By the time she has dressed, eaten, and avoided her mother's plans for a Mortimer-Hyde wedding, filming is already underway. While she has glanced at the queues in the canteen tent each morning as she makes her way to work, starlets obviously as desperate for caffeine as city commuters, she has never stopped to observe.

Her reluctance has partly arisen from her pressing workload, and partly from the wish to avoid Jamie Smythe. She has not seen him since the night of the kick-off party, and although his behaviour was not inappropriate, she could not escape the sense that his intention might have been otherwise. She cannot believe her charms are sufficient to lure his attention in her direction away from more beguiling women, but she does believe it of her status.

If she had wanted him, she might not have shied away from using every advantage but she has never been a fan of men who can transfer their regard so easily from one sister to the next, and she cannot forget he had wanted Anna first. It has happened more than once before, that some suitor rejected by her lovelier sisters has sought consolation with her, but she has always promised herself greater respect for her own esteem than to sink to that.

This morning, as Eleanor leaves the Hall, she turns her steps away from the North Drive and walks along the front of the building to where the formal gardens start. Having checked her emails over breakfast, she knows there is nothing of immediate concern waiting on her desk, and the morning is so lovely it inclines her to dalliance.

As she reaches the corner, she can hear peremptory commands being issued, a forewarning of the presence of the cameras. Perching on the low wall, risking lichen stains to her sprigged cotton empire-line dress, is one of the actresses, obviously waiting for her call. Eleanor stops beside her, and as the stranger turns her head, Eleanor recognises Claire, now outfitted as her character, Charlotte Lucas. When Eleanor had first met the young actress, she had thought her too pretty to be playing the plain, ageing spinster, but now she sees what an unflattering hairstyle, drab clothes, and an artful bit of make-up can do. It is the reverse of what Eleanor achieves every morning.

"Claire, I almost didn't recognise you. Lovely morning," Eleanor remarks, her voice low to avoid disturbing the scene.

"Yes, isn't it?" The actress dips her head.

"Have you been at it long?"

"Hours!" Claire pitches her voice like a bored schoolgirl, waiting for detention to end. Then a smile brightens her face and she says, "Did you hear that your mate, Ptolemy, is due today?"

"Yes, my mother told me at breakfast," Eleanor responds, then adds, to divert the conversation, "I've always felt a bit sorry for your character, Charlotte Lucas."

"I know what you mean," Claire's eyes light up. "She's the best of them, really – wise, perceptive, kind. And yet she gets the worst fate."

"You think? What? Worse than being married to Wickham?"

"Yes, of course. Lydia will have no scruples about sleeping with other men or running up debts her sisters will have to discharge. Charlotte is shackled for life, unless a passing ague carries him off. Although, given her luck, he'll turn out to have robust health while she dies giving birth to a child he's forced on her."

Eleanor, a little taken aback by the vehemence of Claire's words, changes tack slightly like the consummate diplomat she has been raised to be. "I've always thought of Charlotte as a Cassandra figure, prophesising the truth and not being believed."

"Well, if you want a prediction," Claire says with a nod in the direction of the canteen tent, "that's not going to end well."

Eleanor follows her gaze and sees Tom Davey sitting at a table with a woman in costume, their heads a little too close together.

"But Tom's got a girlfriend!" she says, remembering to bite her tongue before she shouts ... *And she's pregnant!* to the world.

"Exactly!" Claire's voice gets a little loud with emphasis, and a couple of the technicians turn around and frown. "And *she's* got a husband," she adds in a mutter. The two of them watch in silence for a moment, while in front of them the scene is reset and the actors move back to their original places. At that moment, a young black-clad woman starts waving to Claire and the actress jumps down. "That's my cue," she says. "I had fun last night. We should do it again sometime."

Ruminating on the perfidy of men, Eleanor watches Claire's scene for a few minutes before leaving the duplicitous couple in the background and heading to the more honest folk with whom she works. Although that adjective may be a stretch if she is to include her wily father.

Nearing lunchtime, Eleanor is considering whether it is worth starting another task when an annoying background buzz rapidly develops into a continuous and overwhelming throbbing which sets every window rattling in their old wooden frames. Running for the exit, Eleanor is in time to see a sleek, bronze hornet settle on the adjacent field. The door retracts, and a tall figure carrying a case climbs out. Ptolemy Hyde.

The field had been cleared of sheep and the electric fence rolled back at the request of the film company, who have earmarked it for some horseback scenes, but Eleanor is still nettled at the presumption. No one asked the Estate's permission to land a helicopter.

With a background theme of the *Ride of the Valkyries* playing in her head, the helicopter slowly rises, swings left, and is gone before Eleanor can even reach the new arrival. It has been many years since she has seen Ptolemy in the flesh, but she recognises him immediately. The lanky frame of the boy she knew is gone, and in his place stands a man, broad of shoulder, strong of chin.

What surprises Eleanor most is his demeanour. Eleanor had been used to Ptolemy's ponderous expression lowered in her direction each time they were in company. If it hadn't been for their first meeting, she would not have believed he could smile. But as Ptolemy strides through the long grass, carrying his case as if it weighs naught, his face is split by a broad grin and his eyes are shining with warmth.

"Tolly, still one for a quiet entrance, I see. Slipping in, unannounced." Eleanor's tone is acidic, despite being pleased to see him. Memories of Oxford and three years of carefree happiness do not outweigh her irritation at the present disruption.

"Well, I ended up contractually bound to be in two places at once today. Lacking a teleportation device, this was the next best thing." Ptolemy nods towards the rapidly receding aircraft.

An explanation, Eleanor notes, is not an apology.

Ptolemy continues, "When I heard Larkford was the location, I'd hoped you'd be here."

"You know me," she replies. "Boring, old Eleanor. Never goes anywhere."

He laughs. "You're hardly old and never boring."

Eleanor's mouth twists and she has to restrain herself from responding.

His eyes roam over her. "You look well." The depth of meaning with which he imbues the innocuous comment makes Eleanor momentarily uncertain.

Eleanor turns to face the same direction as Ptolemy, noting her staff gathered outside the offices, gawping at the spectacle. It is yet another charge to lay at Ptolemy's feet – her stock frightened, her buildings rattled, her workforce idle. "I'll take you to the action," she says, her wish to get her team back to their desks coinciding with the exercise of good manners.

"Thanks. I'm already late," he says with a grimace. "I'll be straight in to make-up and costume."

She moves to the side without the suitcase and they walk in silence to the North Drive.

"You haven't changed a bit." Ptolemy is polite if not honest.

"Really?" Eleanor challenges with a wave of her hand over her short-sleeved shift dress, tailor-made in a silk-cotton mix. "And here I thought I was dressed to impress, but you still think I look like a student?"

Ptolemy frowns. "Not at all. Here I am, *still* in jeans and T-shirt, looking like a student. You, Eleanor, will always make the right impression. You have employed your time much better. No one admitted to the pleasure of *seeing* you can think anything wanting."

"You have been learning your lines," she accuses.

Pride and Prejudice was on her syllabus at school. With that curious ability of teenage years to retain memories, she can still recall huge chunks of the novel she rote-learned for exams.

With a smile at his blatant insincerity, she continues with the superficial cordialities so vital to being regarded as polite. "So, how have you been? I watched your Mancunian series. You were very good in it."

"You think so?"

If Eleanor didn't know Ptolemy well enough to be sure of his innate self-confidence, she might imagine his face pinked slightly at her compliment, but she is surely mistaken. She puts his slight flushed look down to the heart-racing helicopter landing or the rising heat of the afternoon after the air-conditioned journey.

"But I think this dramatisation may make your name." She waves an arm in the general direction of the film set. "At least I'll always be able to claim I knew you before you were famous."

"Yes," the habitually serious Ptolemy replies. "I haven't even filmed it yet, but my agent is already starting to get interest from the US."

"Well, it's a good part for you, a good fit. You'll make a fantastic Darcy – every woman's dream." She fancies she has equalled his insincerity, maybe even topped it. She stops at the corner of the Hall, smiles up at him and says, "This is you. You'll find the action just around the corner." About to turn away, she remembers her manners. "Message me if you need anything."

Then she walks quickly towards the portico, leaving him standing on the tarmac, wondering at the truth of her words.

Mr Wickham Improves

Eleanor has always enjoyed playing sport. Throughout her school years and at university she played netball for fun. Netball in winter and tennis in the summer. Lady Larkford herself had been fond of tennis, and the tennis coach had been a familiar sight at the Hall for many years until with age came a frozen shoulder. Left with a reduced range of movement, Eleanor's mother had finally accepted her playing days were over.

Eleanor had not mourned the departure of the tennis coach, although her youngest sisters had sobbed melodramatically for days. The twins were then fifteen and far more interested in the male species than their schoolwork. To give credit where it was due, there had never been the slightest hint of flirtation from the coach himself. When he stepped in to correct a racquet position on a serve or made an adjustment to a backhand, he had always acted professionally. His hands had never lingered; his body had never touched anyone's inappropriately.

The departure of the coach had coincided with Lady Larkford's slide into indolence. She did not fancy golf, and communal swimming baths were a horror to be avoided at all costs. She was content to do no more than to potter around the estate. Eleanor, though, needed a way to maintain her own fitness and so she had laced up her trainers and started to run, once a week minimum. The aim was never to exhaust herself or to run too fast, for that might increase risk of seizure; she ran in the mornings when her energy levels were high and mainly on weekends when no strenuous working day ensued. She kept to the drives and main paths around the estate, knowing that the monitor on her wrist would summon help if she needed it. She would have liked a running companion, but in this she was yet to find someone whose chatter she could tolerate for an entire hour.

This morning is bright and sunny and promises to end in a blaze of heat. The air still contains the slight chill of the night as Eleanor laces up her running shoes in front of the large entrance door. She hears a clatter behind her and turns to see Annabelle, the newest housemaid, unsuccessfully juggling an armful of cleaning products.

Eleanor's bright and friendly, "Good morning, Annabelle", is greeted with a look of horror and an incomprehensible mutter in return. Eleanor sighs and helps Annabelle collect up her paraphernalia, fetching a can of polish which had rolled away and putting it back in the girl's hands. Annabelle keeps her eyes averted the whole time, and when she has everything within grasp, she flees. Eleanor finds it hard to believe that girls like Annabelle exist anymore; frightened of the world and everyone in it. Would Annabelle really have preferred the old tradition where servants turned to face the nearest wall when their masters and mistresses passed? In an instant, Eleanor leaps from present to future, forecasting a life of mundanity for Annabelle, never leaving this little corner of England, content to live out the entirety of her existence within the security of her family and friends.

Eleanor considers the baffling diversity of families. Annabelle's brother, Matthew, joined the Army with Jacob and is still out there in some godforsaken country. He has seen Afghanistan and who knows what other hellholes, and inspires enough confidence in his soldiers that they follow him into the most dangerous situations. Two children born of the same parents, raised in the same place, subject to the same influences grow to be so different. It mirrors her own family and leads her to the conclusion that parenting is luck, not skill.

Putting aside thoughts of the vagaries of kinship, Eleanor steps outside and begins to warm up, swinging arms and legs, loosening muscles. She begins to plan out today's route and starts to walk, setting the GPS on her other wrist. She has only taken her first few strides when she is startled to hear her name called.

She turns to find a slightly sweaty and very steamy Jamie Smythe, his lithe form lined in tight microfibre and his compression shorts leaving little to the imagination. Eleanor can envision the effect this image might have on his fans, for even she is not unaffected, and is tempted to reach for her phone. This one picture would be guaranteed to go viral, but then she remembers the draconian contract she signed, and her fingers move away from the waistband pocket and instead wave in greeting.

Despite avoiding him for the last week, Eleanor is not by nature rude or churlish, and she cannot bring herself to be discourteous as he falls into step beside her, matching his pace with hers. Eleanor runs at a controlled speed and Jamie has no trouble talking at the same time as running.

"You haven't been to watch the filming yet, Miss Mortimer?"

"Call me Eleanor, please," she answers. "I stopped by for a few minutes on Thursday morning, but it has been quite a busy week for me."

"Oh? What've you been doing?"

Eleanor is a little taken aback by the question, wondering if he is asking for a detailed breakdown of her work calendar, but eventually she goes with, "Estate business."

"What? You work?"

"Yes, of course. What did you think I do?"

"I dunno. Have lunch? Maybe a bit of yoga?"

"My father and I split the running of the Estate. He handles most of the day-to-day maintenance of the hall and park, and I do the commercial side. Although the film company is my responsibility."

"Couldn't you pay someone to do that for you?"

"Well, yes. But the Estate isn't theirs, so their approach may be different."

"How?"

"Maximising short-term gain at the expense of long-term viability, sidestepping social responsibility, exploiting our employees and tenants instead of valuing their loyalty and years of service, remembering this Estate is our home as well as our business."

"Huh?"

Eleanor realises Jamie is having trouble reconciling the person she is with the life he imagines she leads. She dials back her forcefulness and deflects the conversation.

"How is the filming going for you?"

"All my scenes have been good. I thought the producer was going to have a heart attack when Ptolemy Hyde didn't turn up first thing Thursday morning, but we caught up a bit filming late yesterday."

"Yes, I saw his helicopter land."

"The biggest problem has been Amelia, the girl who is playing Lydia. A bee fell down her cleavage and stung her. Her chest has swelled up so much it looks like she's got three boobs. Wardrobe are going mental trying to cover her up, but part of the reason she got the job is because of her assets." Jamie makes a coarse gesture, cupping his hands, which makes Eleanor wince, but she understands. Lydia is by character silly and louche, and the male shorthand for that in a woman is buxom; despite decades of feminism, still big chest equals small brain.

They cover three miles with Jamie's recollections of disasters that have happened while filming and despite her misgivings as to the man, Eleanor has to admit she has not been half so well-entertained at many a party. She begins to understand why he is so popular; she hears him spoken of with friendliness by villager and film folk alike. He may not be clever or cultured, but he is agreeable and he genuinely seems to want to please. She wonders how he gets on with Ptolemy – the two could not be more dissimilar. Ptolemy is all intelligence and refinement and does not care what the world thinks of him – he knows his own worth.

As she turns their path towards home, she asks, "So how do you find the rest of the cast?"

"Most of them are all right. I've not had much of a chance to get to know Ptolemy yet – he's too busy making friends with all the actresses. Every time I turn around, he's in a corner somewhere with a different woman."

Eleanor is surprised. The Ptolemy she knew was never promiscuous. University gave plenty of opportunity to experiment sexually, especially for the rich and good-looking, but he had only dated a handful of girls. His restraint was one of the things she had always appreciated about him, but people change. Perhaps he has become used to being the centre of the attention.

She wants to protest on Ptolemy's behalf but contents herself with a doubt-filled, "Really?"

"Oh yeah! You should hear the noises coming from his trailer."

Eleanor makes a silent promise to herself to stay well clear of Ptolemy's motorhome, just in case. She cannot imagine the embarrassment of interrupting such an activity – Ptolemy with his trousers down bent over some faceless female. The thought alone is enough to make her blush.

But Jamie has not finished. "I hear it's sometimes more than one at once. He has a big appetite."

Aware of the dangers of self-righteousness, Eleanor tries hard not to condemn other consenting adults for their sexual adventures, but at heart, she is a prude. She cannot help but think happiness is more likely to be found in the arms of one sincere lover than in the embrace of many casual ones.

They complete the homeward leg with Eleanor wondering how much of Ptolemy she really knows, while Jamie chatters away giving inconsequential gossip about his fellow actors. When they arrive back at the Hall, Eleanor stretches her muscles and bids Jamie farewell with a reminder of their engagement that evening; her parents have invited the producer, the director, and the top cast to dinner. As she wanders inside, she reflects how the world turns: the upstanding Mr Hyde may not be as respectable as she thought, and the roguish Mr Smythe may be decidedly better than she had assumed.

The Dinner Party

When Eleanor comes down to dinner, she is anticipating a very pleasant evening in entertaining company. While the talents of Mrs Hill, the head housekeeper, aided and abetted by a delicatessen in Bridgetown and some of the more upmarket ready-meal providers, are sufficient for family dinners, Lady Larkford always uses professional caterers for formal dining. They take advantage of the Hall's supplies of linen, silverware, and china, but the food is cooked and served by the company.

On her way to the library, where all are to meet for drinks before dining, Eleanor detours to check everything is as it should be. The formal dining room, with its antique table with inlaid marquetry having been part of the house commandeered by the filmmakers, the catering company have set up a banqueting table and chairs in the great hall. Normally, it is too draughty to use for entertaining, but in midsummer it is delightfully cool, and certainly imposing with its ornate, gilt-encrusted ceiling and the grand fireplace complete with flanking statues.

Eleanor runs her fingers over the curved backs of the Chippendale-style chairs, all precisely aligned. In contrast to the dark mahogany of the chair backs, the table gleams with cream and crystal and polished silver. She glances down at the name cards and finds her own, placed between Ptolemy Hyde and the elderly John Twelvetree. She detects her mother's doing. Her eyes travel onwards to find Phoebe beside Jamie Smythe, and she draws a deep breath. That will never do. A handsome, charming but – Eleanor suspects – possibly mercenary, young man and her silly, impulsive sister is not a combination that is likely to give her any piece of mind. In a moment, Eleanor has switched the two names, hers and Phoebe's, taking care to ensure the cards are placed perfectly central and parallel to the table edge. Satisfied her interference is undetectable, Eleanor hurries on to where the party is to assemble for an aperitif.

She finds she is the first of the women to arrive, the others apparently requiring far more extensive preparations despite their advantage of natural-born beauty, and she joins her father who is sitting in an armchair by the mantlepiece. The fire is unlit, and the windows are cracked to allow the evening air to drift in, bringing the scents of rose and honeysuckle.

"How is young Jacob working out?" Lord Larkford looks up with a calculating eye.

"He's been very useful," Eleanor admits, and she considers how much she has been able to accomplish over the last few days with his help. She hadn't realised how constrained her movements had become by having to ask her family for transport.

"Did you mean to say, '*Daddy, you were right*'?"

"Aren't you always?" Eleanor laughs.

"Don't you forget it, sweetheart. Repeat after me, '*My Papa is the best in all the world*'."

Eleanor is saved from having to reply by the arrival of the first of the guests. Not being naïve enough to place complete trust in Jamie's earlier intelligence, Eleanor has determined to decide on Ptolemy's present-day character only through the evidence of her own eyes. Thus, she is rather nonplussed when the man himself walks in with not one, but two, women on his arms. An actress either side, snuggled in, each with one hand resting on his forearm, another clinging to his bicep, he looks every inch the lothario Jamie painted him to be.

Putting aside her own confusion, she moves swiftly across the room to greet the first arrivals.

"Ah, Tolly! You seem to have your hands full tonight," Eleanor says.

She goes to kiss his cheek as he tries to disentangle himself from his companions with some haste and a trace of embarrassment, as if he is surprised to find Eleanor here, in her own home.

"Eleanor, may I introduce Claire and Amelia?" He nods towards each woman as he mentions their name, stepping backwards slightly, leaving both women in the limelight.

"We've met," Eleanor and Claire say the words in unison and both laugh. Eleanor turns her attention to the other member of the group. While she knows Amelia is an actress with a few roles behind her, she cannot help but be taken aback by her appearance of youth. Despite her well-developed bosom, she looks to be in her mid-teens – no doubt one of the reasons she was chosen for the role of Lydia. Remembering Jamie's earlier tale, Eleanor's eyes drop to Amelia's chest and, although the swelling has diminished from what he so uncharitably described as a third boob, it is still discernibly red and swollen.

Eleanor is about to make a sympathetic comment when she feels the looming presence of her father at her back and changes her words to that of introduction.

"My father, Peregrine Mortimer, Baron of Larkford."

Even as Ptolemy steps forwards to offer a brisk handshake and the words spoken with the assurance of equals, "Lord Larkford", Eleanor sees the rounded eyes and hears the softly breathed *Oh* of Amelia. She wonders if people treat the young actress differently because she is so child-like, thus enabling her to remain so. While Claire is moving with self-possession in accord with the normal rituals, Amelia is immobile. Eleanor would freely admit her father is an imposing figure, but she has never before come across someone who has been struck dumb by his presence.

Her father draws his guests away to supply each with a glass of English sparkling wine, except Claire, who chooses to remain by Eleanor's side.

"Amelia was so worried about meeting nobility. Anyone would think you were royalty, and the penalty for giving offence, beheading. Tolly was very sweet and said he would look after her."

"And does Tolly look after all of you so diligently?" Eleanor asks.

"I wish!" Claire scoffs. "Look at him. He is quite the catch, isn't he? But I don't need to tell you that. I know you've been friends for years." Her intonation changes the statement into a question. "He was singing your praises on the way down from the trailers. I think it unsettled Amelia even more, poor chick."

"Oh?" Eleanor finds she does not wish Claire to elaborate, unsure of what Ptolemy has said.

"Well, his arrival has been like throwing a chunk of steak into a pool of starving piranhas. Don't let that wide-eyed innocent act fool you. Amelia knows exactly what effect she has, and it appears to be working. Leastways he walked her down and he is standing beside her. But while he may enjoy playing, I think he is quite practised at slipping through all those grasping hands."

"And you? Are you also after a tasty chunk?"

Claire laughs, sounding genuinely amused, even though Eleanor is listening for a tinge of bitterness. "Oh, I would tap that ass if I could, but I'm well aware the likes of Darcy is not for such as me. Besides, I have a problem with Daddy issues – I much prefer older men."

The last sentence was uttered *sotto voce* with her eyes on the door as two men, both looking remarkably like they are edging towards their mid-life crises, are shown into the library by her mother. Lady Larkford, despite her age, is looking resplendent in a black cocktail dress and faultless make-up.

"The Producer and the Director," Claire whispers, her finger pointing left and then right, "but I don't recognise the woman." She sounds a little concerned as the one on the right executes a sweeping, courtly bow.

"That would be my mother, Lady Larkford."

The actress gives a tinkling little laugh of relief. With the arrival of her mother, Eleanor no longer has to play hostess, and she steps back to withdraw further into the library. She is surprised to find Claire moves with her, although the woman's eyes remain fixed on Lady Larkford's companions. Over the next ten minutes, the trickle of guests swells with an influx of actors. Eleanor is grateful as Claire identifies each one, together with their character. She recognises Tom Davey, who turns up with his on-screen love interest (and real-life paramour, it seems), Olivia, playing Miss Jane Bennet.

Last, but by no means unexpected, come the twins, accompanied by their aunt Mary. Lady Mary is Lord Larkford's older sister and Eleanor cannot not help but feel sorry for her aunt. With the British aristocracy's views on the equality of women being firmly grounded in the Dark Ages, the Estate passed with the title to the eldest boy, leaving Mary to make her way in a world for which she was less well-equipped than her Eton-educated younger brother. *Her* schooling had focused more on producing well-bred young ladies who could get in and out of cars without showing their knickers rather than future world leaders. The cruellest twist was that, by the time control of Larkford came to her father, Eleanor had already been established as his subsequent heir and everyone was aware the title would separate from the Estate. Excluding Mary had only brought them one generation.

In an attempt to insulate herself from the harshness of the world, Mary had bagged herself a strapping, rugby-playing bastion of the prosperous upper middle-class, unaware these goliaths were soon to be eclipsed in earning potential by the earnest, bespectacled geeks. Further she also failed to foresee these mountains of manhood would soon find themselves rapidly going to seed as their playing days ended, amply assisted by a career of liquid lunches and no activity more strenuous than lifting a few sheets of paper. It never occurred to Mary to hold out for a better offer; she was grateful *anyone* might want to marry her. Unfortunately, gratitude is not a strong enough foundation for a long-term relationship, especially one plagued by the usual afflictions of humanity: selfishness, resentment, and covetousness. As the illusions faded and reality showed her husband to have definite feet of clay, he had looked elsewhere for adoration, and despite being fat, forty and with a nose red enough to rival Rudolph's, he had found it in his much younger, and far more naïve, personal assistant.

A good divorce lawyer of Lord Larkford's acquaintance had ensured an equitable distribution of the marital assets, and Mary had packed up her boys and retired to the country she knew and loved, to live a modest life. Ever since the Dowager Baroness had departed Larkford for Bridgetown, Mary had become a frequent visitor at the Hall, and was the conduit for much of the local gossip.

The advent of Mary and the twins causes a small frisson of excitement in the gathered males. Phoebe and Lily are similar enough in features to clearly denote a close familial connection, but they are not identical. They are, however, both stunning – their faces fair, figures well-proportioned, and they move with a natural grace. Eleanor is so used to their radiance; she forgets its impact on others until she is forcibly reminded at times like these. As each male eye turns towards her sisters, Eleanor looks for Ptolemy, but finds him looking back at her.

He has, though, failed to extract himself from a trio of actresses, one of whom soon recalls his attention to herself by the careful application of a hand on his arm, a hand not removed even after he answers his admirer – her expression plainly shows her admiration. Eleanor can only conclude that if he truly did not want their attentions, he could avoid them easily enough. Some part of him must enjoy the followers, some vanity flattered by their adulation. She cannot not explain why, if she has no romantic interest in Ptolemy any more, it matters if he is sleeping with one, or possibly more, of these women. She only knows it does, and that she does not feel comfortable thinking of Ptolemy in that way. While it had hurt that he might not hold her in high opinion, she was still accustomed to thinking of him as discerning; much better to be rejected by a man of the highest tastes than by one who was indiscriminate. It makes no sense, because her friend of many years, Charlie Fairfax, is well-known as a womaniser and his love life would certainly not bear too close a scrutiny, yet it makes not one jot of difference to her regard for him.

She turns her eyes back to her sisters, and she sees the moment Phoebe spots Jamie Smythe, thankful she switched the seating cards. Her mother cannot have understood the attraction that young man would hold for her daughters; either that or she overestimates the twins' sense. She is saved from trying to intervene by the announcement of dinner. Her sisters have cut it so fine, there is barely time for them to make their greetings before the Baron and Baroness are leading their guests in to dine.

As Eleanor takes her seat between Jamie and Ptolemy, she glances down the table to see Phoebe's expression of disgust at being seated next the portly John Twelvetree.

In days gone by, there would have been a footman behind each chair, but now guests are left to fend for themselves, except where their neighbours graciously assist.

"Thank you, Tolly." Eleanor smiles up at him as he pushes her chair in and takes his seat beside her.

But those are well-nigh the only words she says to him throughout dinner, as Jamie leans over and whispers conspiratorially, "There's a book on which actress he bangs tonight. Do you want in? My money is on Claire *and* Amelia."

Eleanor frowns and shakes her head. She is not at ease betting on Ptolemy's love life, but Jamie does not notice and moves smoothly on. He talks about the weather, and the weird and wonderful inhabitants of Larkford he has stumbled across. He talks about his fellow cast members and the antics of the crew with the junior actors. He is charming and funny, and Eleanor finds him a thoroughly entertaining dinner companion. He seems to know everyone and gets along with all. Except, maybe, Ptolemy. Eleanor can feel Ptolemy glowering at her and Jamie, and for one brief moment, it reminds her of Oxford and the way he used to glare at her. Some things don't change, she thinks.

Jamie keeps her amused as each course is served and eaten. When the waiter comes to clear the debris, he trades good-humoured banter with him, and Eleanor notices Jamie's wine glass gets refilled deeper than others', including hers.

In one of the rare moments when Jamie has stopped talking in order to eat, and while Ptolemy appears engaged in talking to John Twelvetree over Phoebe's head, Eleanor hears her aunt's high clear voice ringing across the dining table. Chief among the talents of the aristocracy is the ability to ensure their voices are always heard.

"Oh, those were the days," Lady Mary cries, "when you could enrol in modelling school and not do much of anything except party and flirt. Nowadays everyone has to have a job – even the old Queen's granddaughters! You can't just be; you have to do! It's quite exhausting!"

Her dinner partner, the one Claire had identified as the Producer, appears less impressed. His voice is frigid as he responds, "Oh, yes. Those days. The days of the miners striking, desperately trying to hang onto their jobs and their way of life. The days when child abuse was swept under the carpet, and perpetrators left free to re-offend and the victims left to rot. The days when gangs went gay-bashing with impunity and when the police thought they could kill black people with no consequences. Those days?"

While Eleanor can understand the frustrations felt by someone who has had to struggle for every advancement in life at the frivolities of those born to wealth, she is also protective of Mary – a job she has assumed from both her father and mother. Lord Larkford protects his wife and his sister from the world, and Lady Larkford protects her husband and his sister from their mother. Mary has been undermined all her life. As she grew up, she was never elegant enough or charming enough or clever enough and the burden of being her constantly carping mother's companion fell to poor Mary more than her brother. He was allowed to escape to outdoor pursuits, to boarding school and on to university. But Mary was kept at home, except for the two years she spent husband-hunting in London. And then she married.

When Mary spoke wistfully of the good old days, she wasn't making a political statement in favour of Thatcher. How can she? For Mary has no interest in politics and is seldom aware of precisely who is the Prime Minister; she would certainly struggle to name two additional members of the Cabinet. Nor is she making a social statement supporting the rigidity of British class system. No, Mary is merely remembering the few years in her life, between home and husband, when she was happy. And for this she does not deserve to be castigated.

The Producer knows nothing of this. All he sees is the braying of a woman of privilege. It has plainly irritated him and while Eleanor is aware he has a point it does not justify such a public put-down. She opens her mouth to defend her aunt even at the risk of giving offense to a guest, but her words are lost as a clear baritone beside her proclaims, "Oh, I think as a young woman in the last century, Mary may well know more about social injustice than either of us. She doesn't need our male-privileged opinions."

Ptolemy raises his glass, the soft light glimmering on the crystal, contrasting with the with deep ruby hue of the contents. "Perhaps we guests should mention instead the fineness of the wine and the quality of each dish. This red is magnificent. I, for one, am glad not to be served yet another Chateau Neuf. Italian, is it?"

The moment passes. The Producer nods and moves on. The guest on Mary's other side makes a comment about the food and engages her attention. Ptolemy returns to his conversation with John Twelvetree, and Jamie, having finished his dessert, starts an anecdote about the last film in which he had a role.

By the end of the meal, though, Eleanor has had enough. Most of the guests are slightly tipsy, some far further along the road to intoxication. Ptolemy is flanked by two actresses vying for his attention and Jamie's chatter has begun to pale. It is not that his stories are dull – quite the opposite – it is more that they are always focussed on him. Eleanor has no chance to supply her own tales of fun and frolics, of horrors and tragedies. She is not used to taking such a passive role.

So, when the first opportunity presents itself, Eleanor slips away. Her parents are the hosts; it is not incumbent on her to stay to the bitter end, and, unlike Jamie, she finds she has no curiosity to discover whom Ptolemy leaves with at the end of the night. Safely in her room, she reflects on the evening. It certainly did not go the way she expected – she had thought it would be an evening of pleasant reminiscences with Ptolemy of their time in Oxford. Instead, she got a glittering show of peacocking from Jamie Smythe. The only redeeming thing was that his show had been viewed by her jaded eyes, not Phoebe's gullible ones. That, at least, is one disaster averted, no matter what else lies on the horizon.

Sunday, Sunday

Eleanor is up early the next morning to go to church. Although Eleanor and her parents are far from devout, patronage of the local church is one of those duties that has traditionally been undertaken by the noble family from the Hall. The three of them pass the baton of familial attendance between themselves, ensuring that representation is never too onerous a duty. Eleanor, herself, finds a certain meditative comfort in the old ceremonies and the current vicar, Aaron Parrish, keeps his sermons pertinent and to a reasonable length.

The building is Victorian, built for the parishioners by a previous baron of Larkford in a faux-Norman style to match other, much older, local flint churches. Constructing it on estate land was not all motivated by charity; the noble family then had only a short walk to their Sunday worship instead of a round trip of a couple of miles, necessitating all the hullaballoo of ordering the carriage. Fortunately, the church and its legacy of ruinously expensive repairs had long ago been passed to the responsibility of the Church Commissioners, and the vicar, to his enormous relief, moved to a more modern vicarage in an unattractive but manageable house with working utilities, instead of the grand, draughty Victorian villa.

Eleanor is still yawning as she enters the porch and walks down the nave to her family's usual seat on a pew at the front. It will not do to fall asleep during the sermon, directly in front of the pulpit, and she is regretting not swapping this morning's appearance with one of her parents.

She has timed her appearance to perfection. The wooden pews with their bolt-upright backs do not entice one to excessive punctuality. Eleanor has barely sat down when the organ starts. The congregation stands and Eleanor fumbles for the hymn book, but she need not have worried; she knows the words to this song by heart. The tremulous tones of a handful of old biddies and the deep rumbling bass of their husbands sing out "*At the name of Jesus, every knee shall bow*". The latest incumbent is not long out of theological college and is still fervent in his faith. His pattern book seems to be to kick off every service, funerals excepted, with a stirring chorus designed to rouse his flagging flock from their torpid belief. It may yet work; attendance has increased and Eleanor is no longer the youngest person in the pews.

The vicar enters, his robes conferring a portliness at odds with his youth. He is accompanied by the choir, an assemblage of worthies of the parish, with an abundance of confidence and somewhat less talent, who seem to view the Sunday service as a competition as to whose note will hit the highest and carry the furthest, regardless of tune.

The procession is brought up with a novelty. Eleanor, who has multiple sources of gossip, would have heard if a new curate had been appointed, but there have been no whispers, and therefore she is puzzled by the identity of the young man, head down at the rear of the procession. Unlike the others, he is not robed, but as he moves to one side and takes his place at the altar, he turns to face the congregation.

Eleanor's heart skips as she recognises the stranger from the pub quiz and, suddenly, she is grateful she did not pass off this morning's duty. As if he feels her eyes on him, he lifts his to gaze directly at her and grins – a heart-stopping, dimple-forming movement that has Eleanor flustered and looking down at her hymn book, concentrating on the words with an attention it has never required before. At points in the service, Eleanor chances surreptitious glances at him, only to find his eyes resting on her. At the Invitation to Confession, Eleanor adds flirting in church to her mental list of sins.

She watches him assisting with the preparation of the sacrament, and he most definitely appears to know what he is doing. When the congregation are asked to draw near with faith to receive the body and the blood, Eleanor joins the queue with more eagerness than usual. When she kneels before the altar to receive the sacrament, her fingertips brush his as she guides the cup of wine to her lips. Never has a touch felt so significant.

After the dismissal, Eleanor slides to her knees, ostensibly head down in prayer. She wants to get up and pursue the handsome stranger, but a surreptitious sweep of the area shows Mrs Fairweather lingering with intent. Married to a Bridgetown solicitor, Mrs Fairweather would desperately like to be Eleanor's friend, not from a co-incidence of characters but rather from an over-appreciation of rank. Eleanor is less keen. Mrs Fairweather, she feels, is one of those women who might only be improved by misfortune – an infidelity on the part of her husband, a chronic illness, or an appalling investment loss. Unfortunately, Mrs Fairweather's luck holds, and the woman continues in her unrelenting self-righteousness, a quality Eleanor finds highly unattractive in others, despite possessing a significant amount herself.

Mrs Fairweather is also persistent. Eleanor waits on her knees, hoping Mrs Fairweather will be called away before Eleanor loses her chance with the vicar's friend. While she kneels with her eyes half-closed, she ponders if there is an otherworldly significance to this event. Was it because she had admitted to Anna she was looking for love? Ask, and He will answer? Or has the arrival of a horde of eligible bachelors into her quiet existence overset her so much, she is losing her head? Or is this a cosmic joke, Fate confusing buses with beefcake? The stranger is certainly agreeable. As a slideshow of the attractive men now featuring in Eleanor's life plays in her mind, she cannot help but imagine he is their equal.

She is forced to wait until the church is almost empty, and then moves towards the exit where the vicar is still doing his duty dispatching his flock with a few kind words for each, the mystery man beside him. The reverend's handshake is the usual brisk up and down, accompanied by the polite enquiry as to her well-being, but when she moves on and gives her hand to his friend, he holds her fingers as if he would raise them to his lips, and all Eleanor can see is the whiteness of his teeth and all she can feel is the warmth of his hand. Then the brief contact is broken and she moves on, out into the bright June sunshine.

There is a tradition of tea and biscuits after the service, usually in the rear of the nave, but with the fine weather, the tables are being set up outside by the churchwardens. The urn, manned by the stalwart Mrs Fairweather, is already dispensing hot water for cups of stewed tea or weak, bitter coffee. Eleanor does not ordinarily linger, but today, with her aspiring friend safely imprisoned behind the tea table, she finds she has the time to enjoy a bourbon cream or rich tea biscuit. She is busy deciding between the two when she hears a quiet voice in her ear.

"Do you have so many people to pray for, or so many sins to confess?"

Eleanor turns at the teasing words. The handsome stranger is close enough that she can confirm her first impressions; there is nothing immediately displeasing about his appearance or his manner.

"I'm sorry?" Her confusion comes from spending more time registering his presence than his words.

"You were a long time on your knees at the end there."

"Oh!" Eleanor smiles at him, her heart skipping at the thought he had been waiting for her. "Both. It is a good thing, isn't it, that the Church of England does not require us to list our sins out loud? I sometimes wonder how Catholic priests can look some of their parishioners in the eye, privy as they are to the darkest secrets of their flock. Even I hear enough on the gossip grapevine to make me uncomfortable at times."

"You make it sound like I've landed in Gotham. Surely a quaint English village like this cannot be so godforsaken?"

"Even in beautiful countryside there is misery: there is poverty and disease; there are feuds and drugs and domestic violence. But I don't want to frighten you away. I can assure you, you will be safe in your bed at night." Eleanor briefly imagines him in his bed, and then schools her mind away from the subject.

"Don't worry, I am made of sterner stuff than that," he says, his trademark grin lighting up his face. "I've just finished a stint doing Youth Ministry in Birmingham. That was by turns hair-raising and inspiring."

"Ah! You are a man of God then. I wondered. But you are out of uniform." Eleanor gestures to her throat.

"I'm on holiday, staying with Aaron for a bit. I'm in mufti."

"And what are you hoping to do on your holiday?"

"Apart from chatting to delightful women?"

Eleanor pinches her lips between her teeth at his blatant flattery.

"Yes," she says. "Apart from that."

"A little bit of fishing, a little bit of sightseeing, and a lot of not much."

"I can help with recommendations for sightseeing," Eleanor offers and they proceed to talk about churches and stately homes, tea rooms and fine gardens and open-air theatre. Then they move on to music and books and things they like best, and neither of them notices the other worshippers have left and the tables have been put away until the vicar comes over to clear his throat.

"Ah, Harry! We're heading over to the Blue Lion for lunch."

Eleanor checks the time and realises she has missed her opportunity for a nap before the exigencies of the afternoon, but she counts the company worth the sacrifice.

"I must be going too," she says quickly. She nods to each in farewell. "Reverend, Harry."

Eleanor's short walk is scarcely long enough for her to marvel at her new acquaintance. While Jamie is beautiful, she doubts he is trustworthy, and although Ptolemy is the epitome of manliness, he thinks her dull. But Harry is a minister – the very essence of dependable – and he found her interesting enough to talk to for over an hour. What *she* finds so engaging about *him*, apart from his appearance, is his openness, his enthusiasm for the world, as if life were a big adventure and he could scoop you along for the ride.

Her daydreaming does not long survive her entrance to the Hall. Within minutes, she is called upon to arbitrate some quarrel between the twins, a role abrogated by her mother and one Eleanor has fulfilled since they learned to talk. She barely has time to eat some lunch before Jacob is waiting for her for her afternoon's test of endurance.

Eleanor directs Jacob to stop by the patisserie in town, and she selects four perfect cakes, pictures of continental sophistication, with light fluffy sponge, plump berries, and whipped cream mousse, dusted with icing sugar. Each delectable morsel is purposefully picked to neutralise the bitterness steeped in her grandmother's soul.

Lady Jessica, the dowager baroness, chooses to live in Bridgetown so she can more easily visit with friends and spend her afternoons bemoaning the inadequacy of her daughter-in-law despite that ship having sailed decades ago. Her eldest son had cheerfully left for boarding school at seven, happy to be anywhere but in her close vicinity and had avoided returning home until he had a bride and could no longer shirk his responsibilities. While his sister also fled the family home as soon as possible, it was determined Peregrine and his new wife, Sarah, should live at the Hall as they started their married life together and produced the next generation. Her son and his undisciplined family had lived in the North Wing, while their parents, Jessica and Percival, had occupied the South Wing until the sudden death of the Baron, her husband.

If ever Eleanor required a cautionary tale about the dangers of marrying for money, she has only to look at the example of her grandparents. While fond of her own mother, there is little about her that Eleanor admires, but that she stood squarely between her grim mother-in-law and her own husband and his children has to be acknowledged. Lady Jessica, the product of the affluent upper middle-class, was raised in an era where rank held far more meaning than today, and Lady Larkford has used this as a weapon. She would dismiss any of her mother-in-law's attempted meddling with the efficacious phrase, "Well, if it was good enough for my father, the Duke, it is good enough for me."

After the death of her husband, finding herself unable to tolerate the noise and clamour of her granddaughters, Lady Jessica had asked her son, the newly endowed Baron, to find her different accommodation. When a detached house close to the centre of Bridgetown had become vacant, he had had it hastily refurbished and the entire family breathed a sigh of relief as Grandma moved in there, finally ending her time of tyranny at the Hall.

Lady Jessica refers to the house as a cottage, although it is a grand, double-fronted, Victorian villa with spacious rooms and high ceilings, and enough bedrooms to accommodate her grandchildren if any of them were ever foolish enough to want to stay. She enjoys the peace of her cottage, but she is also wise to duty and a weekly visit from one or other member of the family is required. Much like church, today's visit has fallen to Eleanor.

When they pull up outside the cottage, Eleanor asks Jacob, "Are you coming in?"

"No, thank you," Jacob says with a grimace. "I remember your grandmother. Dad's always said she was a great believer in a good birching for recalcitrant servants. Besides, your mother has given me a few errands to run, and when I'm finished, I'm happy to wait out here in the car."

Eleanor cannot blame him. She reaches into her bag of goodies and extracts a fat-soaked paper bag and hands it to him.

He peeks inside. "Doughnuts!" he sighs happily.

"Just don't get any jam on my leather seats," she warns as if he were a two-year-old, and Jacob grins in return.

Eleanor times her visits to her grandmother precisely. Less than an hour is a snub, two hours far too taxing. Ninety minutes is the ideal. When Lady Jessica opens the door, Eleanor gives her the requisite peck on the cheek and proffers the ribbon-wrapped box of delights.

"I've brought you a present, Grandma." Grandma, not Gran or Granny, and, on pain of disinheritance, Nan.

"Oh, thank you, dear. I'll save them for later."

God forbid the old misery would share teatime treats with her visitors. Eleanor knows she can expect nothing more than a cup of tea and a single plain digestive, two on the plate, one each.

On these visits, Eleanor appreciates the ritual of tea-making, laying the china on the tray, boiling the kettle. She spoons first flush Darjeeling from the tin into a warmed pot, puts a shot of milk in a jug and a slice of lemon on a saucer before turning all the handles to face the same way. Each of these jobs eats into the allotted time. Today, because the weather is so pleasant, she carries the tray out into the garden to where her grandmother is waiting. One of the estate workers is charged with keeping the lawn and flowerbeds in order, an afternoon every fortnight, and Eleanor is well aware they draw straws for the task.

Before she begins her visit with the usual enquiry into her grandmother's health, she is forestalled by an enquiry from the dowager.

"Who was that man in the car with you?" she asks with her usual abruptness.

"My new driver," is Eleanor's calm reply. "He's Robert Winter's lad," she continues, aware her grandmother will know him immediately. The Dowager has only been gone from the Estate a few years, and it was the previous Baron who had had so much faith in Robert as to make him Head Gardener.

"Hmph," is all the response she gets.

Eleanor knows she is in no danger of the dowager making further enquiries into her health despite being aware of the reason Eleanor needs a driver. Her grandmother has always felt Eleanor is flawed by her illness, and if primogeniture were not so fixed in her psyche, she would have advocated for a different heir. It occurs to her now, maybe her grandmother had, specifically for Eleanor to be disinherited and the Estate to pass with the title to her male cousin.

Perhaps it is a little petty, but Eleanor skips the usual *How are you?* and goes directly to "What have you been doing this week?". She follows this up with a request for an update on the successes of the offspring of her grandmother's friends, because she knows her own family's achievements can never yield as much pleasure. It is also Eleanor's job to give highlights, judiciously edited, of the Estate affairs, adding in rather more detail about village gossip, together with thorough particulars of who has died recently. Lastly, and compressed in the final five minutes, she updates her grandmother on her own family.

It is with great relief Eleanor draws the visit to a close. She carries the tea tray into the kitchen and leaves it for the housekeeper to deal with tomorrow morning. She gathers up her things, places a respectful kiss vaguely near her grandmother's cheek, and escapes out of the door, glad to get away unmauled.

"So, how was the old trout?" Jacob asks as she climbs back into the car.

Eleanor is mindful that propriety would dictate she pull him up on his rudeness, but she cannot find it in her to care. "Same old, same old," she replies.

"It amazes me someone like that managed to produce two children who are both so compassionate in their own ways." Jacob is referring to her father and his sister.

"One has to be grateful for excellent nannies and the English public school system," she says dryly. "Much better at raising children than the aristocracy."

As Jacob delivers her safely back to the bosom of her family, she finds as usual that she has a renewed appreciation of her own mother for resisting the termagant and her father for surviving. She feels free to indulge the warmth of her feelings. Confident they won't long survive the next interaction with her parents, she enjoys them while they persist.

When Eleanor lies in her bed that night, she thinks over her day and every minute of her interplay with Harry, and for the first time in years, she has hope for her heart.

The Incredible Serena

Lady Larkford's youngest brother, Augustus, known familiarly as Gus, had been something of a rising star in the Foreign Office. After a few relatively undemanding postings, he had achieved his goal. The celebration of his attainment of the rank of ambassador to Georgia was offset by the dire state of the political situation in his destination, with deepening tensions between Russia and Georgia threatening to erupt into war. Gus could have rejected the posting, but using the clear logical reasoning that had led to his elevation, he decided a little pain now might lead to much gain later. Everyone gets one bad posting – to have his so early in his career was actually fortuitous. Three years in a miserable post meant he would never end up in such a position again.

The only intractable issue was his wife, Anima. Early in his career, Gus had been posted as Vice Consul to the British High Commission in Dhaka, Bangladesh. A chance meeting at an embassy party had led to both Gus and Anima leaving without their respective dates and with each other. And a whirlwind courtship had led the normally cautious Gus to acquire a wife in under six months and a child within the year.

Anima – while happy to put her own security at risk in order to stay at her husband's side and reduce the chance of his eye wandering – had flatly refused to endanger their only child, a daughter Serena, then only thirteen years old. Things were at an impasse and the whole scheme looked set to dissolve when Lady Larkford stepped in.

The girl was old enough for boarding school; she could attend with her cousin Eleanor when she went later that year. While the situation in the Georgia remained unsound, Serena would spend her holidays with them at Larkford Park, where Gus and Anima could visit at will.

Serena had been ecstatic with this solution. All her short life, she had prayed for one thing only – something all her compatriots seemed to have and yet she did not – brothers and sisters. The two years she subsequently spent with the Mortimers were everything she had dreamt they would be. Even after a peace treaty was brokered between the rival factions and she could safely go to Georgia, Serena connived to get a further summer with her cousins. Finally, though, she could no longer avoid the inevitable and it was with a heavy heart that she boarded the plane at Heathrow to be re-united with her parents.

She and Eleanor continued their friendship through their boarding school years until their separation was enforced at eighteen. Gus, having achieved the dizzying heights of the ambassador extraordinary and plenipotentiary in Washington DC, had decided his daughter should return to the bosom of his family and attend an American university. Serena's future for the next four years was set. The cousins said farewell, Serena departed, and their lives took different paths.

When her father returned to the United Kingdom, now as Sir Augustus, to take up a very well-rewarded, non-executive directorship with a multi-national corporation and an advisory position with an investment fund management company, Serena did not return with her parents. Serena went to Hollywood.

Eleanor had often reflected if there was anyone who was ironically named, it was her cousin, for Serena was a stranger to tranquillity and calmness. Naturally inclined to obedience, the only times Eleanor had found herself facing an irate parent was always with Serena by her side. She often wondered whether her mother had regretted her offer to her brother all those years ago, but the offer once made was not the type that could be rescinded, and Lady Larkford had never made the attempt.

Eleanor, herself, had once envied so much about Serena – her warm, russet skin, her large, umber eyes framed by long, black eyelashes, and her nomadic life, every few years a new country, a new language. As Eleanor grew older, she had begun to understand her own nature and realised her roots were very firmly fixed in the soil of Larkford. Although Eleanor had tried to maintain a correspondence, it was not in Serena's nature, and the superficiality of social media posts had been the limit of their involvement for half a decade.

Serena has put her upbringing to good use in a career as a film location scout. If her own stratagems do not work on an intractable, unbribable foreign official – a rare concurrence – she can reach out through Daddy's network of contacts. It makes her a formidable force and a very successful one. Eleanor is glad her mercurial cousin has managed to find a role in life that suits her temperament so well, but occasionally she misses her old co-partner-in-crime.

Eleanor comes out of the Hall on Wednesday morning, expecting to find Jacob waiting to take her to her meeting, and is shocked to find Serena on the top step about to lift the heavy metal door knocker.

The effusiveness of their greeting takes a good five minutes. When Eleanor discovers her cousin arrived the previous night, she is, at first, hurt. "Why didn't you come here?"

"I went to see Frankie," is Serena's guarded answer, but Eleanor understands.

She cannot for the life of her fathom their relationship, but she can see each of them is drawn to the other, even as they cannot seem to find a way forwards. She hopes she is never in the same position, perhaps forced to choose between love and Larkford.

Eleanor is recalled to the present and her own pressing responsibilities by Jacob clearing his throat.

"I'm sorry, Serena," she says with real regret, "but I'm due at a meeting with a tenant. I don't want to be late; it would be rude. Will you still be here later?" She briefly contemplates cancelling her meeting if the answer is negative, but she does not have to make this sacrifice.

"You go off and do your business. I'll be around all day and I'm staying for dinner tonight," Serena glances across at the waiting Jacob and then her eyes widen.

"Oh my God …" Serena's gaze flicks back to Eleanor. "It's him, isn't it?" She walks a circle around Jacob, inspecting every inch. "It's been a long time and he's wearing clothes, but it's him."

If ever there were a moment Eleanor wished she could silence her cousin, it is now but Serena has never been biddable, and God isn't listening either.

"He's filled out well."

Jacob, tired of being examined like a prize bull in an agricultural show, interrupts, "I don't think we've met." In the absence of Eleanor's customary politeness, he makes his own introduction. "I'm Jake," he says, and he doesn't forget the epithet to pinpoint his identification, "Eleanor's driver."

"Serena. Cousin," she replies and turns to Eleanor with mischief in her eyes. "You haven't told him."

"Time to go!" Eleanor chirps, and to Serena, "I'll see you when I get back."

For once, Jacob does not comply. "Told me what?"

Eleanor, her delight in her cousin's presence rapidly fading, debates getting into the car herself, but she dare not leave Jacob and Serena alone together.

"I used to come for summers when I was a teenager. Eleanor and I would sneak off through the woods, down to the river. We used to hide in the undergrowth and watch you from the trees. You and your friend …" Serena says with a pause between each sentence to heighten suspense. She has always known how to tell a tale, and Eleanor waits for the axe to fall. "… skinny-dipping!" Both Jacob and Eleanor flush and Serena cackles at her own wit.

Leaving her cousin almost capering with glee, Eleanor flees for the safety of the car, hearing the driver's side door thud closed moments after her own. Jacob has the car moving and has left the Estate, turning onto the public highway before he even thinks to ask the destination.

"There is no excuse," Eleanor's apology is quiet. "It was a terrible invasion of your privacy, yours and Matthew's. But we were both very young and very silly." She doesn't add, *And very curious*.

“I don’t think we need to mention this, ever again,” Jacob says gallantly, but he knows seeing someone naked and knowing someone has spied on you to see you naked cannot be put back in a bottle.

As Jacob focusses on guiding the big car through the twists and turns of the narrow road, Eleanor closes her eyes and lets the memories surface.

Just down from the Hall but before you get to Home Farm, there is a place where trees on both sides of the long lake grow down to the bank. Many decades ago, some enterprising youngster had slung a rope over a sturdy bough which protrudes over the water and it remained there, often forgotten, hidden as it was from direct view. One hot summer, when they were both thirteen, she and Serena had stumbled across Jacob Winter and his friend, Matthew Greene, swinging on the rope and launching themselves into the cool water, totally naked.

Serena was an only child and Eleanor the eldest of five girls. While they had both seen men unclothed on screen and paper, neither of them had seen nude male bodies in the flesh. The two naïve girls were fascinated, their voyeurism driven by curiosity rather than arousal, the jocular interaction between the boys as interesting as their bare flesh. Neither of them had given a thought as to the boys’ wish to privacy nor how violated they might have felt had the roles been reversed. Having come across the boys by accident, they should have retreated. They hadn’t. They had crept through the trees on the opposite bank, getting as close as they’d dared. Even though it was clear to both of them by then that Serena’s preferences were for her own sex, they sat and fantasised over which boy they would choose, safe in the knowledge that sixteen-year-old boys would barely register their presence.

Jacob pulls the car to a halt outside the home of one of the Estate’s tenant farmers, and the brief foray into her memories of the lazy days of summers long gone is replaced by the details of Carl Taylor’s scheme for an anaerobic digester before the last of the government grants is removed. Having only taken over from his father in the previous couple of years, Carl is youngish, in his early thirties, the seventh generation of his family to farm at Whitehill but the first to do so professionally. With a degree from one of the country's top agricultural colleges, Carl is determined to bring farming into harmony with the environment. Eleanor finds talking to Carl is always refreshing and often instructive. Not only is he passionate, he is also careful and thorough. His innovations are well-researched and costed, supported by spreadsheets and pilot projects.

Eleanor exits the car and steps forwards to greet Carl with her hand outstretched, but is astonished when he ignores her and wraps his arms around Jacob instead.

"I was wondering when you were going to get round to coming to see us." Carl drops his hug and thumps Jacob on the arm. "I guess it takes an order from the Boss." Belatedly noticing Eleanor's outstretched hand, he takes it in a firm grip and continues, "Jake and I go way back."

Jacob is wearing a rather sheepish expression as he answers, "I haven't really seen anyone from the old days since I've been back."

It is a pitiful excuse and Eleanor is left wondering why. His work for the Mortimers is hardly onerous; it involves some unsociable hours but seldom exceeds a normal working week. Jacob should have plenty of time to fit in an evening with friends, and it's been a couple of months since he came home from the Army, so he hasn't lacked opportunity. The only conclusion she can draw is Jacob is actively avoiding them. Eleanor is her father's daughter; she cannot resist the opportunity to interfere. She went through a similar process herself, coming back into a world, knowing people view you differently. She knows that the longer Jacob leaves it, the harder it will be. Jacob has had long enough to mend in his mental cave; it is time for him to emerge into society, no matter his reluctance.

"I think," she says quietly to him, "you should come with me on these visits and not wait in the car. If something were to happen to me, I would rather you were close by. After all, farms are dangerous places."

Jacob ruefully looks at his shiny Oxford shoes but nods. Having set her scheme underway, Eleanor enjoys herself, tramping over fields in her waterproof country boots, looking around at the improvements Carl has already made. The farmer explains his plans, talking as much to Jacob as to her, and then invites them in for tea and homemade cake. There are not many mornings that pass so pleasantly. The visit ends with Carl extracting a promise from Jacob to meet for a pint in the Blue Lion, and a promise from Eleanor to review his figures as soon as the farmer emails his reports. Eleanor understands the urgency. There will be a planning process and grant application to be undertaken with all speed if they are to beat the deadline. Mercifully, Carl will be shouldering most of the burden, but that does not mean it won't be another item added to her To Do list.

Jacob and Eleanor grab lunch on the go and continue with visit after visit. Eleanor tries to keep tenant inspections and meetings to one day so her entire week is not disrupted. The final scheduled visit of the day is the Mulwood farm. Jeanette Mulwood has run the place since her husband took his own life five years ago. People view farming as idyllic, but it is hard work for an uncertain fortune. The difference between profit and loss any year is dependent on factors entirely outside your control – a wet harvest can leave your grain worth a fraction of its value compared to previous years because of the high moisture content. At the other end of the scale, a long, fine, dry summer of a kind celebrated by the general public results in far lower yields and consequently less income.

When her husband died, Jeanette's boys were only young and of limited help on the land. Eleanor and her father held off any increase at the last rent review and have helped where they can. Her farm neighbours have all rallied round and lent equipment and manpower when needed, but even so, the Mulwoods would not have survived without the additional income from a small bed-and-breakfast business. Jeanette bunked her boys up together and moved herself into the box room in order to have two rooms to rent out. Eleanor made sure Larkford's wedding brochures listed Jeanette's as one of their local approved hosts. It was never going to generate a huge income, but it is enough to keep the wolf from the door, and with their next rent review coming up, Eleanor's visit is more of a courtesy call to ensure they know a rise is on the table.

Eleanor has always thought of Jeanette as a strong, sensible woman. Despite still struggling with her husband's death, she had come to Eleanor and her father with a list of measures for the support she needed and a business plan for bringing the farm back to full profitability long-term. Which is why Eleanor's head jerks up when she hears Jeanette giggle. As they walk the land, Eleanor becomes increasingly suspicious as Jeanette plays with her shirt collar and spends rather more time looking at Jacob than her landlord. When Jeanette lays her hand on Jacob's forearm, doubt disappears. Eleanor looks at Jacob again. He is certainly handsome enough and he has a kind of charm, if you like being mocked at regular intervals. Having both grown up on the estate, throughout her childhood Jacob had usually been around somewhere, like part of the scenery. She had never thought of him one of the eligible bachelors of the village, but it is clear Jeanette does. And Jacob is doing nothing to discourage her – quite the opposite, in fact, if his cheerfulness is anything to go by.

The visit is interrupted by a minor family crisis – the youngest lad comes back from school with a black eye. Eleanor uses the drama to terminate the inspection, leaving Jeanette free to deal with her troublesome child. As she straps on her seatbelt, she says to Jacob, "You should be ashamed of yourself! She's old enough to be your mother."

"Your mother perhaps, not mine," he responds with a twinkle in his eye. "But you should be ashamed of yourself. If it were a forty-year-old guy hitting on you, no one would bat an eyelid. But because she's an older woman, suddenly you have a problem. Besides, it's harmless. Jeanette's been through a lot, and if I can make her day a little bit brighter by giving her a smile, I will do."

Eleanor subsides. There is not much she can say. She has never considered flirting as a charitable endeavour, but Jacob is a free agent – he can do what he wants with whomever he wants.

Having finished earlier than expected, she directs Jacob to drop her at his house instead. He usually leaves the car at the Hall and walks home when his day is done, but with Serena home, no one will be driving anywhere tonight. Besides, Jacob has been on his feet most of the day beside her and could probably do with resting his leg. The day is glorious, and Eleanor contemplates the enjoyment of a slow stroll homewards. This close to Midsummer, the days feel long and lazy, the heat heavy, the land somnolent. The big gates at the end of the West Drive are kept permanently locked, but the small pedestrian gate is always open, so she slips through and makes her way around the broad head of the lake. Here, where the water tumbles over the weir and on into the river, the rushes and duckweed are kept at bay by the movement. Past the weir, the lake curves around and a little way up a jetty leans out into the water. In the summer months, a little rowing boat is tied there, and it is possible to row out to fish for carp in the deepest part of the lake.

Eleanor is ambling along following the course of a family of ducks, the ducklings paddling obediently behind their mother, when she notices someone sitting on the jetty. With an short-brimmed sunhat low on his head, it is hard to be sure, but she has a suspicion as to the angler's identity. She calls out "Hello", and watches him slowly get to his long legs.

The chance of running across Harry might have influenced her decision to walk back today, and the broad smile that creeps across his face as he recognises her makes her glad she made the effort.

"You caught me!" Harry says. "I confess I was asleep on the job."

"And why not? You are on holiday. What is a holiday without a few snoozes in the sun?"

"Have you finished for the day? Have you got time to sit for a bit?" He indicates his camping chair, and as she takes the seat, he perches against one of the jetty supports.

Eleanor looks around and asks, "Are you all alone? Where's the Reverend?"

"Aaron? Off administering to his flock – I may be on holiday, but unfortunately, he isn't."

With no shade on the jetty and the sun reflecting off the water, Eleanor begins to understand the need for a sunhat, no matter how unflattering. She screws up her eyes, regretting leaving her sunglasses in the car.

"It's hot out here," she comments.

"Yes, but I'd better get used to it. When my holiday is over, I'm headed to Africa."

He is watching her intently.

"Oh?" Eleanor can hear her own disappointment lacing that one syllable, and she struggles to regain her composure.

"Whereabouts in Africa?" she asks, although that is not the question she wants to ask.

"Mali."

"Mali?" she echoes, stunned. "It's not exactly safe over there at the moment!"

"Precisely why I'm going. I'm single with no dependants. I'm more expendable."

Is this, Eleanor thinks, *meant to warn me?* Trying to sound unconcerned – as if her curiosity comes from politeness rather than feeling – she says, "Expendable? What on earth will you be doing out there?"

"I'll be working as a missionary on a refugee station," Harry replies.

He's no longer looking at her but at his feet.

Finally, she asks the question she wanted answered from the start: "How long will you be gone?"

He looks away, over the water staring directly at the old folly on the island, just visible among the trees. "Three years."

Eleanor hears the words echo hollowly inside her mind, a death knell to her fantasies. Three years is a long time, as long as she was at Oxford. In three years, she will be thirty, hopefully starting a family.

In case he fancies her affected by his words, she rouses herself enough to say, "So what have you been doing with your time off?"

He tells her where he has been and what he has done. They discuss what he might do with his remaining holiday and he thanks her for her recommendation of the little patisserie. It is inconsequential chatter when all she wishes to do is ask, '*Is it just me? Do you not feel it too? That connection between us?'* After a while, when they reach a pause, Eleanor stands and makes her excuses to leave.

The day feels less beautiful. The comfort of being alone in her room is calling to her, and she suddenly regrets getting Jacob to drop her at his house. She contemplates retracing her steps and having him drive her home, but then she would have to walk past Harry again. She has no option but to go on.

As she clears the copse by the lake, the path winds through the landscaped park. Big stately oaks and fine specimen trees from around the world, given space and time to spread their boughs to their full majesty, stand strategically placed in the rolling grasslands. Eleanor can see, in the distance, two figures, each astride a horse, surrounded by the paraphernalia of the camera crew. An occasional breath of air brings the whir of the drone overhead as it swings to and fro, capturing a bird's eye view of the action.

The baking heat is causing her feet to swell in her shoes, making walking uncomfortable, and a cloud of midges keep pace above her head. The light, cooling breeze seems to have disappeared, and her shirt is sticking to her back. Never has a mile felt so long, and Eleanor is thankful when she finally steps into the cool vestibule of the Hall.

Her spirits are lifted a little to find a cold drink awaiting her in the living room, and she perks up considerably when she sees Serena already curled up in a big armchair. But her cousin's first words cause her mood once again to drop.

"Frankie tells me you fancy someone."

Eleanor, for a moment, wonders what gossip is circulating around the film set, but she is too disheartened to care.

"Who?" she asks flatly.

"Some guy in the pub?"

"Huh!" Eleanor scoffs. "Well, you needn't worry you'll have to pick out a hat – he's off to Mali for three years at the end of this week."

"Bummer!" Serena is all sympathy. "But I think it is interesting your mind leapt to weddings."

Eleanor doesn't respond. She knows it is the safest course with her cousin. Dissembling will only lead to teasing.

"You could just bone him like hell for the rest of the week?" Frankie suggests.

"He's a man of the cloth!" Eleanor protests. "Forget about it. I already have."

"You know the old adage – the best way to get over a man is to get under another. There is an army of men out there to help you forget. If you want, I'll put in a good word for you. Frankie will, too." Serena nods towards the open window where more of the film crew still work outside, and sounds of them packing up their equipment drift in, together with the occasional ribald comment or swear word.

"You sound like Anna," Eleanor laughs. "Thank you for your offer, but I'm not looking for a quick, easy lay."

"Ah! Frankie was right."

"What about?"

"You're looking for love."

"Isn't everyone?"

"Maybe. Maybe not. Some people get to a stage when they tire of the game and they long to settle down. You're tired of the game."

"I'm also tired of this conversation," says Eleanor with some asperity. "Let's conclude I will die an old spinster, and tell me instead what have you been doing?"

Serena does as told and changes the subject. The rest of the family wander in as their day's engagements end. When the twins enter, the noise level picks up. Their cousin has long acted as a bridge between them and their stuffy oldest sister, Serena being closer in temperament to the youngest two but with the benefit of a maturity and worldliness Eleanor has always admired.

Frankie joins them briefly for a genial family dinner, but excuses herself, citing work commitments as soon as dessert has been cleared away. Eleanor has the chance to see her cousin and lover together at last, and she notes how often Serena's eyes rest on her girlfriend. Once more, she considers their life and she wonders if they have made the best choice of work over love. The rest of the family retire to the library, bringing with them bottles of wine and, in Eleanor's case, soda. Their expectation of an agreeable evening, passed in a company where there is much affection, plentiful wit, and good humour but with infrequent contact, is interrupted by the doorbell – a great jangling thing, very effective at alerting the entire house to visitors.

Eleanor, as the sole sober occupant, makes her way to the entrance hall and is surprised to find Ptolemy on the doorstep.

"I hope I'm not intruding?" he says with a courtly nod. "Your mother invited me."

"Not at all," she answers holding the door wide to grant admittance, but she can't help feeling a little disappointed at the thoughtlessness of her mother. It is a family party of people who know one another well; Ptolemy will be bound to feel left out of the in-jokes and family references. Despite her ambivalence towards him, she determines to do her best to include him. When she leads him into the room, she takes him by the elbow and guides him to a seat beside her. For the rest of the evening, she makes a real effort to involve him in the conversation, taking time to explain the various aunts, uncles, cousins, and their spouses and offspring, and all the obtuse allusions to past Mortimer clan events.

Whenever she leans towards him to explain who the protagonist of a story is, he rewards her with a smile that says he is grateful for her attempts at inclusion, and each time she smiles in return. It is hard work, though, not being able to relax into the ebb and flow of the chatter, and she is relieved when Ptolemy rises and thanks everyone.

"You may as well go out the back door," she says, opening the French doors and stepping onto the gravel path. "Here, I'll show you."

Ptolemy follows her out, and she stops by the big conical topiary bush, to point north towards the wrought iron gate set in the garden wall. The moon is swinging overhead in a cloudless sky ablaze with stars. Almost full, it bathes the formal garden in an ethereal light bright enough to pick out any obstacles. Eleanor can hear Ptolemy thanking her but her attention is caught by a bat, probably a common pipistrelle she thinks, zipping erratically in the air.

Then a mouth crushes onto hers and as her lips open in surprise, a slug crawls in. Momentarily stunned, Eleanor freezes but only for a second. As reason returns, she recoils in horror and she pushes Ptolemy away with as much force as she can muster.

"What the fuck?" Eleanor is not given to using profanities, but never has she felt a profanity more called for than now.

Ptolemy appears puzzled. "Eleanor! What's wrong?"

"What's wrong?" Eleanor's temper explodes. "You kissed me! That's what's wrong. Why on earth would you do that?"

"Because I thought you liked me!"

"I do like you. But I don't *like* like you." Eleanor isn't even sure she is making sense to her own ears, but she is remarkably discombobulated by this turn of events. *Discombobulated.* She has always disliked the word, but here, now, she can think of none other more fitting.

"But … I thought …" Ptolemy's face, clear in the bright moonlight, shows only puzzlement.

Eleanor recalls Jamie Smythe's description of Ptolemy and how many women might have thrown themselves at him, and she thinks maybe his reality has become a little distorted.

She orders her thoughts and makes her words as clear as she can: "I see you as a friend. Nothing more."

"But—" he begins.

"No buts, Tolly!" she hisses, exasperated. "In fact, just go. Go!" She is suddenly very tired. Far too tired to deal with this latest complication.

Ptolemy looks at Eleanor, hands either side of her head, fingers cradling her temples and he turns to leave. His footsteps crunch on the gravel as he makes his way to the wrought-iron gate. It opens, falls shut with a clang, and he is gone, swallowed by the shadows.

Eleanor waits for a minute or two. Then she shakes her head, straightens her spine, and turns to re-join her family. When Eleanor steps back inside, she draws out the process of locking the double doors because she still needs the time to recover. Her hands are shaking and her thoughts are skittering. Instead of sitting back down, she makes her excuses and heads to bed.

She is undressing, feeling a little calmer in the familiar surroundings of her room, when a tap on her door quickly followed by Serena sliding in, is enough for her to realise she has not escaped undetected.

"I never had you down as sly," Serena says, indirect as ever.

"What do you mean?"

"All that stuff about your missionary in Mali? Meanwhile you're getting down and dirty with Tolly. There's me offering to set you up, but it looks as if you don't need my help at all."

"I'm not getting down and dirty with Tolly." The frostiness in her words should be warning enough, but Serena's conviction is overriding her perception.

"I saw you made sure he sat right next to you *and* you proceeded to monopolise him all night." Serena looks at Eleanor with her eyebrows arched and a knowing expression on her face.

"You took quite some time out there in the garden, showing him the way out. It's not that difficult. What were the two of you up to?"

Eleanor colours, and Serena leaps to the correct but wrong conclusion.

"Well, well, well. Slyness seems the fashion. You go get him, girl!"

All the time they were growing up, it was Serena who set the pace and Eleanor who followed. Serena who found the route to the cupola, Serena who discovered the hidden cache of sex books in the library, Serena who instigated the spying on Jacob and Matthew.

As Eleanor grew older, she began to realise she herself was a leader in the best sense of the word. Out of the two, she was the one with vision and purpose, whose honesty was above reproach. Most importantly, she was the one who made better decisions. She stopped following her cousin's ideas and started to think for herself. The more she thought, the more she realised Serena was impulsive, flicking between fads, and her cousin did not always choose wisely. Like her relationship with Frankie – Serena enjoys travelling and though she loves Frankie, making relationships work is hard graft requiring compromise and sometimes sacrifice. So, Serena picks the short-term gratification over what would give her long-term happiness.

"You've got it wrong. Tolly did kiss me, out in the topiary, but I don't think of him like that."

"Why ever not?"

Eleanor is silent, partly because she does not want to explain the whole of her history with Ptolemy and partly because she cannot actually answer the question. *Why ever not?*

Serena tries to help out.

"He's hot?"

"Obviously."

"He's rich?"

"Yes, but that shouldn't count."

"Don't be naïve. Of course it counts. Marilyn Monroe got it right in *Gentlemen Prefer Blondes* – '*a man being rich is like a girl being pretty*'."

"Not at all," Eleanor shakes her head, decidedly. "You lived with us. You saw my grandparents. I will never marry for money."

"Who's talking marriage? I'm just saying money makes a man easier to love."

"Marriage *is* the endpoint. I don't want to play-date anymore. I want someone in my bed every night, someone by my side every day. I want children, and my biological clock is ticking."

"So why not Tolly? You're friends, right?"

Eleanor has not yet considered how the incident in the topiary garden might have changed their friendship. It is something she will need to process herself, before she shares her thoughts with others. She defaults to acceptance. "Yes."

"Why? What do you like about him?"

"He's interesting and, for all his grumpiness, he's not unkind, and despite the fact he lies for a living, I think he's a sincere person."

"So, you're single and you don't dislike him and he's evidently into you. I don't get the problem?"

The problem is he kissed her without her consent. The problem is he told everyone nine years ago that she was boring, and even though it was a long time ago, that's not the sort of opinion you change. The problem is, he's witty but not fun. The problem is, she realises now for the first time, he reminds her of Sebastien.

"Are you staying here tonight or with Frankie?" Unwilling to let her irritation with her cousin spill out, Eleanor changes the topic with a question designed to end Serena's interference.

Serena looks at Eleanor as if her wits have slipped. "With Frankie. Which reminds me, I'd better be going."

When Serena finally leaves, Eleanor slips under the lightweight summer duvet and tries to sleep. But despite the lateness of the hour, she finds she cannot. The scene in the garden replays constantly in her mind. Serena's words weigh on her. There had been a time when she would have given anything to kiss Ptolemy. She inspects every move trying to be fair to both parties. Should her behaviour have been different? Should she have been more aware out on the path and forestalled him? She is close to acquitting Ptolemy of all misconduct when she finally pulls out her phone and texts her sister Anna.

When a reply arrives instantly, she connects a call.

"Tolly just kissed me without asking. Serena thinks I am silly for being upset about it. I was angry at that too, but now I don't know if maybe I was." She proceeds to fill Anna in on her evening.

"Did you want him to kiss you?" Anna asks.

"No!"

"Not even a little?"

"No!"

"Then you have your answer," Anna is brusque, for to her the logic is clear. "You didn't lead him on. Even if you had, consent is still required, Eleanor, and he didn't stop to ask first. He made a mistake – a colossal one from the sounds of it."

"Serena thinks none of it matters. He's hot and rich and into me."

"And there you have it!" scoffs her sister. "He's an arrogant, entitled arsehole. People want to think that inside every arrogant entitled arsehole, there is a Mr Darcy trying to get out. But the truth about arrogant, entitled arseholes is …"

"They really are arrogant, entitled arseholes." Eleanor finishes her sister's prompt.

"Who kiss women without being asked," Anna says with finality, then changes the subject. "I saw Jasmine tonight."

"How is she?"

"Still angry with the world."

"It's been a couple of years." It has been a long time since Jasmine has come home. Eleanor would tell her she misses her, except Jasmine is unlikely to listen.

"She always did feel things deeply."

"Is she seeing anyone?" It would have to be a very brave man, if so, one with great self-confidence.

"What do you think?"

"No."

"What about you?"

They chat about Anna's love life and by the time the call ends, Eleanor is feeling better. Her self-recrimination for the fiasco that evening has been obliterated by her sister's forthright rebuttal. If she wants to consider a bright side, at least the events in the garden have driven the meeting with Harry out of her head. Instead of mooning over him, when she falls asleep, the only thing she is wondering is how on earth can she avoid Ptolemy for the rest of the filming when her mother is determined to push them together?

The Music Festival

The next weekend, Eleanor starts her Saturday morning run half an hour earlier than normal. After the unpleasantness with Ptolemy earlier in the week, she doesn't want to risk being alone with another suitor. She is wary of giving off the wrong signals and Jamie is the type to take the smallest sign as encouragement. Men, it seems, routinely over-estimate friendliness from women, and Eleanor is unwilling to risk another embarrassing encounter.

Returning home, sweaty but feeling pleasantly buzzed, she sees a man lazing on the steps of the grand entrance, legs stretched out in front of him. For a moment she worries it might be Jamie, but as she gets closer, she notices the hair is lighter and tinged with gold. He hears her approaching footsteps light on the tarmac and looks up. She cannot help but smile in response to his open-hearted grin, and she forgoes her normal stretch routine to sit on the cold stone beside him.

"You're a little on the early side for a visit."

Harry looks embarrassed but says quietly, "I'm leaving in an hour. I wanted to come and say goodbye."

Eleanor holds his eyes and smiles again, trying to telegraph her genuine good wishes. "Well, I hope you've enjoyed your holiday. It doesn't sound like you will get one again for quite some time."

"It's been more than I hoped for. I will miss this place, and I'll miss you."

He opens his mouth to continue, but Eleanor forestalls his words. She really does not want to be told how much he regrets or does not regret his commitment. He is free to go and she is free to carry on with her life.

"I expect there will be a lot of wonderful experiences awaiting you. I suspect you will soon forget the lot of us." She stands up and dusts herself down. Then she holds out her hand and says, "It was good to meet you."

Harry, understanding he is being duly dismissed, takes her hand and replies, "Likewise."

Eleanor watches Harry until he takes the fork down to the church and disappears from sight. For one mad moment she longs to call him, to tell him she will wait, but she resists the inclination to run after him. He will be gone too long and the man who returns from such a venture will not be the man who left. She tells herself she is being stupid. An affection of a few hours' acquaintance is but an affectation – it is a foolish girl's fancy. He is gone and he will not be back for years. If she is still single on his return, and he happens to visit his friend? She takes a deep breath … The thought of being alone at thirty is horrifying. She shakes her head and continues in to shower and breakfast.

Eleanor is aware she needs a break. Her normal good humour is disrupted, her tolerance for the pretensions of others low. Unfortunately, when you live with your boss, within sight of your office and among your employees, even time outside of work is not a respite. If you want a rest, you must leave home. So today, Eleanor is going to visit her old friend, Charles Fairfax.

Charlie was the first boy Eleanor had ever kissed. In the same town as Eleanor's girls' boarding school, there existed a prestigious boys' public school. Unfortunately, playwrights do not inhabit a single sex world, and when their schools' respective drama clubs needed actors of the wrong sex, they would borrow them from each other.

A direct result of this policy was that fraternisation was common, especially among the older teenagers. More than one girl of Eleanor's acquaintance had had her first grand love affair, closely followed by her first big heartbreak, courtesy of the boys in drama club. Charlie and Eleanor met when he played the male lead and she the female in a house production. On stage, in front of two hundred parents including their own, they had shared a fervent but poignant kiss as Charlie bid his dying fake wife farewell.

Perhaps because they had met thus, with a sanctioned kiss lacking any true passion, they avoided the pitfalls of romance and became friends. Charlie was a boy to break any girl's heart, and it is to Eleanor's credit she was cognisant of the danger. Tanned, blond, lithe, Charlie had no shortage of bedfellows over the years of their acquaintance, but they never included Eleanor. It was not hard for her to resist; Eleanor's taste has always run to tall, dark, and sardonic. And Charlie himself seemed to find her eminently resistible.

That fateful night of their kiss, the Fairfaxes had met the Mortimers and both generations had enjoyed each other's company. They had met up through the years at garden parties, ski parties, and the occasional villa in France. The Fairfax family had a large estate a good three-hour drive from Larkford, so meetings weren't frequent. In a move which Eleanor considers appropriately apt, as all these grand houses were built to entertain, every year around midsummer the Fairfaxes give over a portion of their park to host an open-air, family-focussed music festival. At the same time as the public festival is going on, the Fairfaxes invite their friends and family to join in the fun at a private event. The two parties run side by side and the Fairfaxes' guests can wander between both camps, although a hefty bouncer makes sure the festivalgoers are excluded from the private party.

Eleanor has been a few times, sometimes with her parents or sisters, only once before by herself. While she generally enjoys the event, chatting, dancing and generally making merry with friends, the last time she was there alone, there was more unwanted male attention and it was decidedly less pleasant.

Whenever Eleanor attends an event with Anna or Phoebe or Lily, the men are like moths to their flame and Eleanor is sure to be left in peace. Eleanor has often been grateful she was not born beautiful; beating off unwanted attentions with good grace would be beyond her. She does not have the patience for it, but then neither does she have Anna's pitiless nature. Naturally empathic, the guilt she feels over each disappointed lover erodes her equanimity.

Eleanor is mindful of the latest debacle with Ptolemy and the attentions she has been receiving from Jamie. It seems a single girl, in possession of a stately home, is never in want of unwelcome suitors, and it is this problem which is occupying her thoughts as Jacob turns off the motorway and begins threading the car along the country lanes leading to the Fairfax manor. How to have a good time without being constantly harassed? The idea that sneaks into Eleanor's mind is deceitful but not so much that it troubles her scruples.

"Pull over!" she instructs.

Jacob brings the car to a halt in the first safe place he can find, the muddy entrance to a field, the gate set back. His body twists towards hers and his concern is clear in his eyes.

"Are you all right?"

The weight of the question gives Eleanor pause and she experiences a tendril of guilt at his alarm. Of course, such an instruction from her can have many meanings.

"I'm fine," she replies quickly to alleviate his evident concern. "Take off your jacket!"

The request is given as an order and Jacob finds himself obeying before sense returns. He slides his jacket off his shoulders, folds it neatly, and twists to lay it on the back seat.

"And the tie!" This time his hand goes to his neck but halts before the action is completed.

"Why?"

"I'm going to need you to come with me." Eleanor's explanation is as clear as her intent.

"No, thank you," Jacob declines firmly.

"Yes!" Eleanor is emphatic, as if tone alone can win an argument where reason is lacking. "Take off the tie!"

"No," he states yet again, calm but unyielding.

Eleanor draws a breath, finally attempting to move by reason what she could not move by demand. "If I go in there without you, I'll spend the entire evening dodging unwanted advances. If you're with me, they will leave me alone. I'll be free to talk to my friends, listen to the music, and have a good time."

"I'm not going to be your fake boyfriend, Eleanor."

"I'm not asking you to be my fake boyfriend," she replies, slightly affronted. "You don't have to kiss me or even touch me.

You just have to be my babysitter – which is, after all, what Daddy is paying you to do?" The rise in her voice at the end turns the statement into a challenge.

She gives him a few minutes to think about it and then reinforces her request with a quiet, "Please?" She debates fluttering her eyelashes, but while Phoebe can seem to get acquiescence from any male within a few feet of her eyes, Eleanor is not sure she can achieve the same effect.

Jacob takes longer to consider her words, and she is beginning to believe her cause lost, when he begins pulling the knot of the tie down until it unravels in his hand and he throws it onto the backseat, on top of his jacket.

She relaxes back into her seat and muses, "You're going to need a suitable backstory. I think you should be an accountant – that's appropriately boring."

Jacob frowns. "Why can't I be who I am?"

"Really? You want to go in there as a wounded war hero? Novelty is rare in my friends' lives and you would be new. If you were ugly, it would be bad enough – they would still be slavering over you like a pack of hyenas with a freshly killed water buffalo. But you're not, you're a handsome guy. You'd be harassed by all sexes the entire evening. Of course, no one would be bothering me so my objective would be met. You, on the other hand, you'd be lucky to come out intact! Trust me. You're safest being an accountant." Then a thought strikes her. "But not tax, or you'll have people trying to pick your brains all evening." She thinks for a moment, her head on one side. "Company administration, maybe. A receiver? Yes! Bankruptcy is properly tedious. That'll work."

Eleanor is happily asking and answering her own questions. "That will be how we became friends. We were looking at buying the assets of a failing business from you. What do you think for a business? A cheesemaker would fit our portfolio. I don't think you'll get many questions, but it's best to be prepared. We only met recently … That covers all the stuff you don't know about me."

She looks at him for a moment, studying his face. "A pity you don't wear glasses." She drops her eyes and runs them over his white shirt and dark grey suit trousers, critically. "But your clothes will balance that out. Rather staid. I mean, who wears suit trousers to a music festival."

Jacob makes one more attempt to protest. "I'm really not sure—"

But Eleanor is not going to give him a voice. "It's nothing, really. You just have to stay by my side and block all those wankers who think they are entitled to my hand and my land. Is that too hard?"

"Won't your mates do that?"

Eleanor shrugs. "They'll probably be too drunk."

When Jacob doesn't respond, she continues, "Daddy hired you to look after me, didn't he? How are you going to do that if you're sitting in a car park all evening? Surely you can do this one little thing? After all, what else are you going to do? If you come with me, you can listen to the bands, and there'll be a barbeque and a free bar – not that you can drink because you're driving … And I'll owe you."

Eleanor is not sure which of these arguments wins the day, but Jacob starts the engine and pulls back onto the road. She gives him directions until he turns into an entrance, where stone lions growl from atop substantial piers, the towering wrought black gates folded back to give free passage. He gives Eleanor's name to the attendant, and then follows the signs to park to one side of the manor house, in among a host of other pristine off-road vehicles, all looking as if they've never left tarmac.

They wait for their drinks at the bar, and when the overworked barman slides them over, Jacob takes them from Eleanor's hands and steps back to give her room to move. Two hands curl around his biceps and a refined voice says, "Steady." The hands drop, Jacob turns to apologise, but the person has already veered away, moving swiftly through the crowd, a companion following closely in their wake.

When Eleanor steps up beside him, she whispers, "Close your mouth and stop staring. You're *not* cool."

"But that's …" Jacob falters "… that was the Prime Minister!"

"Mm. I know," Eleanor agrees. "Charlie's father is a Tory peer. He's something of a mover and shaker in the House of Lords, if that's not a contradiction in terms. There will be quite a few politicians from both sides of the House around. They all went to school or college together anyway. It's really not a big world."

She leads a stunned Jacob away and goes in search of her friends. Knowing them well, she had planned on arriving early in the day, in the hope most of them would still be able to maintain a sensible conversation, but in this respect, she has severely underestimated her friends' predilection for gin in the sun. If Eleanor wanted to be kind, she would describe them as squiffy, although Maria is already well on her way to catatonic.

"This is Jake, everyone." Eleanor is holding Jacob's arm, after towing him through the crowd, so she feels his start of surprise. She ignores it and instead points to each in turn naming, "Charlie, Sophia, Bertie, Freddy, Adelaide and Maria."

As one, they turn to inspect the new addition, each giving a greeting in their own way, a "Hi, Jake", or a lethargic wave or a finger lifted. Eleanor guides Jacob to two vacant chairs and they settle themselves down.

"You look like you came straight from work," Sophia drawls lazily from underneath Charlie's arm.

"I did," Jacob replies, the precise accuracy of his statement evident only to Eleanor.

"Jake's doing an urgent pre-pack," Eleanor chimes in, smoothing out the wrinkles in their plot, given it is the weekend. "It's hard work, but it's commercially sensitive so he can't really talk about it."

"You're an accountant?" This comes from Bertie, his head in Freddy's lap, the two of them lolling on a rattan divan.

Jacob nods.

"Which firm?" The obvious question forces Eleanor to acknowledge a career in espionage will never be her destiny. She freezes. She can't answer for him without making Jacob appear a half-wit, but does Jacob even know of any accounting firms?

"KPMG."

With Jacob's quiet lie, Eleanor can breathe again.

"Uh," is the eloquent response and the interrogation lapses with the same languid interest with which it began.

"So, Ellie, what's news in your neck of the woods?" Freddy is alert for gossip.

"They're filming at Larkford."

"God yes, I'd heard! I got a text from Tolly saying he was there," exclaims Charlie. "He said he'd try and come this weekend, but he wasn't sure he'd get away, what with learning lines and practising his stately stride or whatever actors do. I take it he's not with you?"

"No. I haven't seen him recently." Eleanor is sincerely hoping Ptolemy is afflicted with a troublesome case of short-term but acute forgetfulness that keeps him in his trailer, his script in hand. It hadn't occurred to her Ptolemy might make the effort of the six-hour round trip given his heavy filming schedule.

"Do you realise, the three of us haven't been together since we had that punting party on the Thames?" Charlie rambles on, unaware of the niggling fear his words have created. Eleanor is reminded of a beautiful day in May, when she was still madly in love with Sebastien and everyone had taken a break from studying for finals to have fun. "Tolly was going out with that awful girl … Caroline? … Clarissa?"

"Clara," Eleanor supplies.

"Yes! Clara. And she insisted on punting, and got the pole stuck and then let go! The rest of us were pissing ourselves thinking Tolly would have to swim back, but you made Seb row over and get it for them."

Jacob smiles at Eleanor and says, "You've always been soft-hearted."

And Eleanor realises the danger is not from how little he knows her, but rather how much. Fortunately, alcohol blunts the senses and those within hearing are well-libated.

"Soft-headed, more like," Charlie responds and Eleanor retorts with a story of one of Charlie's idiocies, of which there were many, and time passes with them trading stories and drinking and laughing. Sunshine dims to dusk and Eleanor is relaxed and happy for what seems like the first time in months.

Situated as they are, close to the entrance and opposite the bar, the group of friends keep up a running commentary as the guests arrive, a commentary that is by turns witty and scathing, charming and caustic.

"Oh my God!" Freddy drawls in mock disgust watching a middle-aged man with a girl half his age. "Look what Alasdair's just dragged in. Men who like big boobs are so working class!"

"That from a man who's averse to all boobs," Adelaide mocks but still turns to gawp at a familiar TV personality – the recent subject of a very bitter, very messy divorce – and his companion, a pneumatic blonde baby doll.

"Not true ..." Freddy trails his fingers along Bertie's sculpted torso. "I've been captivated by the occasional man-boob at times." The disparagement continues, "But look at her. She must be just out of school. That's just desperate!"

Eleanor, though, is no longer focussed on the scandalous couple because behind them she has glimpsed a tall, imposing character, a familiar and unwelcome figure, momentarily caught in conversation at the entrance to the marquee.

"Oh my God! He's here!" Eleanor, keen to avoid another awkward encounter, this time in public, puts her mouth to Jacob's ear, and in a furious whisper, says, "Dance with me!"

"I haven't mastered dance," Jacob says her with a meaningful look at his feet.

"Look, it's a slow ballad," she points out. "No fancy footwork required. You just have to stand close and sway a bit. Please! Ptolemy Hyde just walked in."

It's a rare man who can resist being a saviour and Jacob is no more proof against it than the average person. He holds out a hand and leads Eleanor onto the dancefloor, as Charlie's raucous, inebriated greeting rings out: "Tollerz!"

Eleanor steps in close, sliding her arms up to rest loosely around Jacob's neck. He keeps his hands on her hips, holding her body a centimetre apart from his. She sways gently, careful to stay in one place and, despite the gulf between them, appearing to the world as if they share the closest intimacy.

"What's the story?" he asks, but this close his breath whispers along her neck, adding to her discomfort.

"I thought he was a friend. Then he kissed me."

"I can see how that might be a little tricky." He draws her fractionally closer, turning them so his body is between her and Ptolemy, effectively screening Eleanor from notice.

The song ends on a long note and the opening bars of a much livelier number bounce from the speakers. Jacob stays in place and attempts to sway more vigorously, but his performance is interrupted by a deep, bass voice.

"You can't avoid me all night, Eleanor."

"Oh, Tolly," Eleanor manages to sound innocent of the accusation, "have you met my friend, Jake?"

"I don't think we've been formally introduced, but I've seen your *driver* around a few times."

Driver. The word drops between them like a grenade, the threat implicit in them wasted on none. Jacob looks at Eleanor; Eleanor looks at Ptolemy. Then she nods, and Jacob's place is taken by the other man, who moves with considerably more style and grace, although Eleanor experiences markedly less enjoyment of his presence.

Eleanor feels, as Ptolemy has imposed his unwelcome company upon her, it is not incumbent on her to start a conversation; she is fully prepared to endure the dance in silence. But the quiet is not about to last. Ptolemy clears his throat, and what he has to say comes as a surprise to Eleanor.

"I wanted to apologise," he starts. "For our last meeting."

"And so you should!" Eleanor replies with some spirit. She gives him credit for the apology; she hadn't thought he had it in him to admit fault. "Your behaviour was nothing less than assault. You're lucky I didn't slap you!"

"I accept that. And I'm truly sorry. I thought you felt the same way," he continues, and he does look remorseful – as much as Ptolemy could ever look less than self-assured. "But I've had time to consider, and I realise I must have misread the entire situation."

"You did." Eleanor is firm, but she acknowledges the sincerity of his words and she does not require anyone to grovel for her forgiveness. "I accept your apology," she says graciously, but cannot resist a reprimand. "In future, perhaps a little hesitancy when moving in for a kiss might be appropriate? An indication of consent is not just good manners but a legal requirement."

Ptolemy nods and Eleanor, deciding their business must be concluded, apology made and accepted – what more is there to say? – makes ready to exit gracefully.

"I'm sorry, but I need to use the ladies," she provides the convenient excuse, not wishing to prolong this moment, but Ptolemy has not finished. He catches her elbow as she turns away.

"Eleanor! I know you said you see me as a friend, and I know I've made a hideous mistake, but please will you consider letting me try again?"

"What do you mean?"

"Let me take you out on a date? Let me see if I can change your mind. I promise I won't touch you without your consent. Eleanor! You have to know! I've always liked you, since the very first time we met at Oxford. That night you sat beside me in the pub and we talked all night – you were so wise, so confident, like some modern-day Athena. But then the next time I saw you, you were cold and distant and I didn't dare ask you for a date. I'd just got up the courage to approach you when you fell for Sebastien and I thought that was it, I'd lost you forever. I only heard from Charlie, a year later, what had happened in Morocco and by then I was filming in Scotland.

"When I found out where we were on location, I thought Fate had finally given me a chance, and when you seemed so happy to sit with me, even though all your family were there that evening, I thought it was destiny. I wanted to believe you felt something for me, the way I feel for you. I realise now I screwed it up, but Eleanor! I have loved you for so long, I cannot let this pass without trying to make it work, to get you to understand, to tell you how I feel. And I'm pleading with you, give me another chance?"

Eleanor is stunned. It is not pleasant to see a proud man begging, and Eleanor is not ignorant of the courage it must have taken, for him to abase himself with this full confession of his unreciprocated feelings. But she is also aware her own inclination is not the same as his. She is not minded to agree, but neither does she want to deny him right here, right now. She is not cruel enough to crush him, perhaps reduce him to tears, surrounded as they are by all their mutual friends. There is only one thing she can say.

"I'll think about it," she promises, looking him directly in the eye so he can see her candour. Mercifully, it appears to be enough for Ptolemy. With one last sigh, his hand drops away and

Eleanor walks off. She is so disconcerted, though, that when pushing through the door of the ladies, she barges into the backside of a well-known politician's wife, head down – quite literally powdering her nose on the vanity unit housing the hand basins – and Eleanor does not even apologise. She locks herself into one of the cubicles until she can calm herself enough to face the festivities with her oblivious friends and the conscious curiosity of Jacob.

It is some minutes before Eleanor can school her unruly mind to stop focussing on Ptolemy's words and put them aside for consideration later. When she finally leaves the safety of her temporary sanctuary and goes in search of Jacob, mindful of the fact she has abandoned him among strangers, she is relieved to find him at the heart of the group of her friends. Ptolemy, thankfully, is nowhere in sight.

Charlie and company have not moved from their spot except to re-fill their balloon glasses with gin, but when Eleanor joins them, she finds another couple are now occupying her chair. She casts about for a spare, but everywhere is fully occupied. She sees Jacob about to stand to offer his seat when Charlie intervenes.

"Don't be a prima donna, Ellie," he drawls languidly from the sofa, Sophia in his arms. "Just sit on Jake's lap."

Eleanor hesitates, not because she minds sitting on Jacob's lap, although she does have a moment's fleeting awareness he may not be so enthusiastic, but because she cannot work out which of his legs is the false one. She has no idea how much damage might be caused by dropping her entire body weight onto the wrong limb.

As if they are of one mind, Jacob pats his right leg and the moment passes. Eleanor takes the indicated side with no one the wiser. She leans back against his torso, conscious of the burden she is, but taking advantage of the support and shelter he offers, grateful there is one sober person she can trust, even if it is only because he is being paid. Jacob's arm steadies her in place and Eleanor finds she can turn to her friends and be as witty and entertaining as normal, with no sign anything remarkable, like a profession of nearly a decade of silent adoration, has ever taken place.

Aware how much she has imposed on Jacob's goodwill, Eleanor tries to make the rest of the evening enjoyable for him. She makes good on her earlier promise, and takes him to listen to some of the stage sets. Among the crowds, Jacob pulls her closer to his side to keep her safe. Eleanor has to admit, he makes a good bodyguard, going from genial to flint-eyed in half a second, frightening away gropers and chancers with one stare. They even have fun together, jigging to the music, eating kebabs and watching the bands. Eventually though, the drunken revelry begins to worry Jacob, especially when some festival-goer, waving his Zippo lighter around with vodka-soaked carelessness, almost sets Eleanor's hair alight. He tries to persuade her to let him take her home, but it is almost midnight before she agrees. So determined is she to ensure Jacob enjoys himself, she entirely misses he has long been wishing for his bed.

There is no need to say farewell. Charlie and Sophia are slumbering on the sofa, and the rest have disappeared into the enveloping night. Jacob helps Eleanor into the car before he climbs into the driver's side and sets off. Eleanor feels the night surround them, herself and Jacob enveloped within the big car, the engine humming low, and she shuts her eyes to think.

Now she has time, she replays Ptolemy's words from earlier and reaches back through the years to recall the night they met. She had felt it too, that attraction, that sense of connection. Which is why she had been so hurt to find out what he really thought of her; to be boring is the most damning of all judgements. If his words tonight were true, his words then were false. She is inclined to believe the older, wiser Ptolemy – although in most cases age brings an ability to lie better, and he has never lacked that skill. She considers what might have been if she had never heard of his unflattering comment. She would have dated Ptolemy, there is no doubt in her mind. He was everything she wanted. There would have been no Sebastien, no hurt, no hesitancy to trust, no aversion to headlong passion. She might well have been married to Ptolemy by now, if things had been different.

If. But the past cannot be changed, and she is no longer the wide-eyed innocent she was at eighteen. Ptolemy's request must be considered in the light of the present, not what might have been. While she is drawn to Ptolemy's strength of character and his passion, she knows from bitter experience that these qualities, untempered, do not make for her own happiness.

Eleanor is jolted out of her musings as the car hits a pothole, and she realises Jacob faces a long drive in the dark. She rouses herself to conversation.

"How did you like my friends?" she asks.

Jacob is slow to answer. Then he says, "They all seem fond of you."

"Ah. How very politic. You didn't like them, then?" Eleanor lays her head against the seat rest and watches Jacob squirm.

"I didn't say that. They just seem like sparkly people."

"Sparkly?"

"Like their lives are perfect. They don't have any worries. They live in a world apart from the rest of us."

"Because they have money?" Eleanor is surprised Jacob is naïve enough to believe money does not have its own set of problems.

"Money and advantage."

"Advantage?"

"Private education, financial security, international travel."

"There are many types of neglect," Eleanor begins, mounting her soapbox. "Sometimes neglect is being left with nannies or stuck in a private boarding school while your parents jet off around the world. And the chance of a world-class education doesn't make up for never being held or tucked up in bed every night. You can be rich and miserable. Misery is no respecter of class."

"Is that how you felt about being sent away to school?"

"No. I always knew I was there to get the best education money could buy, and I was relieved to get away from my grandmother. But some of my friends – they are all clever and it was hard for them to believe they were boarding for their benefit when there were great schools around the corner from their homes. They knew they'd been dumped. Often the housemasters or housemistresses are better at parenting than their own parent, but it is no substitute for the real thing."

"Are you saying your friends were dumped?"

"Freddie's father took his own life, and his mother remarried a wealthy man who didn't have time for children. Maria's mother is an alcoholic mess, and Maria is in danger of following in her mother's footsteps. Adelaide's parents had one of the bitterest, protracted divorces I've ever seen, with her and her sister being used as ammunition by both sides. Most people can't afford long divorce disputes. The rich can. Adelaide was only put in boarding school as a way of hurting her father, by forcing him to pay out more."

Eleanor watches the shadows on Jacob's face and is satisfied from his expression that she has got her point across. Then she relents. "Before you get too carried away with sympathy, let's remember Freddie's father did leave his family with a fortune of fifty million securely salted away in offshore accounts and trusts. Maria's mother goes on a bender in Bermuda, not Bermondsey, and when Adelaide's mother wanted to wound her husband where it hurt most, she gave each child cans of silly string and shaving foam and told them to go make Daddy's red Ferrari Testarossa look like Santa. It was left out in the baking sun for days before he got back."

Eleanor is silent a moment, and then she continues. "I sometimes think Adelaide has it the hardest. While I have every sympathy with a woman scorned, her mother weaponised her kids without an iota of shame and has continued in the same vein since."

Jacob is feeling uncomfortable, like she is playing with him, pulling his empathy this way and that merely to see how he reacts. Defence or offense. He goes with the latter.

"What did Ptolemy want with you?" Jacob expects evasion and is surprised when Eleanor answers.

"He told me he's been in love with me for nine years. He wants me to go on a date."

"Do you want to?"

"Not particularly …"

"Did you tell him that?"

"I said I'd think about it."

So much for trying to avoid thinking about Ptolemy. It seems all roads lead back to him. Eleanor remembers the desperation in Ptolemy's voice as he spoke, the look of wretchedness in his eyes, the turn of his head as he gambled all his pride to try to win her. She realises she is flattered. By anybody's estimation, Ptolemy Hyde is a man of substance, and to have a man like that, an intelligent, rational man, profess his passion for her, a long-lasting, enduring desire, is a compliment of the highest order. She was certain that, had she noticed Ptolemy's intent that night he kissed her and forestalled him, he would have respected her denial; he would never have attempted to force her. And motive had to be considered. He was not attempting to dominate her, to take what he regarded as his entitlement, nor was he trying to control her. What he had done was wrong, but he had clearly acknowledged that. Could she now put it behind her? Could the two of them start again with a clean slate? Cocooned in the warm car, surrounded by the darkness, with Jacob beside her, she thinks maybe she can.

Jacob drives in silence, his own thoughts on the matter contained inside his head. It isn't his place to influence Eleanor; that decision is hers alone. Eleanor doesn't speak again, not until she is clambering out of the car and telling Jacob to drive himself home rather than parking up and walking back.

When she enters the haven of her own bedroom, she breathes a sigh. The trip to Charlie's was supposed to calm her troubled mind, but Eleanor finds it has only increased her confusion. That night, when she slides between her smooth cotton sheets and closes her eyes, she reflects on each part of the day. She seems to have a revolving door of suitors, but as she considers the choices before her, she finds all her thoughts centre on one man.

Lazing on a Sunday Afternoon

Eleanor sleeps late. It is nearly noon before she wakes, and even then, she finds she is sluggish. It is of no matter; she has no engagements today. Her mother did church duty and the twins are taxed with visiting their grandmother. It is hunger and the need to take her medication that eventually gets her moving. She has missed breakfast, but lunch will be served early today as the village cricket team are playing at home.

Lord Larkford is a stalwart of the Larkford Cricket Club. A fairly decent fast bowler in his university days, he still retains enough pace to make a satisfactory showing. It must be allowed, though, if it were not for the desperate shortage of players – the team even press-gangs some of the local teenagers – Eleanor's father might have found himself on the receiving end of a gentle hint to hang up his bat. The club is very inclusive in its membership – the youngest is only twelve and, while the age of the oldest is uncertain, there are some thoroughly grizzled veterans.

Lady Larkford is thankful she has a prior engagement with her friends. Through the passage of years, she has failed to find anything remotely interesting about the game of cricket, whether played at the Oval or on a local pitch. Out of love, she has sat beside her husband at internationals, Twenty20 matches, and inter-village cricket, the only redeeming feature of the game that it is played in summer.

With the twins away on dowager duty, her father turns to her at the lunch table.

"Are you coming along to support us today?" he asks, and Eleanor, tired from the previous day, cannot find a reasonable excuse quick enough.

"Okay …" She shrugs her acquiescence.

And so it is that Eleanor finds herself approaching the little white pavilion. Her progress is slow because it is necessary to say a few words to each person she passes in order to avoid the accusation of arrogance. The club itself is situated on a field to the south of the village, with stunning views over the surrounding countryside. It is over a hundred years old. One of its first members had been Thomas Mortimer, Eleanor's ancestor who died at the Somme just short of his twentieth birthday. If her father had not already been a keen cricketer, he would have still supported the team out of ancestral duty.

The weather is fine, and a goodly number of villagers have turned out, either as players or supporters. Eleanor sees Jacob talking to his father and Jeanette Mulwood, whose oldest boy is on the team. Robert Winter is another long-time player. Although he has a decade on her own father, a lifetime of physical labour has left him with the upper body strength to add pace to the ball.

Eleanor avoids that little group, certain she does not want to see any more of Jeanette's attempts at seduction, and heads for her father. When she finally reaches him, she finds him in good spirits.

"We've got a full team," he says, obviously chuffed. "Stan dropped out because he's too hungover, but little Lola has agreed to step in." He nods towards the sixteen-year-old daughter of the landlord of the Blue Lion, who is, herself, making eyes at the Mulwood boy. "And looking at the opposition, I reckon we've got the edge." Lord Larkford's beady eye is fixed on one of their players, a man of substantial height *and* girth.

The opposition win the toss and go in to bat first. The Baron's estimation of the portly player is proved incorrect when he steps up to the wicket as their opening batsmen and proceeds to whack the ball all over the ground. His impressive innings are aided by the complete inability of the Larkford wicketkeeper to catch a ball. They are coming to the end of the twentieth over and the big batter is still not out when Eleanor feels someone materialising at her elbow.

"Oh, Mrs Fairweather! How are you? Are you enjoying the cricket?" she says politely.

"Julia, please," the woman simpers. "I wonder if you could help me? Please could you find someone to help me carry my cucumber sandwiches back from the car? I was running a little late today."

Eleanor gazes at the mounds of golden-headed scones and clotted cream, cake and quiche, and the inevitable mountain of malt loaf, and doubts anyone will miss the cucumber sandwiches.

"Of course," she responds, but she is not about to ask someone to leave the final overs of the tense innings. "I'll give you a hand."

She indicates for Julia to lead the way and follows along, listening to her companion twitter about trivialities. As they near the car – a great black monster – the slightest breeze brings Eleanor the sound of a moan. It's a short groan – as if cut off – but there is no mistaking the sensuality it contains.

Eleanor turns to her companion and says as loudly as she can without seeming demented, "Have you got your keys? Do we need to go back for them?"

But Eleanor's efforts are for naught. Julia answers, "It's not locked," before continuing with her anecdote, a story showing her stepping in and saving the day for some tiny drama. A clearly audible grunt follows and Eleanor, who is only too aware what the sounds portend is desperate to halt Julia before they become the most embarrassing interruption. She swings around, trying to put her body between Julia and the car, but her foot gets caught in the long grass. Before she can right herself, she falls against Julia and the two of them go down, Eleanor on top. Momentarily winded by Julia's elbow in her midriff, Eleanor lies still until a shriek echoes in her ear.

At the scream, the copulating couple final register they are not alone. The man who is on top disengages, and in the blink of an eye he has slipped between the parked vehicles, one hand clutching his jeans closed so he can run. Vaguely, Eleanor notes he is running in the wrong direction for the exit.

Julia finally finds words. "Help!" she calls, "She's having a fit!"

Eleanor rolls off the mildly hysterical woman. "I'm fine," she clarifies as Kylie, the barmaid at the Blue Lion, dashes over to help, unaware that her shirt is partly open and her ample breasts are threatening to spill out of her bra. "I just tripped." She takes the hand Kylie extends and pulls herself upright.

Eleanor is annoyed by Julia's overreaction. It demonstrates some people still see her epilepsy before they see an ordinary human being and that annoyance taints her words with asperity.

She whispers "Your shirt" to Kylie before helping Julia off the ground as Kylie turns her back and quickly tidies herself.

Wanting to get rid of Julia's company as soon as possible, Eleanor prompts, "Sandwiches?"

Julia opens the car's rear hatch, and Eleanor passes one foil-wrapped tray to Kylie, picks up the other and turns back to the pavilion.

"We'll take these straight there," Eleanor says and strides off, leaving Julia to balance the last tray while she locks up her car.

"You must be mad," Eleanor mutters to Kylie. "I don't think Julia saw anything, but if she did, you are in trouble."

"Please say you won't tell Hank! He'd go mental," the barmaid pleads.

"I won't say anything," Eleanor promises, "but your husband deserves better than this. Were you trying to get caught?"

Kylie looks truly downcast as she contemplates what she has done. "It was all so exciting … I think I got carried away."

Eleanor is no marriage counsellor. She hopes Kylie has learned a lesson today, but beyond that, she won't get involved. She realises Kylie came to her aid when Julia was screaming to the world, and for that kindness, Eleanor will keep her silence.

The two of them deposit their burdens and part ways. Eleanor joins her father, who is waiting his turn to bat.

"How's it going?" she asks.

"Praying for rain," he replies. "It's the only chance we won't be annihilated."

He doesn't get rain but he does get something almost as good. The first sign of a problem is a gentle *moo*, not unusual in the countryside. Except it is followed by a chorus of moos as one after the other a herd of Ayrshires crosses the pitch, ignoring the players and the on-going game and heading straight for the mound of food awaiting the final wicket. The stumps are flattened and the batsmen scramble to get out of the way as the cows converge unerringly on the cricket tea.

At the tables, platters go tumbling as each cow tries to snatch a delicate morsel and noses through the piled goodies in search of a treats.

Hank, Kylie's husband, a big brute of a man who works as a cowman for Carl Taylor, wanders over to Lord Larkford.

"Can't you do something?" Eleanor asks, looking at the devastation.

"Not much to do," he says laconically. "Ayrshires are right contrary buggers. Looks like the match will have to be abandoned."

"Yes, indeed," Lord Larkford agrees happily, rubbing his hands. "It's a draw."

"But what about the cows?" Eleanor protests.

"I'll move them back when they've had enough. Not a man here strong enough to move a cow when she doesn't want to go," he looks around the pitch. One heifer has managed to nose a bowl of potato salad all the way to the infield. "I wonder how they got out?"

Eleanor closes her eyes for a moment. She is pretty sure she knows the answer to his question.

The captain of the opposing team has finally made his way to Lord Larkford. "Sabotage!" he cries.

"Oh no, no, no," Lord Larkford placates. "Some townie has left a gate open somewhere." He looks around at the mutinous faces of the opposing team and wisely decides some amelioration is necessary. "Still we must apologise to your team. As the tea is gone, I think we should repair to the Blue Lion. I'm sure they can rustle up some food. And first round on me, for you and your teammates."

That is all it takes – the promise of free beer. Lord Larkford asks Robert, Hank, and the Mulwood boy to take care of the cows, ensuring they are safely returned to their field and the farmer alerted to their adventure. He also sends Lola running ahead to warn her father of the sudden influx of customers and the need to fire up the chip fryer.

The two cricket teams and a large number of villagers, including Jacob and Julia Fairweather wander up to the pub, in search of sustenance and to continue discussion of the afternoon's events. Eleanor hangs back, her sense of responsibility not allowing her to abandon the work party who remain behind until Robert Winter says gently, "We've got this. Why don't you go and give your dad a hand?"

As Eleanor set off, she notes that Kylie has opted to stay with her husband, picking up and binning the debris whenever possible, removing anything that might be harmful to the livestock. She hopes it is a good sign. When she enters the pub, the first person she sees is Jamie Smythe, sitting with a coterie of villagers, looking quite at home. She has absolutely no wish to join that table but she finds herself at a loss. Jeanette Mulwood is stuck to Jacob's side and that is a tête-à-tête she definitely doesn't want to witness, her father is busy being the convivial host to the opposing team and Julia has monopolised the affable Aaron Parrish. She finds herself in the awkward position of being surrounded by people she has known her entire life and wanting to avoid them all. She contemplates a quiet withdrawal, wondering if anyone would notice when a friendly voice says, "Come on Eleanor. You're blocking the doorway and there's a G & T calling to me."

Relieved she turns to find Claire, accompanied by Mia, two saviours in designer denim. Soon they are ensconced in a little nook having scrounged three stools from around the crowded pub and Eleanor is telling the tale of the cricket match, omitting all mention of the al fresco fornication, when she hears a male voice interrupting her.

"Afternoon, lovely ladies. Can I get any of you a drink?" The invitation is general but Jamie Smythe's predatory gaze is fixed on Eleanor. Perhaps, she thinks, he was running too fast to realise she had recognised him. From barmaid to daughter of the baron in the space of a few hours. Jamie really was a piece of work.

When all the women indicate their fresh drinks and Eleanor pointedly does not invite him to join them, Jamie retires back to his circle of fans. Mia, who notices Claire blushing says, "You didn't? Oh, you did! But I thought had other interests?"

"I do but he caught me at a weak moment." And Eleanor wryly reflects it seems a speciality of Jamie's.

"Well, I don't think you have to worry about him getting in the way of the producer. He seems to have moved on," says Mia. "He was looking at you, Eleanor."

"He was, wasn't he?" Claire turns to Eleanor, who shakes her head.

"Don't care. Not interested."

As if sensing this is a delicate issue, Mia steps in and turns the talk to Claire's abortive pursuit of the producer and the moment passes.

Later, Eleanor and her father walk back home together in the afternoon sunshine. Her father, still in his cricket whites, throws his arm around her and says, "Are you okay, daughter?"

She pauses before answering and then she decides she has to tell someone the truth. "I know how the cows got out of their field."

"Was it deliberate? I would hate to think we cheated to avoid defeat. Happenstance is one thing, sabotage quite another. Definitely not cricket."

"No. I caught Kylie *in flagrante delicto* with Jamie Smythe. I'm pretty sure he left the gate open as he legged it."

"Hm, Hank is a good guy but he does put his wife on a pedestal and worships her. He would go off like a rocket if he suspected Kylie of being unfaithful."

"You won't tell him, will you?"

"If Kylie carries on like that, I won't have to. If she doesn't, I won't need to. Either way…" He leaves the words unsaid. He will not break Eleanor's confidence.

Relieved, Eleanor gives her father a hug.

"Jamie Smythe is that actor fellow?" Her father's brow wrinkles. "That boy is trouble, Eleanor." But he's preaching to the converted.

Despite his charm, or maybe because of it, Eleanor has long had her doubts as to Jamie's sincerity, but even so, he was starting to overcome her natural caution. Now, no matter how brief the glimpse, Eleanor is not going to forget the sight of his condom-covered member being hastily rammed back into his trousers as he legged it to freedom. Sadly, it seems as soon as someone crops up on her list of potential suitors, she has to cross them off. At this rate, Ptolemy will win by virtue of being the last man standing. After all this time, he has definitely proved his persistence.

Jamie's easy charm and even easier morals paint Ptolemy's character in stark relief. One faithful, the other faithless. While Eleanor shies away from the intensity of Ptolemy's emotions, Jamie is a lesson in the dangers of too much lightness in a person – someone who plays at relationships, leaving devastation in his wake, even as he seems to emerge unscathed.

The Baron pulls Eleanor on again, and the two continue discussing the minutiae of the match up until its disruption until they reach the Hall, where they part, each to their own diversion. Her father, relishing the unusual quiet of the afternoon, makes his way to the library, where a particularly complex crime novel awaits, and Eleanor goes to her room. She feels some time spent practising her harp might help stop her fixating on the vagaries of men.

The day has long since ended and all sensible workers are in bed, ready to face the week ahead, bright-eyed and bushy-tailed on the Monday morning. All except Eleanor. It has been an eventful weekend, and tonight she has need of some calm.

Eleanor has always been glad that the room she had been assigned, by chance, at birth, faces west. She has enjoyed many sunsets, sitting at the window, the sash pulled up, the room bathed in shades of red and orange as the day winds to a close. She has developed a habit, when it is late and she needs time for quiet and reflection, of sitting there, the window cranked, her feet pulled up in the big Bergère and letting the forces of nature fill her soul.

The moon is full and the sky almost cloudless. It is bright enough that a slightly inebriated gardener and his soberer son can make their slow way home from the local hostelry without the aid of additional illumination. She sees the two figures separate, the older, drunker one wending his way down the hoggin-covered track, while the younger, spritelier figure takes a seat on the low, lichen-covered wall that separates the manicured gardens from the wilder parkland. If she had any doubt as to his identity, a flare of light from his phone briefly destroys the timeless darkness, clearly illuminating his features before the silvered night descends again.

Eleanor watches for many minutes as he sits staring into the dark woods, looming on the opposite bank. Then she sees his body twist and she follows his direction. A slender figure approaches from the direction of the house, a figure with long hair and a short dress, a woman. She sits beside him, her back to Eleanor. The distance is enough to prohibit the sound of their conversation, but when it is over, the woman lays her head on his shoulder and his arm comes around her body, circling her waist. Then his head dips and Eleanor senses, rather than sees, the tender kiss he places on the top of his companion's head.

"Oh!" Eleanor releases her breath in a whisper that carries into the still night air to wither and die. The feeling of being a voyeur, an interloper in their moment of intimacy, is strong. Eleanor quietly closes the window, draws the curtain and goes to bed.

Mr Darcy Again

When Eleanor opens her eyes the following morning, she regrets her cowardice in letting her scruples send her to bed, for her curiosity about Jacob has been replaced with intense nosiness as to the identity of his lover. Over breakfast, she remembers the way he placed his kiss, gentle and comforting. It speaks of a loving affection, deeply held, far more eloquently than any fervent French kiss.

As her father sits in silence, turning the pages of his paper, she considers the candidates in her head but soon realises there is a vast pool of women it could be. Slender with long, dark hair – the description even matches her own sisters. It occurs to her that, although the girl approached from the direction of the Hall, she may not be from it, but could have come from the village or even from the film encampment. One person it isn't, Eleanor is perversely pleased to note, is Jeanette Mulwood. The farmer has close-cropped hair, the perfect style for a woman with no time to spend tending her tresses every morning.

As Eleanor walks out into the fresh morning air, she forces her mind to put the puzzle aside. She is known to have an open face to those who know her, and Jacob is waiting to take her to her first appointment: signing papers at the firm of solicitors the estate uses – a general practice called Cobb, Cobb and Hoyland. Most of Eleanor's dealings are with their property department, as they draw up the contracts of sale and tenancy documents the estate uses.

Fortunately for Eleanor, Jacob is pre-occupied with the events of the previous day and the village's speculation on who let the cows out. Instead, she remains silent, until Jacob runs to a stop and notices that fact.

"It wasn't you, was it?" he asks, jokingly. Then a thought seems to occur to him. "You were there, I saw you."

She wants to say *I should hope you know by now, that I would never put people, livestock or property at risk by reckless behaviour* but she contents herself with a scathing, "What do you think?"

Although the need to keep his eyes on the road prevents more searching scrutiny of her expression, he flicks a quick glance towards her.

"I don't think it was you. But I think you know who it is."

Eleanor, who prides herself on her honesty and integrity in all her dealings cannot find the words to deny it. She feels she is slowly being drawn into a web of lies to protect a cheating spouse from the consequences of her actions.

Fortunately there is no time for further deliberation as Jacob pulls up in front of the offices of Cobb, Cobb and Hoyland on the High Street. She stands on the pavement and straightens her jacket and trousers – even a linen-mix tends to crease at the slightest provocation in this heat – before marching up the steps into the old Georgian building to start her day's work.

With a full schedule of visits, Jacob and Eleanor are out of the office all day. Between destinations, she is careful to read over the copies of the papers she signed at the solicitors, although she already knows full well what is contained within them – she would never put her signature to a document she has not thoroughly reviewed. So it is, when they pull up outside the Hall at the end of the afternoon, there has been very little conversation. All well and good with regards to the salacious affairs of Sunday afternoon but not so beneficial for uncovering the identity of Jacob's lover.

As she gathers her things and steps out of the car, Eleanor spots Jamie lurking, presumably hovering with the intent of speaking to her after having heard from Kylie. She hurries to intercept him, for this is not a conversation she wants Jacob to overhear. Without waiting to hear what Jamie has to say, what manufactured excuses he has or false protestations, she cuts him short with a furious whisper, "Yes, I saw you. No, I didn't say anything. But *you* need to stay well away from Kylie. She's a married woman!" When Jamie opens his mouth to respond, she overrides him again, pointing a finger at his chest and emphasising every word with a little jab. "This isn't town. This is the country – and jealous husbands have shotguns. If you want someone to shoot off your crown jewels, go right ahead. Otherwise, I repeat, stay away from Kylie!"

The shock on Jamie's face says her words have finally registered. He lifts his hands in a gesture he obviously believes will placate her, finally getting to speak. "Okay! Okay."

It is just as well. Eleanor feels Jacob coming up behind her, adding his presence to bolster her words. Jamie turns on his heel and scurries back to the trailer park. Jacob crooks one brow and asks, "Nora?"

She waves a hand, "Minor problem." Then she gives him a broad smile and bids him good day before trying to escape to the safety of the Hall, where the most heinous crime is who has stolen whose eyeliner.

Even if the hand that closes around her forearm lacks force, Jacob's words are enough to stop her. "Why must he stay away from Kylie?"

The blast which took his lower leg obviously failed to do any lasting damage to his hearing and patently, he was paying more attention to her interaction with Jamie than his mileage records. Eleanor runs through a series of excuses in her head but finds all unconvincing. Meanwhile Jacob, never deficient in sense, makes the connection.

"What's going on, Eleanor? What does it have to do with Kylie? And don't even think about lying to me."

She notes the full use of her name. Her first inclination is to ignore him and stalk inside, then her shoulders slump. This thing with Kylie isn't worth discord between herself and Jacob.

"I caught him and Kylie at it in the car park at the village cricket. Kylie knows it was stupid. Please don't say anything! Especially not to Hank," she stresses and then, remembering Robert Winter's propensity for gossip, adds, "nor your father."

She watches Jacob's expression change as he processes her words. She can see him considering each point and she notes the exact moment he seems to accept her request. "Promise?" she prompts, as if they are standing on the playground and trading cards, not discussing a sordid affair.

Eventually he grinds out, "Okay, I promise."

"Then let go of me." His fingers unpeel from her arm and she rubs the area deliberately, although he was not holding her tight enough to cause pain or even to mark her skin. Accusation in her eyes, she walks away, her feelings in confusion. She engaged in this duplicity to keep a faithless woman and her reckless lover safe from further village gossip. It has not been one day and already two more people know this secret. How long before it is the entire village?

The following morning Eleanor is surprised, and somewhat disconcerted, to come face to face with Ptolemy as she makes her way down to breakfast. With the bulk of the filming until now taking place outside, she had quite forgotten they also had access to the house. Today, the fine summer weather has been interrupted by a series of squally, blustery showers, and the film crew have been driven indoors to shoot the Bennet family scenes.

It is the first time Eleanor has seen Ptolemy in costume, and she is taken aback by how transformative the clothing is. Handsome enough in jeans and shirt, he is the epitome of manliness in Regency wear. The high collar emphasises the strength of his jaw, the form-fitting riding breeches and cut-away jacket seem to frame his assets for the world. Eleanor is momentarily speechless. She has no doubt when this Mr Darcy hits the screens, the collective women of the world – and a fair few men – will swoon.

"Wow ..." The word comes out in a gentle expulsion of breath and then she recollects everything that has passed between them over the last few days. Her head drops in embarrassment. She had come down the stairs with all the clatter of familiarity; there is no way he can have missed her.

They stand frozen in a tableau for a moment and then Eleanor makes to move, with understandable alacrity, towards the door which leads to the safety of the breakfast room. She is chiding herself – she should have used the servants' stair and avoided all this unpleasantness.

"Eleanor! Wait!" Ptolemy holds his hand out as if to stop her, even though the distance between them precludes his touch. His words are enough, though, and she turns back to face him. "I don't want things to be awkward between us."

"They aren't awkward," she lies. "I promised to think about what you said, and I have been doing that."

"And what are your thoughts so far?"

Eleanor forces a lightness into her speech she doesn't feel. "I'm wondering how your co-stars manage to remember their lines when presented with such magnificence!" Sometimes, the only safe way to flatter is to excess. Everyone suspects insincerity, all while the comment is heartfelt and sincere. Ptolemy laughs and the danger is passed.

"How long have you been at it this morning?" she asks.

"Not long – I've been in hair and make-up. I'm waiting for my cue to go striding through the door. They'll be a little while setting up the scene."

But Ptolemy is proved wrong as a black-clad production runner slides around the door and beckons him over.

Eleanor is relieved to have an escape – and not just because her stomach is growling. She smiles and says, "I'll leave you to it", and makes her way to the breakfast room, fairly hopeful she acquitted herself without disgrace. The room is empty, her father having eaten earlier ahead of a meeting with Robert Winter. She anticipates a lonely meal with only her thoughts of Ptolemy for company, but no sooner has she taken a mouthful of granola than she becomes aware of an altercation in the grand stairway; a voice raised in anger drifts through the open doorway. While the twins' squabbles are common, it has been rare to hear a male voice full of fury since her grandfather passed, and even he was only provoked by his wife.

Eleanor abandons her breakfast and goes to intervene. She finds Annabelle, the young housemaid, cowering behind a vacuum cleaner while a man, almost puce in colour, bellows at her. Eleanor slides between the two, physically shielding the girl, even though it puts her uncomfortably close to the irate shouter. Despite his rage-distorted features, she recognises the Producer from her parent's dinner party – a man in mid-life and surely old enough to control his tantrums.

"That is quite enough," she says. She does not raise her voice, but she uses her frostiest inflection. "You are scaring her. Be a gentleman and step back." She flaps her hands at him until he obliges. "Now what is the problem?"

"The problem," he snarls, "is they didn't have vacuum cleaners in the early eighteenth century! We're halfway through a difficult scene and she starts up with that fucking racket."

Eleanor is aware the grand stairway tends to amplify noise – all the limestone and solid walls with no soft furnishings – but such behaviour is not warranted at all.

She makes a show of looking around. "I am aware we gave your production team *Quiet Zone* signs. I see none of them around. Annabelle can hardly be faulted for doing her job if you have failed to do yours. Now we know you need quiet, I'm sure we will oblige, but in future please ensure the signs are used. I suggest you waste no more of your valuable time bullying my staff. After all, you have a scene to re-shoot."

With a visible effort to control himself, the Producer heads back towards the sitting room to find the doorway thronged with crew, eagerly watching the drama unfold. They part before him, and when the door is closed, Eleanor turns to Annabelle and finds her weeping quietly. With a sigh – so much drama to deal with even before breakfast – she takes the young girl by the elbow and guides her to the breakfast room. There she pours a cup of Assam – her father favours strength over complexity of flavour in the mornings – and places it in front of the young housemaid.

Annabelle seems to think she is in trouble. "I told him it's Tuesday morning, Miss. I always do the Grand Stair on Tuesdays and Fridays," she insists.

"Drink your tea, Annabelle." Eleanor hopes her tone conveys kindly reassurance. "I know it is not your fault – you were just doing your job. But I'm afraid you will have to fit things in when the film crew are not around. While they are in the house, there will be some disruption, but we will all just have to bear with it."

Eleanor is relieved to see Mrs Hill appear – the woman has a useful nose for trouble – so she can hand off her charge and return to her breakfast.

While the housekeeper shepherds the maid, still clutching her teacup, out of the room, Eleanor finishes her rather soggy cereal. She still needs to make a decision about Ptolemy, but it seems time to think is a scarce commodity.

When she makes her way to the office, she takes care to avoid the main staircase and any chance of an accidental encounter with an aspiring lover. She reflects if she is to evade an increasing number of men – first Harry, now Jamie and Ptolemy – very soon she will not be able to leave her room.

As soon as she walks into the office, thoughts of Ptolemy are overlaid by the exigencies of work. Suzy, her assistant, is already waiting with a couple of requests from the production company and a cup of overly weak tea. The inconsistency of Suzy's tea-making skills is more than compensated for by her organisational masterwork. Eleanor likes an orderly office – if she goes looking for a tenancy agreement, she wants to find it quickly. She likes suppliers and subcontractors' invoices checked and processed in good time, and she doesn't want to turn up to meetings to find the room double-booked or half the participants missing. Suzy's efficiency makes Eleanor more productive, and both of them understand that. They have settled into a relationship of mutual respect, un-tempered by intimacy. A divorcee with two young children, from what little Eleanor can glean, Suzy's personal life seems chaotic – a stark contrast to her work. It may explain why she is always cheerful on a Monday morning.

When Eleanor first started work at the Estate, she had seen the reverence which characterised her father's dealings with his employees, and determined she would be different. Time had moved on and she felt a friendlier, more collegiate approach would be appropriate.

That lasted a few months, until the office Christmas party. Eleanor, with two glasses of wine more than was wise, had succumbed to the pressure from her workmates and climbed on the stage to sing karaoke. Together with Kevin, one of the groundsmen, she had sung a duet from *Grease*, with all the actions. Three weeks later, her father and mother away on a skiing break, Robert Winter had come to her as head of the Estate. Kevin had been caught smoking dope in his lunch hour. He might have got away with a stiff warning if he had been office-based, but Kevin's job involved driving big tractors and using chainsaws. There was no choice but immediate dismissal and Eleanor had to do it.

Eleanor sat in the room, looking at a face she had drunkenly stroked while she had sung, as she told him to empty his locker and leave the premises under escort. Unwanted memories kept creeping in. In the biggest irony of all, the duet they had crooned that night had been '*You're The One That I Want*'. From that moment on, she realised her staff could never be her friends.

Several years later, and Eleanor has long been disabused of the notion that the Estate staff were a merry band all coming together to pilot Larkford through the troubled economic times. That may be her vision and they may be her priorities – they certainly aren't her workers. Some are loyal; some are not. Some are honest; some are not. Some are competent; some are not. Unfortunately getting all three to co-exist in one individual is uncommon. And, as anyone who has managed a team will attest, many of them are inclined to idleness unless directed otherwise. Employees the calibre of Robert Winter and Mrs Hill are a rarity, and both are approaching retirement in the next few years. Succession planning is one of Eleanor's biggest headaches, right up there with the East Wing roof.

Marooned as she is by her position, Eleanor struggles for friends. The village kids she ran around with as a child have grown. Those who stayed would find her life as alien as she finds theirs. Those who left for university, never came back. There is family, of course, but while she wouldn't hesitate to take her work woes to her father, she shies away from discussing her love life. The twins would be no help, communication with Jasmine is still mostly monosyllabic, and Serena is good for fun but not life advice. Even though Eleanor loves Anna deeply, she is not blind. As a junior doctor, although Anna might have previously been inexperienced in the hardships of life, the pandemic has not left her unscarred. There is a hardness to Anna that prohibits Eleanor from exposing her most vulnerable self. Besides, when you unload your troubles, it is much easier face-to-face, and Anna has already paid her obligatory visit for the next half year.

She has begun to talk to Jacob – having left and returned like her, he seems to straddle both worlds – but while she hopes she can trust his discretion, this would be a level of intimacy beyond her comfort. Besides she has already told him too much, involved him too deeply in her life. As for Charlie and her Oxford friends, they would all be overjoyed to see her with Ptolemy. They would not understand her hesitation.

Although Eleanor tries to tackle her day's tasks, and despite Suzy's best endeavours at keeping her on track, her productivity declines. It is not surprising when half of her mind is preoccupied with thoughts of men, and one in particular. Having successfully ignored the problem of Ptolemy Hyde for two days, she now finds it has only become more pressing. She needs to give Ptolemy an answer, but she currently has no answer to give. On Friday, it would have been a firm no. On Saturday, it was a no but with sympathy. Yesterday, probably no. Today, not sure. She hasn't forgotten the kiss in the topiary but she knew Ptolemy long before that moment. Should she condemn him completely for one ill-judged act?

Morning passes to afternoon. The wind drops, the sun comes out, and still Eleanor has no insight into her own mind. When she takes some paperwork back to Suzy, she sees her assistant staring fixedly out of the window, and crouches down to see what has caught Suzy's attention. Outside, Jacob is valeting the big four-by-four. He stretches across the car to buff the paintwork, his work polo shirt plastered to his lean body with the damp, a breeze ruffling his hair, and it is a scene straight from a soft drink advertisement.

"I think he's taken," Eleanor offers helpfully.

"Uh? Who?" Suzy appears a little discomfited at having been caught daydreaming.

"Jacob."

"Oh my God!" Suzy turns her head and her mouth drops open in astonishment. "You can't be serious! Imagine going to bed with him at night – when he takes his foot off! Eww! Gross!" She gives a fake little shiver, as if something nasty slid down her spine. "Not him. Him!"

Eleanor lifts her eyes to see one of the production crew who has obviously been unloading equipment from one of the trucks. He is in a vest, patches discoloured with sweat, and while he has clearly been working hard, he is now skiving a sneaky fag break, lounging on one of the equipment cases with his feet up.

Obviously Suzy is no rival for Jeanette Mulwood or Jacob's lover, but Eleanor can't help but feel offended on Jacob's behalf. With a shock she realises if she were to have a seizure here, now, Suzy's reaction might well be the same; a shiver and the pronouncement "*Gross!*".

Eleanor's tone is distinctly sharp as she replies, "Well, that's enough ogling for today. Let's get back to work. I need that finished before you head off tonight."

Even if a level of confidence existed between her and Suzy that would allow her to discuss her dating dilemma, she wouldn't be taking dating advice from a woman who chooses a partner purely on looks, with complete disregard for character. That is surely the road to unhappiness. The hard truth is, Harry is gone. Unless she is prepared to wait three years, the brightest prospect she has seen in half a decade has been essentially snuffed out. Out of the single men available, Jamie, from an inauspicious start, had been growing on her. He was charming and witty, but Sunday had revealed he was also feckless and deceitful, for he must have known Kylie was a married woman. Eleanor does not think she could ever contemplate being with a man who places no value on the bonds of relationships. How could you ever trust such a person with your own heart?

No, indeed, Ptolemy may be the best prospect. The repulsion she felt that night by the topiary has abated. She acknowledges she had once felt some sort of attraction for him ... Could she again? But Ptolemy today is not the young, unformed version she'd known at university. While he has had wealth all his life, he is now a man who is worshipped by fans, and adoration can turn heads. She just has to look at herself – the only reason she is contemplating his offer is because he has admitted to loving her for so long. Such an obsession, while flattering, is dangerous. She does not want to encourage him if there is no prospect of loving him in return. He is handsome, certainly, interesting, too, but he is also the type of man to demand all of her. After Sebastien, would she want to give it? Of that, she is doubtful.

By the time Suzy brings her afternoon tea, a cup so stewed it is almost undrinkable, Eleanor has resolved on a way forwards. She will send Ptolemy a message, but even that is not simple.

I need to talk to you. No. *I want to talk to you.* No. Eventually she sends: *I would like to talk to you.*

There is no instant reply – Ptolemy is, after all, on set and phones will be silenced. It isn't until Eleanor is gathering up her papers to lock them away for the night that her phone chimes with the message, *Come to my trailer tonight.* A second text gives directions and a time.

The rest of the workday passes with Eleanor mentally rehearsing the questions she wishes to ask Ptolemy so they are less likely to give offense.

It is with some trepidation that she makes her way to the parked trailers as the sun is lowering in the sky. Not only is this a difficult conversation, but Jamie's lurid descriptions of Ptolemy's love life have left her slightly nervous of arriving early. While she doesn't give Jamie much credit for truthfulness, sometimes the most improbable allegations turn out to be correct, and she does not wish to come face-to-face with one of Ptolemy's conquests. Reality though, as is often the case, is far more mundane than imagination. When Eleanor knocks on the trailer door, Ptolemy opens it with a smile. He is clearly alone – there is no lingering waft of perfume, no articles of women's underwear peeking out from under the furniture, no wine glasses smeared with lipstick by the sink. It is tidy and clean, with nothing other than a few pages of marked-up script lying on a table.

Like any host, Ptolemy offers a choice of beverages, and Eleanor accepts tea with a nod. She does not know how to open this conversation, and she grips the mug he passes her with both hands to stop her uneasiness showing. She takes a seat, ensuring the table is between them. Ptolemy himself seems comfortable, as if having made his declaration on Saturday he is at peace, content to let the future unfold.

"Before we start, I just want to say I still haven't made a decision, but there are some things troubling me and I thought communication was a much better way of resolving them."

Ptolemy bends his head in encouragement and Eleanor continues. "I wanted you to know that the night we first met, I felt the same way, too."

He breathes out a large sigh and she realises that, contrary to appearances, he is not as relaxed as he looks.

"But a little later, I was told you did not like me, that you thought me boring."

"I didn't! Who said that? I would never have told someone that!" protests Ptolemy.

"It doesn't matter," Eleanor says. She is fairly certain of her information for she had had it confirmed by more than one source at the time, including Charlie. She is not surprised his recollection of a nearly decade-old conversation, especially one that does not paint him in a favourable light, is not as accurate as hers. *Her* memories were seared into her brain by the humiliation she felt at the time. "What matters is that, from that point, we each followed a path that leaves us as very different people today. You are a star; I am not."

"In essence, I am the same person I was then."

"In essence, I am not," she replies. "I cannot love blindly. I have learnt to trust my doubts."

"And what do you doubt about me?"

"I doubt whether I can care for you again. I doubt you truly love me as I am now."

"As to the first, let's at least try. For the second, I have said I do. What makes you think it's a lie?"

"You scarcely know me now. Besides, I find it hard to believe you are in love with me when you're busy sleeping with so many other women."

The look of disbelief on his face would be hard to fake, but Eleanor has always known Ptolemy is an excellent actor.

"What other women?" he splutters.

"Cast, crew, anyone." Eleanor makes a vague gesture with her hand, encircling the world.

"Who told you that?" he demands, convincingly insulted.

This time she has no scruples about naming her informant. "Jamie Smythe, mostly."

But his information is backed up by hearsay from her weekly nights out with Frankie and company. A significant number of the female crew are boasting they have slept with Ptolemy Hyde.

“I might’ve known,” he spits. “If that prick spent as much time practising his craft as he does peddling his drugs, he might get somewhere in the world.”

This piece of information leaves Eleanor momentarily aghast. She was reconciled to Jamie’s immorality regarding the sanctity of marriage, but in that he is hardly alone. While her opinion of Jamie has never been high, this new accusation against him shocks her. Faithless, yes. Mercenary, yes. Criminal, no. But the casual way Ptolemy says it, as if it is common knowledge, makes her realise how naïve she still is. Ptolemy was never the sort to repeat idle gossip. He would only have made the accusation if he were certain of its truth. Once she thought she was a good judge of character – then she met Sebastien. Now she believes that anyone who thinks they are a good judge of character is only someone who hasn’t been conned, yet.

“Is this what you truly think of me? No wonder you pushed me away! I swear to you, Eleanor, I have not slept with a single woman since I came here. Not for want of offers either. Chloe from make-up says it’s because they know I have a trust fund – though how they found out about it is anyone’s guess!”

Eleanor drops her eyes and looks at her half-drunk tea. She wisely stays silent.

“You cannot imagine how irritating it is to have some woman forcing her attentions on you irrespective of your own wishes.”

Eleanor almost chokes. People are quick to recognise faults in others while their own go unregulated, but she cannot allow this to pass. “Isn’t that what you did to me?” she asks quietly.

He stills and sits in silence for a moment. “I have already apologised. If you need me to beg, I will.”

“I don’t need you to beg.” Maybe, just a little.

“Do you believe me when I say I have not been screwing half the cast?”

She shrugs and then answers, “I’ll admit I was surprised when he said it. You’ve never needed to bolster your ego with hordes of one-night stands. You could have done that easily enough at Oxford and I never heard that of you.”

"Thank you."

"Although at the dinner party, you did not seem averse to their attentions."

"I'm sorry. I was annoyed you spent so much time flirting with Jamie. I thought to pay you back. It was juvenile and stupid and beneath me. I regretted it as soon as I left."

"What you call flirting, I call chatting. I'm not interested in Jamie Smythe."

"And me? Are you interested in me?"

And just like that, they are back to the crux. After all the discussion, all the straightening out, Eleanor still does not have an answer.

"I don't know."

"Can't we try? Can't we go on a few dates? Take it slowly. Get to know each other again."

"I wish …" Eleanor lets the words trail off, struggling to pick apart the swirls of emotion.

"What do you wish?"

"I wish things had never gone wrong. I wish you and I had sailed off into the sunset, that I had never met Sebastien, that I had never learnt caution, that I am not who I am now."

Ptolemy cannot possibly understand how many red flags he carries for Eleanor. Everything that makes him profoundly attractive to others, frightens her. His passion, his trade, his status. None of these quiet her hesitation. A man who lies easily, indeed, one who essentially lies for a living and does so very convincingly. Someone who inherently believes he is better than others and who has never been disadvantaged in his life. The parallels between him and Sebastien leave her gasping. They have the same strong self-belief, the same disregard for those they see as weaker, the same intense focus on what they want in life, and her instinct is to run in the opposite direction.

She also knows her fears are unreasonable. She knows Ptolemy is not Sebastien, his childish behaviour at the dinner party and the incident in the topiary notwithstanding. He has acknowledged his fault in both, a thing her former lover would never have done. But whether it is age or experience, what she values in a man today is not what she looked for at eighteen. She would take a man now with an appalling taste in music and art, who is colour-blind in his dress sense, but who in essence was decent and kind and clever and witty. The last man she dated, a solicitor in Norton, managed the first two, but was woefully short on the last. Harry, she was sure, possessed all four. Ptolemy, she fears, might only have one.

There is silence between them, Ptolemy waiting patiently for Eleanor to come to a decision. Eventually she says, "I'll let you know. In any case, I'm busy the rest of this week and I'm away for the weekend, looking at a wedding hotel. I'll text you when I'm back."

She stands to leave and he rises with her. There is a moment of awkwardness when neither of them knows what to do. A handshake feels too formal. Eventually, Ptolemy leans towards her and gently places his cheek next to hers, his strong hands closing on her shoulders. There is a moment of contact, a brief sensation of evening bristle, and it is gone. Eleanor nods and makes for the door. When she is safely outside, she gulps in the night air and walks home the long way.

A Wedding Takes Place

Unable to identify Jacob's lover through close observation, Eleanor concocts a plan to ask Jacob, somewhat indirectly. While cunning is to be deplored, of course, tact in approach is to be admired. How she asks the question will be critical, and she has a strategy which needs to be put into effect at the earliest opportunity.

But while Jacob is nominally Eleanor's driver, the entire family seems to usurp her privilege. Her mother, who has never been keen on steering anything mechanical, whether it be a lawnmower or a Lamborghini, has been happily commandeering Jacob from the start. Her sisters, more interested in Jacob's strong back and large hands, have press-ganged him into their numerous shopping trips as bag-carrier, and even her father has occasionally seized the advantage of having a sober chauffeur.

Unfortunately for Eleanor, this week her family seems intent on conspiring to prevent her ever having a quiet, confidential moment with Jacob. When he drives her to lunch with their old nanny, her mother comes along, and when she goes to her book club meeting in a Bridgetown pub, the twins hitch a ride as well.

Eleanor considers manufacturing an occasion which will require Jacob's attendance, but even that is not without difficulty. It is getting later into the week and dangerously close to the point at which Eleanor's plan becomes unusable when an opportunity finally presents itself.

After Jacob picks her up, she waits until they are safely underway before she begins with her seemingly innocent query: "Are you all packed for the weekend?"

"Not really," he shrugs. "I don't need much time to pack. I'm used to having to shift without much notice."

"You know," she says artlessly, "you will be in your own room. If you wanted to bring someone else with you, you could."

"Someone else?"

Oh my God! Eleanor thinks. *How obvious do I have to be?* Aloud, she says, "Yes, someone. Like a girlfriend? She might like a free weekend in a swanky hotel. There's a spa too."

Eleanor is watching Jacob's reaction and he looks puzzled. Not at all what she was going for.

"We'll be working," he says, glancing across at her. "I'll be on my own." He has the most peculiar look on his face, a mix of suspicion and interest, as if he thinks *she* might proposition *him*. She realises now how her enquiries about his lover may be misconstrued and she decides the wisest course may be silence, to avoid Jacob interpreting her natural inquisitiveness as personal interest. No sense in digging herself any deeper.

So it is, when Jacob collects her after work on Friday, there are only two cases in the boot – one for her and one for him. She gives him instructions for the journey, then settles back in her seat, grateful she doesn't have to undertake this drive herself, following a full day of work. They have a long journey ahead, made more difficult by the summer holiday traffic fleeing the hot, choked city for crystal seas and salty breeze. For the first part of the trip, until they get to London, they will be going against the main flow and the driving will be easy.

"What's the point of this visit?" Jacob asks after steering onto the dual carriageway and setting the cruise control.

"Ellingham Hall is one of the top ten wedding hotels in Britain. It's extremely profitable, pandemic aside. Daddy has arranged for us to meet with the hotel manager and the events team. There's a big wedding tomorrow taking over the entire hotel, and we'll be able to see exactly what happens behind the scenes." Eleanor has become so used to Jacob accompanying her on visits, she has never stopped to consider his presence is not required on this one.

With the prospect of being able to renovate the East Wing born out of the *Pride and Prejudice* series, comes the debate about what to do with it. It will need to earn its keep, becoming an asset rather than the enormous liability it currently is. The family does not need it to provide housing, being amply accommodated in the North and South Wings. One proposition is to use it as a wedding venue, massively expanding their current business. But running a hotel successfully is a far more complex business than renting out a few rooms and linking in external caterers and marquee erectors.

Lord Larkford counts among his old school chums the owner of Ellingham Hall and has reached across his nebulous web of friendships to arrange this fact-finding mission. Eleanor is unconvinced the wedding business is the correct answer – she feels it will be disruptive to the family still living at Larkford and doubts, even with the East Wing, whether they could operate at a scale that would turn a profit. She also believes the development funds required to convert it into a luxurious hotel will be astronomical and the interest on those loans, crippling.

Still, she is open to being persuaded. *Fortis Fortuna Adiuvat* – fortune favours the bold – is on enough coats-of-arms in stately homes that Eleanor has no doubt as to its efficacy, and she knows her natural inclination to caution is a drawback in business. She is not averse to taking a risk, provided it is a well-researched, thoroughly calculated risk.

In order to fortify themselves for the horrendous traffic ahead, they stop for a rather lacklustre fish and chips at a pub just off the motorway, before they hit the London Orbital. Despite being close to midsummer, it is dark by the time Jacob finally turns the big car in at a grand entrance, huge buff stone pillars tastefully uplit, and follows the signs directing them towards the hotel reception.

Valets in uniform lurk at the entrance, and Eleanor smiles to herself at the echo of days long gone when liveried footmen would have awaited the carriages of guests. She leaves Jacob to manage the cases and walks inside the reception area. There are other guests waiting, so she takes the time to look around. They have eschewed the traditional chest-high reception counter in favour of reproduction antique desks which complement the overstuffed damask sofas and high-backed winged chairs framing the fireplace. When the receptionist is free, Eleanor approaches, giving her name and the Larkford Estate, unsure as to how this was booked.

"Oh, yes! We've been expecting you. The manager will be down right away. She will take you to your suite."

Suite? Eleanor is surprised. She had thought they would have been in the two smallest rooms, probably tucked away just above the kitchen extractor. A few moments later, a neatly coiffed, petite, middle-aged woman joins them, smiling warmly, her hand outstretched. "I'm Lara Chen, the manager here. I'm pleased to meet you."

Eleanor introduces herself and Jacob, and the manager chirps on, "I hope your journey wasn't too horrendous. The traffic on the roads with this fine weather, every weekend it's just choked." She continues her chatter as she leads them up the wide stairs, fingers trailing the mahogany handrail. Lara Chen proceeds at some pace for a woman with little legs, finally stopping at the end of a corridor to open a door with a flourish. They walk ahead of her into a large lounge area with what promises to be jaw-dropping views over the countryside in the daylight, distant lights glittering in patches. Doors on either side of the room presumably lead to the bedrooms.

Lara Chen follows them in. "I hope this is satisfactory? Lord Ellingham was very clear we should give you every assistance."

"It's lovely. Thank you," Eleanor murmurs, full of silent admiration for the strength of her father's old-boy network as the manager crosses the room to open one of the bedroom doors.

"The suite has two bedrooms, both with en suite bathrooms, of course. We find it is very popular with Mother and Bride, but the bride tomorrow lives locally. Although the hotel is full, this suite wasn't required."

"How many rooms do you have?"

"Fifty-three, but they aren't all in the main house. A lot of the outbuildings have been converted. The guest list tomorrow runs to four hundred, but not all the guests stay with us." Lara Chen carries on running through the features of their bedrooms and the hotel facilities. One of the rooms has a four-poster bed complete with canopy which Eleanor feels is quite frankly over the top, but she realises it probably helps a bride to feel special, waking up in such splendour on her wedding day. She directs Jacob to put her case in the simpler room. Four-posters make her feel claustrophobic.

"What time do things start tomorrow?" she asks the manager.

"I'll be in at six."

"We'll see you then."

Lara Chen nods and withdraws, leaving Jacob and Eleanor alone.

"It's certainly impressive," she says, looking around. She sits on one of the chairs, "And comfortable."

Jacob murmurs agreement, hovering in the entrance to his room. "If you don't need anything, Nora, I'd like to get to bed."

Aware he is probably tired after the long drive, she nods. He closes his door but Eleanor stays put for a while. The twinkle of lights from a village on the horizon disappear as, one by one, the villagers go to bed. The night is clear and country-dark. The stars are bright, like diamonds strewn across black silk. She can see the vague vestiges of star clusters or nebulae, hinting at the immensity of the universe.

The hotel is as she had expected, for she has stayed in many such before, but never with an eye to emulating them. Now she notices the smooth competence of the staff, the quality of the finishes, and the unobtrusive luxury. She considers how Lara Chen makes Eleanor's own staff, even the redoubtable Mrs Hill, look gauche and inept, and she despairs of ever achieving this standard. But Lord Ellingham started with nothing, albeit forty years ago, as the boom in the City funded the rise in popularity of the country house hotel. Perhaps there is still hope. What she needs is to stop fretting and get some sleep, in preparation for the next day.

If Eleanor had admired Lara Chen's poise and ability on Friday evening, by lunchtime on Saturday her admiration for the woman is positively overflowing. After a breakfast courtesy of twenty-four-hour room service due to the early start, Eleanor and Jacob are in the reception area by six. Jacob appears unaffected by the premature start to the day, but Eleanor, who had trouble getting to sleep, is realising she will only make it through the day with copious coffee. The manager joins them, looking as fresh and composed as she had been the night before. Lara Chen has arranged for them to spend time with every section involved in the day from housekeeping to events management. And through all the chaos, she moves, leaving staff calm and industrious in her wake, solving crisis after crisis as the day progresses.

The treacherous British weather plays its own part, too, with a downpour requiring the outdoor bar to be moved to an indoor location at the last minute. Still, the bride and groom and their four hundred guests slip happily into inebriation as the day winds into evening, unaware of the frantic efforts of the hotel staff to ensure their every dream is realised.

Lara Chen has finally ended her shift, an extraordinarily long day which speaks to her dedication, and gone home. Eleanor, with Jacob at her heel, is ready for a rest. They are making their way back from the marquee when they pass the door to the spa. The manager had requested they avoid the spa earlier, as a lot of guests had booked treatments. Tired as she is, Eleanor is tempted to skip it, but then her annoying sense of responsibility kicks in and she turns towards the glass doors in the gothic-arched entrance. She feels a little guilty as she does; she and Jacob have been on their feet all day, and she has seen him surreptitiously rubbing his left leg a couple of times.

"It won't take long," she says, unsure whether she is reassuring Jacob or herself.

They give their names to the teenaged girl on the desk and are waved through. "Feel free to look around," she says. "There's no one around now – they're all at the wedding. The therapists have all gone home, but I can't leave until closing time. You can take your time." She turns her attention back to her phone.

Eleanor wanders through the spa, Jacob trailing behind her while she checks out the treatment rooms and notes the finish in the bathrooms and changing rooms, taking photos to aid her memory. When they come to the pool, Eleanor's intake of breath is sincere. A vast glass dome is held up by square columns in tones of cream to offset the deep turquoise of the water, and which complement the honed limestone floor. The pool is immense but has none of the chlorinated starkness of a municipal bath. Instead, the effect is like the Great Roman Bath, but as if newly built in Aquae Sulis. With the night sky and the soft low-level lighting, it seems like swimming under the stars. Once more, Eleanor is impressed with the design elements of the hotel and realises the magnitude of the task of building the equivalent at home.

"It's magnificent," she sighs. "You can feel the calm. Can you imagine swimming in this at the end of a long working day, stretching out all your muscles, letting your cares float away?"

While Jacob believes the calm owes more to the absence of people than the construction, he registers her tone of wistful longing and instead he says, "Why don't you?"

"We're here to work not play, Jacob," she reprimands swiftly and is startled by his laugh in response.

"Something got twisted in your ancestry, Nora. You're supposed to be the feckless, fun-loving Cavalier nobility, but you've ended up as a Puritan with an overdose of work ethic. Most adults only work in order to have fun, but you – you work instead of fun. I'm sure when you were a child you knew how to play." He looks directly at her. "If you want to swim, then swim."

"I can't."

"Can't?"

"Water is lethal with epilepsy." And doesn't she know the truth of that statement. "Unless there is a lifeguard close by."

"I'm here."

"Can you swim?"

"You tell me, Nora? Apparently, someone spent one summer checking that out." She blushes and he continues, "My leg is not swim-rated, and anyway it would act like an anchor, but I can take it off. I can swim without it – enough to get you to safety."

Eleanor gnaws her bottom lip. "I don't have a costume."

"I thought you were the problem-solver? You're wearing underwear, aren't you?" Jacob asks, desperately hoping the answer to the question is affirmative and that he has not just laid himself wide open to a charge of workplace harassment. "What's the difference between a bikini and a bra and knickers?"

The water beckons, one more longing look at the pool enough to make the decision. She starts to undo the buttons on her shirt, but some Victorian ideal of modesty has her turning her back to her companion. When she turns around again, Jacob is sitting on a lounger with his prosthetic laid beside him and he is rolling down the gel liner and sock. He doesn't bother with the buttons on his shirt, removing it simply by hauling the collar over his head.

With some measure of tact, Eleanor turns her attention back to the water and slides in from the side. She begins her warm-up with a gentle breaststroke, enjoying the feeling as the blood starts to flow through her muscles. She is halfway down the pool when Jacob catches up. As she switches to crawl, he matches her stroke and pace. Several lengths later, she's feeling pleasantly exhausted, so she moves to the hot tub in the bottom corner and lets the jets work on her body. Jacob doesn't join her; he sits on the side with his legs in the warm pool water.

"Thank you," Eleanor sighs, and Jacob nods in acknowledgement.

They sit in silence for a minute, listening to the soft lap of the residual waves in the pool and the quiet bubble of the tub.

Eleanor's gaze ranges across his body. One arm and thigh is flecked with scars, although the rest of him is unmarked. When she reaches out with her hand, she lightly brushes his knee with her fingers. It seems the most impersonal place to touch; she doesn't want to lay her hand on his thigh or – god forbid – his stump, but not to touch him while she asks her deeply personal question seems impossible.

She keeps her voice low, almost a whisper. "How did it happen?"

Jacob grimaces, and for a moment she thinks he won't answer. Then his eyes meet hers and he says, "I actually don't remember." The truth was he tried very hard not to remember. He didn't want to be one of those ex-servicemen who woke every night screaming, to find their wives pinned beneath them, terrified. He draws a breath. "One moment I was in a village in East Africa, standing by a wall, talking to a government soldier. We'd just been briefed about local activity by a sergeant, a guy called Ethan Cooper, and I was watching him walk away from us. The next I knew, I was waking up in a hospital bed. A rocket came out of nowhere, hit the wall. I was told Ethan pulled me out, put a tourniquet on me, kept me alive. The other guy wasn't so lucky.

"It could've been worse. I was partly shielded by the guy who died – he caught the worst of the blast – and I'm eternally grateful the Army issues us with ballistic boxers and pelvic protection." He chuckles and splays his hand across his crotch. Eleanor blushes. She knows she started this intimate conversation, but Jacob has demolished her carefully set boundaries. Nothing new there.

"Does it hurt?"

He shrugs. "If I'm on it too long, yes. And my leg aches a bit sometimes because walking with a prosthetic is harder. But by and large it doesn't give me any trouble." He pauses and then continues, softly. "Still a shock, though, when I look in a mirror."

Unwilling to push the confidence any further, Eleanor leans back in the water and closes her eyes for a few minutes, leaving Jacob in peace.

Then she says, "Well, I think we'd better get going. They'll be wanting to lock up soon."

She stands and makes her way to the steps at the end of the hot tub. Jacob slips back into the pool and swims across to where he left his leg. To give him privacy as he struggles out of the water, Eleanor turns to the stack of towels. Winding one around her body and another around her hair, she picks up a third and makes her way over to Jacob, now perched on a lounger having heaved himself out of the water. She hands him the towel and walks over to her own clothes. A shimmy and a wriggle, and her wet bra and knickers are off, the towel still in place. She slides her shirt over and her skirt under before unwinding the cloth. It would normally take no time for a veteran of school changing rooms, but she draws it out, carefully folding the wet towel and wringing out her underwear, giving Jacob the privacy she feels necessary.

When she can no longer avoid it, she turns around. Jacob is clothed on his bottom half and his prothesis is attached. While he is unbuttoning his shirt to put it on again, Eleanor busies herself taking the used towels to the labelled bin. They leave the spa with a chorus of '*Thank you*'s to the receptionist. As they re-enter the hotel lobby, busy with wedding guests, Eleanor fancies they look like the same professionals who started this morning – apart from their wet hair – until Jacob leans over with an impertinent whisper, "Oh my, Miss Mortimer! Are you going commando?"

She pins him with a glare. "It is a mystery to me, how you survived over a decade in the Army. Impertinence seems to be embedded in your bones."

But the comment is enough to reinforce Eleanor's own sense of propriety and impropriety. She feels self-conscious, walking down corridors and past inebriated wedding guests with her breasts unrestrained and her skirt lining sliding over her bottom, until they finally reach the safety of their suite.

As she prepares for bed, pulling on her pyjama bottoms and buttoning the top, Eleanor knows she has overdone it. She feels odd, as if she is disconnected from her own body, and she knows what this portends. She takes a step towards the centre of the room and calls out urgently "Jake!" before she falls.

Jacob, with two closed doors and a lounge between them, cannot hear her cry but the peaceful routine of his evening ablutions is indecently interrupted by the siren emanating from his phone. Without pausing to spit his toothpaste, he grabs a towel and hurries to Eleanor's room. He does not bother with a knock but rushes to kneel by her side, stopping only to kick away anything in her reach. The towel, he folds and places under her head before he glances at his watch to check the time. Two minutes go by while her body trembles and shakes. Jacob watches and waits and speaks a stream of soothing nonsense as the electrical storm takes over Eleanor's brain, lighting up her synapses like a firework display. If any part of her brain is registering, he hopes she is reassured.

"It's okay, sweetheart," he whispers. "I'm with you. It's just a seizure. I'll be here. Don't worry, you'll be okay in a bit. I won't leave you." And he repeats the words over and over and over until she stills.

He blows out a sigh of relief. From the start, he has known this was a possibility – his training in the Army as a combat medical technician was the reason Lord Larkford had been keen to have him for the job, the reason for his enhanced pay. He had hoped, for Eleanor's sake, this part of his employment would never be required. Jacob has experienced the trauma of men wounded in all sorts of situations, both in battle and on the base, and has borne it with a quiet composure. What he is unprepared for is how much he is shaken to see Eleanor, whose competence and decorum is in her very soul, lying vulnerable and helpless.

Jacob is conflicted; it will distress her to know he has seen her like this, her clothes soaked in urine and saliva drooling from her mouth, but he is also sure she would not want anyone else to see it. He processes these thoughts even as he continues, mechanically checking her tongue is intact and rolling her over into the recovery position to prevent her from choking. He goes back to his room to grab his pulse-oximeter from his suitcase, clipping it onto her finger to check her heart rate and blood oxygen levels. Finding all is normal, reassures him. Unless she has another seizure tonight, she won't need an ambulance.

He needs to clean her up; leaving her in sodden clothes until she wakes tomorrow might cause sores. Covering her with a towel, he strips her clothing from the waist down. He moves her out of the patch of dampness she is lying in, sliding her along the carpet until she is clear of body fluids. She moans at the rough treatment and then slips away again. He wants to find her another pair of pyjamas, but he hesitates to rummage through her suitcase; he feels he has violated her enough.

He fetches his own spare pyjama bottoms. They are too large for her but the drawstring waist just about holds on her hips. He stands back to consider. She would be far more comfortable in the bed, sleeping deeply, brain and body exhausted. Unfortunately, the risk of another seizure in the night is non-zero, and even though her wrist monitor will message his phone, there is a chance she could fall out of bed before he can get to her. Moreover, he is not sure he can lift her; he has never before tried to raise such a weight from down on the floor wearing his prosthesis, especially after the long day he has already had. It would do neither of them any good to have him incapacitated as well. In the end, he straddles her body, squats, slides his hands under her armpits and pulls her to him. It is enough to take the few steps to reach the bed.

She stirs again with the jostling, mutters, and falls sleep once more, leaving him to position her in the centre of the bed. Once she is safely settled, he collects his phone from his room and calls her father. The epilepsy monitor will have notified him as well, and Jacob is aware that if she were his daughter, he would be gnawing his arm off in desperation by now. The call doesn't take long; Peregrine Mortimer just needs re-assurance Jacob is with her and she isn't hurt.

Jacob also contacts Reception and requests breakfast in the room for the morning. He doesn't know how Eleanor will feel when she wakes, but he guesses that she won't be in the mood to deal with other people. She is a private person, so his automatic reaction is to keep news of this confined. Instead of calling housekeeping, he mops up the urine on the carpet with a towel and dabs over the area with watered-down shampoo before he starts to take care of himself. He takes his toiletries to her bathroom so he can be close by. He dare not take a shower or leave her too long, but he has to care for his stump and clean the socket and gel liner of his prosthesis. He packed a couple of changes of sock for his stump. For the moment, he tosses the used one in the corner, and lays the limb flat, away from where it could do damage to Eleanor if she wanders in the night.

Jacob is thankful he thought to pack his folding, carbon-fibre crutch. While he can manage well enough without it, he is vain enough not to want Eleanor witnessing him hopping, crawling, or bottom-shuffling if she needs anything in the night. There is bottled water by the bed and he adds painkillers before he seats himself on the mattress beside her. Over the years, there have been far worse places he has slept, and his body has no problem finding oblivion.

Eleanor wakes in the morning to birdsong and sunshine and the feel of another form next to hers. Her movement disturbs Jacob and he sits bolt upright, before swinging his legs off the bed, grabbing his crutch and lifting up. In an instant, they are once again employer and employee.

"I'm sorry," he mumbles. "I needed to sleep if I was to drive today, but I didn't think you should be left alone."

Eleanor lies back on the pillows. She takes note of the pyjamas she has on, the mismatching bottoms, and the bed she is lying in. She can hardly meet his eyes.

Jacob is silent, waiting for Eleanor to process all the information, her quick mind following each implication. She will know she has had a seizure, but it is one thing to know and another to witness. Jacob is grateful for small mercies; that epilepsy removes her consciousness means she will never have to see herself.

"Apparently," she exhales, "in the matter of private parts, we are now equal. I know quite how small you get when submerged in cold water and you know how overdue I am for a bikini wax."

Jacob leaves her alone to dress. She takes so long in the shower that by the time she emerges fully dressed, he has already set up the breakfast trays in the lounge. Eleanor has no appetite, but she needs to eat. She forces some small pastries past her lips while she considers how best to proceed.

Eventually, she looks Jacob directly in the eyes. "Now you know," she says. "You might be broken on the outside, but I'm broken on the inside and neither of us can ever be whole again." Then she folds up her napkin, places it carefully on the tray, and escapes to her room.

While Jacob is arranging for the car to be brought around, Eleanor sits on the arm of a sofa in the hotel lobby. Lara Chen is off today, but Eleanor has left a note of thanks at the reception desk. She pulls out her phone from her jacket pocket and sends a text to her father. It simply says, *I'm okay.*

Jacob is waiting by the passenger door of the big, black car, but as she arrives by his side, he doesn't move. He looks at Eleanor with styled hair, flawless make-up, and impeccable outfit, the very picture of organisational efficiency, and he understands.

"It must be hard," he says, "never knowing when you will lose all control of your body. But for the record, I don't think you are broken."

There is a subtle difference between pity and sympathy, and Eleanor understands what is being offered here. She nods. Truthfully, she too does not see either of them as broken; her words had only been prompted by the frustration she feels as the clock resets. She needs to be a year seizure-free. When he opens the door for her, she takes her seat with a smile. She will let him have this win in their endless game of Who Gets to the Car Door First.

Once the journey is underway, she lies her head back against the seat. Eleanor wonders if Jacob's lover knows how lucky she is. Then her thoughts turn to her own situation. Perhaps it is time to be more pragmatic – to stop ignoring what is right in front of her. She fishes out her phone. She has one more message she needs to send, to Ptolemy Hyde: *I'm free Wednesday evening*. Then she turns it off, drops it back into her bag, and sets about bracing herself for the long road home.

It's a Date

When Wednesday evening rolls around, it's not without trepidation that Eleanor awaits Ptolemy's arrival. Dressed as instructed in jeans and shirt, she sticks her hands in her back pockets to keep them still. She is nervous for more than one reason. She dreads her mother happening on them and imbuing the whole date with a level of meaning that would have her picking out a wedding hat the next day. And she very much wants to avoid the twins, for they would not hold back from teasing. In truth, she would rather be seen by no one: staff, cast, family, or villager.

She is watching the North Drive for any sign of Ptolemy coming from the trailers and jumps when his voice calls from the side. He seems to have come from set – although filming finished a while ago and the technicians have almost finished packing up – for he is still in costume, albeit much stripped down. His jacket, waistcoat, and cravat are gone, and the shirt is open-necked but he still wears breeches tucked into riding boots.

He is clearly pleased to see her, as if he doubted to the last whether she would be here. "Come," he says, holding out a hand. She considers for a second, and then places her fingers in his – this is a date after all, understood as such by both parties.

He leads her around the corner and along until they round the catering tent, and she sees two horses being held by a groom, one a magnificent bay mare and another, two hands shorter, a chestnut. Ptolemy is watching her closely as she approaches the horses.

"Oh," she says, "aren't they beautiful?" She strokes her hand down the nose of the chestnut mare and murmurs some more nonsense, just sounds to introduce herself to the animal.

There haven't been horses on the Estate since her grandfather started to decline. The old Baron had been keen on outdoor pursuits, probably because his wife was not. Although raised in the hunting, shooting, fishing tradition, and able to handle both sixteen hands and twelve bore, her father did not have the same enthusiasms, and equably excised the expense of stable-hands, farriers, and vets. Eleanor has not mourned the loss of odour of horse and dog ingrained into the soft furnishings of the house. Still, she is fond of both riding and horses.

"Is this our date?" she asks, eyeing the tack.

"I thought we could go for a picnic," he says with a nod towards the saddlebags on the bay.

Eleanor considers her epilepsy for a moment; the day has been relatively easy and the few seconds of sensation that precede a seizure should be sufficient for her to dismount. The chestnut mare appears to have a calm temperament and she has ridden many times before without incident. When the groom hands her a helmet, she takes it. He holds her horse's bridle, while she mounts, foot in the stirrup and hand on the pommel. The stretch is enough to make her muscles protest, and she anticipates she will ache tomorrow – sitting at a desk for years has probably shortened critical muscle groups used in riding – but it does not dampen her delight.

Ptolemy indicates she should lead, and he follows behind until the path widens enough for the two mounts to walk side by side, their riders conversing. Eleanor heads for the heath to the north-west of the Estate, where the sandy grass is ideal to let the horses have their head. Then she urges the mare forwards, and the little chestnut picks up her pace until she is galloping, Eleanor perched in her stirrups. The bay easily keeps pace, and she sees Ptolemy beside her, grinning widely.

They pull up just before the bridleway enters a covert. Eleanor knows better than to go thundering through the woods, knocking walkers, runners, and cyclists aside. It seems like an age since she had such fun, and she is looking forward to the return journey.

After an hour, Eleanor guides them to a hill, a grassy clearing in the forest, but the tree on its summit blew over in a storm a long time ago. The trunk has been left, home to millipedes and earthworms, but providing an ideal backrest for a picnic. They tie the reins to a branch, and Ptolemy unrolls the blanket strapped behind his saddle, spreading it on the ground. From one side of his saddlebags, he starts to extract food.

"I've gone quite traditional," he says. "Pork pies, scotch eggs, cheese, and some crudités. Chocolate and flapjacks for dessert. I was afraid less robust fare would not survive the mode of transportation."

"That all sounds perfectly wonderful to me," Eleanor announces, shaking out her hair from her helmet. "I'm ravenous."

He pulls out a couple of soft drink cans. "I know you don't drink much," he says, and Eleanor wonders if he knows why. As far as she is aware, her epilepsy is not widely known outside of her inner circle of friends – unless, like Charlie, people happen to know her from her schooldays when it was not well-controlled.

Ptolemy pats the blanket next to him and she sits, stretching her legs out before her. He passes her a wipe for her hands. "You thought of everything," she comments, handing it back to him to put with the rest of the rubbish, and taking a pork pie in exchange.

"Ah!" she breathes at one point, between the eating and chatting, tipping her head right back and looking up at the sky. "It feels so good to get away from it all. Just for a bit."

"You could appoint an Estate manager," Ptolemy remarks. "Then you would be free."

Eleanor makes a non-committal noise. They could indeed replace her with an Estate manager, but the money for the post would mean the lake was not dredged nor the pot-holed drives repaired. Above all, if someone else did the job she loved, then this place and its people would no longer be hers; it would become nothing beyond a holiday home. She would no longer belong to them, and then what would be the purpose of her life? The link that binds her to this land, that defines her, would be broken. The Hydes have money and property on every continent but not *land*. How can she explain all this on a first date?

So, she passes off his suggestion with "Can't afford one". And, Ptolemy takes her at her word and leaves it alone.

He tips his head back to match hers. "We'll be leaving soon."

"Yes, I know. End of this week."

"We're shooting the village scenes next, then Pemberley and Hunsford. I shall be sad to go."

"Me too," says Eleanor, thinking of the daily hire fee, but then Ptolemy's hand closes around hers and she realises her words have been misconstrued. She thinks about correcting him but changes her mind. Let his understanding be; despite everything that has passed between them, she *will* be sad to see him go.

They sit in silence this way for some time until Eleanor, noting the sun lowering toward the horizon, says, "We should get going before we are riding through rough country in the dark. There's little moon tonight."

Ptolemy packs the rubbish back into the saddlebags, now much reduced in bulk. He folds the blanket, and then rolls it and secures it before he halts. Eleanor has already mounted, and he is forced to stare up at her as he asks, "Have you enjoyed it?"

She smiles at him, her face full of genuine warmth. "I have, Ptolemy," she says. "In fact, I think this may be the best first date I've ever had."

"Good," he replies, but he's already turned his back to place his foot in the stirrup and so she cannot judge the impact of her words. When he wheels his horse around to ride beside her, his face is inscrutable.

By the time they reach the heath, the light is failing and Eleanor knows a full-out gallop would be madness. Feeling carefree, she risks a canter, the horses' hooves throwing up little clouds of dry, sandy soil. Eleanor is laughing as they reach the other side. Even though there is no way her chestnut mare could beat the big bay, Ptolemy has let her win.

By the time they arrive back at the ancient oak tree behind the catering tent, night is underway. Eleanor slides off her horse and gives it a pat and words of gratitude. She hands her reins and helmet to Ptolemy, but he puts them down and closes the distance between them.

This is it. The moment has been building all evening. Eleanor looks up at him, invitation in her eyes, but he stops. After all that has happened between them, she understands his hesitation. She reaches a hand to slide her fingers along his jaw, curling them around the curve of his neck, gently pulling his head down. His lips touch hers, the kiss soft, uncertain, but hiding a depth of passion. Then she steps back and turns for home.

His hand catches hers. “Eleanor,” he calls, “may I see you again?”

“Oh yes,” she breathes. “Most definitely.” Then she pulls her hand from his and disappears into the night.

She has no sooner closed the massive oak entrance door behind her, than she hears her mother’s dulcet tones raised in query, “Eleanor, is that you?”

Closing her eyes and muttering a fervent prayer for fortitude, she walks into the Great Hall to find the Baroness. Her mother must have been lingering on purpose, waiting for her, for there is no other reason to be standing here, alone. Which means she suspects. Eleanor could have sworn it was too dark for her mother to have observed her return, unless she is the possessor of a pair of night-vision goggles, which may not be too much of a stretch.

“It’s very late,” Lady Larkford says. “Where on earth have you been? You missed dinner.”

“I ate out.”

Eleanor is familiar with this routine. Her mother prompts for information; Eleanor dissembles. She does not know why she does it. She could easily be open and honest, but some part of her delights in it.

“Your father said he saw you with Tolly?”

“Did he?” Eleanor is moving quickly, across the room towards the exit to the Grand Stair, but she is not going fast enough to avoid her mother’s next question.

“Oh, Eleanor,” she says, oozing with delight, “are you dating Tolly Hyde?”

Eleanor pushes the door open wide. She considers her answer. Any attempt to evade or mislead may get back to Ptolemy and cause him pain.

“I guess so,” she says as she steps through and lets it fall closed behind her.

Despite Eleanor's best attempts to avoid her mother's questions, when Friday evening rolls around, her mother is on the porch steps to see her clamber into Ptolemy's car. Lady Larkford's cheerful, "Tissy and I are so pleased to see you two hitting it off," starts the idea that, maybe, her mother is getting her information from the other side.

As they pull up outside the best hotel in Bridgetown, Eleanor can't help but feel a little disappointed. The first date set the bar high, but this is very *ordinary*. She has been here on dates many times before, for drinks in the bar or food in the restaurant and once, memorably, for sex in the superior suite. She smiles, remembering the double-ended copper bath, and Ptolemy takes it for approval.

"I thought it would be good to talk, especially as we leave tomorrow," he says, as the maître d' guides them through the restaurant.

"I hate to say it, but I shall be glad to get back to normal. It has been harder work than I anticipated having your lot around," Eleanor says as she takes her place and the maître d' goes on to seat Ptolemy.

The early part of the evening goes smoothly; they have many acquaintances in common and similar tastes in a lot of matters. But the relaxed tone hits a bump when Ptolemy mentions a cousin of his who has been appointed to the board of a FTSE 100 company.

"That can't be right?" Eleanor questions. "He's far too young."

Ptolemy shrugs. "People like us – we were born to lead, born to be the best."

Eleanor is familiar with this sentiment; she has heard it many times before, phrased in different ways but always coming down to the same thing. The rich are rich because they are better, and the poor are poor because they deserve to be.

Trained as a historian, she is well-aware of the fallacy. There are plenty of displaced royals and younger sons of the nobility who are sunk in ignominy – proof there is nothing inherently superior about the genetics of the nobility. The persistence of the wealthy classes is rather more about the robustness of primogeniture in preserving money and control of valuable assets like land, ports, coalfields, and latterly, banks. The advantage of providing a well-fed start in life, a sound education, and the confidence to take risks knowing someone – parents, siblings, friends – will likely bail you out, is also incalculable.

Unlike some noble families, the Barons of Larkford have lived lives of quiet indistinction. Apart from her great-grandfather's brothers, travelling back through the centuries yields no tales of Mortimer heroics, of astounding leadership. Even the honour Percival, Thomas, and Samuel achieved in dying for their country was shared with a dozen others from the parish.

During the English Civil War, the then Baron of Larkford had wisely kept his head down, until forced to make a choice. Reluctantly, he came out on the side of the Parliamentarians – although that itself had repercussions for them during the Restoration. Eleanor often wonders about the twists and turns of history. For if her family had not been excluded from royal favour and the award of lucrative civil offices, they would not have turned to trade and investment before other noble families. The vast growth in their fortune which led to the expansion of the Hall and the acquisition of assets that have sustained them over the last penurious century can be directly linked to that one hesitant decision.

Eleanor is a student of history. She understands well her family's fortunes were built on the back of a legacy of misery from colonial imperialism and slavery. Apart from a scattering of notable Abolitionist peers, there were few noble families in Britain not so tainted, a shameful distinction that also applied to a large number of clergymen, businessmen and a horde of widows. She knows – it is a matter of record – that to her family's shame, her ancestor put profit before principle and voted against the Slavery Abolition Act.

No one can change the deeds their ancestors have done; sinner to saint, hero or coward, their stories are already written. Eleanor and her father make sure to practise compassion in their own business dealings. Perhaps because most of Eleanor's ancestors failed to distinguish themselves, while she has a deep sense of the continuity of her line, she has no particular pride in her ancestry. She has always felt her position is her good fortune rather than her right and her due. After all, if the twins had been boys, would she be heir now?

The conviction of upper-class supremacy is so ingrained in society at all levels that Eleanor seldom bothers to correct it. Tonight, though, she is unwilling to let it pass. If Ptolemy is to persist in loving her, he should love the reality, not some illusion conjured by his imagination. Eleanor's views on this are influenced by her father and the two of them have worked together to improve matters on the Estate, providing long leases for security of tenure and opportunities for further education while employed.

"Really?" queries Eleanor. "You don't think we are born to advantage? Given the best nutrition from the cradle, sent to the finest schools, introduced to the world beyond our own doorstep? You don't think it makes a difference that we have always been expected to succeed, never labelled with failure?"

"Not particularly, no. Those factors play a part, but in the end, you must admit, you and I and people like us succeed not just because we are clever but because we apply ourselves. We have self-discipline. Anyone can do anything they want, if only they want it badly enough and work at it hard enough. That they don't, is their own choice."

"Oh," says Eleanor angrily, "that old lie. Funny, I've never seen a colour-blind pilot, or a female imam or a poor judge."

"You're being absurd! We are not talking about disability here, just normal, everyday people."

Eleanor's eyebrows shoot up. He has riled her now. "Being a woman is a disability?"

"No! You know I didn't mean that."

"My point is that society imposes constraints that hinder most and help the already privileged few. You don't get judges from poor backgrounds because barristers get paid a pittance in the early years, neatly eliminating anyone who does not have other methods of financial support. They just don't get the opportunity!"

"We have state schools and state-supported universities. The opportunity is there, and anyone who wanted it enough would still do it!" Ptolemy mistakes Eleanor's exasperated silence at his protestation for potential surrender. He moves in for his coup-de-grace. "We are here and they are there. Take that driver of yours."

"Jacob?" Eleanor frowns.

"Him. He's with you a lot of the time. He sees who you are, what you do, but even so, given a choice between you and some pretty face, he'd probably choose the other woman."

This evening, it seems where Eleanor is concerned, Ptolemy has a particular talent for offending. It takes him a moment to discover his mistake, amply aided by the expression of affront evident on her face. Then he hurries to make good.

"What I meant was, you are wonderful. You are fascinating – clever and insightful and kind – and he probably can't see that. I can see it, but men like that cannot."

Eleanor ignores the flattery and says, "I believe he appreciates rather more of my character than you allow."

"Has he asked you out?"

"No. He has someone."

"And she's not you," Ptolemy points out. "I rest my case."

Eleanor's vanity is happier with the idea that the local bachelors don't make the approach from a lack of any expectation of success, rather than their inability to perceive her good qualities. Or the subjugation of those qualities to beauty – a characteristic that was notably missing from Ptolemy's list.

"You underestimate Jacob," she says briskly. "And there are plenty of examples of leadership, innovation and integrity from the working class, and cowardice, corruption, and stupidity in the aristocracy to undermine your theory."

"I don't want to argue with you tonight." Ptolemy finally finds wisdom and retreats.

He takes her hand, but Eleanor is not prepared to let him off the hook yet.

"You don't think I'm attractive?" she needles. "Clever, insightful, kind. But not attractive?" She holds her breath, waiting for his answer. If he tells her she is beautiful, she will not believe another word out of his mouth.

"Eleanor, I've stood opposite beautiful women on screen and kissed them without the slightest feeling of longing. But you," his fingers trace along the line of her hand, tipping it palm up, closing his fingers around it, "I'm attracted to every single part of you."

Well done! Eleanor couldn't have scripted a better answer herself. She allows him to change the subject, and they move on to a discussion of the latest prize-winning novel to be televised.

Later, when the last drop of coffee has been drunk and the last scrap of dessert savoured, Ptolemy walks Eleanor out into the cooler night air, his arm around her shoulders. Since their argument, he has been charming and attentive, and Eleanor cannot help but be seduced. They stop by his car, and Ptolemy brings his other hand up to rest on her hip.

This time when his head lowers, he doesn't pause waiting for her to demur. He brings his mouth very, very slowly to meet hers. She tingles with anticipation, recalling their last kiss. His lips are soft and warm but firm, and she responds, letting hers part. Ptolemy, almost trembling with the effort of holding back, allows himself to savour her, tongue embracing tongue, for a few moments and then he pulls away. Emboldened by her acceptance of his kiss, he draws her in closer until her head rests on his shoulder and her body is pressed between his and the car door.

He soaks in the sensation of being in contact with her body, her entire length touching his. Eleanor feels his warmth disappear as he steps back to open the car door. She understands why he is going so slowly – he does not want to spook her – but it is slightly frustrating. Maybe, she realises, that is his intent, to tease. If so, he is slyer than she imagined.

The journey home is quiet, as if the kiss has superseded conversation. When Ptolemy pulls up outside the Hall, she expects him to lean in for another, but he gets out of the car. She follows his action and clambers out just as he arrives to help her.

"We leave tomorrow," he says, and Eleanor doesn't bother to respond. They both are aware of this fact.

He takes both her hands in his and looks straight into her eyes, every detail of her face clear in the harsh, white glare of the security lights. "May I come and see you next weekend?" he asks. "I can stay somewhere locally if your parents would prefer."

Eleanor privately thinks her mother would be pushing Ptolemy through her daughter's bedroom door if she had a chance, but it is too soon to complicate this nascent relationship with sex. Eleanor is still not sure of her feelings for Ptolemy. She feels the attraction, but she is not about to abandon herself wildly to his passion.

She senses the effort it takes him every time to pull back. If she were to open the floodgates, how would either of them survive? She does believe he is in love with her, but it is a perfect version of her, one far from reality. He thinks her clever, compassionate, strong but there is also weak, selfish, snarky Eleanor, hiding from scrutiny, but there nonetheless.

So, she sets out the parameters clearly in her reply. "Don't be silly, Ptolemy. I would love to see you, and my parents would be very happy to have you stay. It would be no trouble at all to get one of the guest rooms ready."

He smiles. He has what he wanted, and he understands exactly what is unsaid. He draws her closer and his hands move to her body, sliding around her waist and up her back. His kiss is more fervent than earlier; he is growing bolder.

Footsteps force them apart. "Good evening, Miss Mortimer."

The gruff tones of Robert Winter steeped in the local accent contrast with the younger, more moderate cadence of his son as he echoes, "Evening, Nora."

"Robert, Jacob," Eleanor acknowledges the two men as they continue on their way home. She turns for her door, suddenly unwilling to linger. "Good night, Tolly. I'll see you next weekend."

Ah well, she thinks as she closes the door behind her. They were bound to learn of it sooner or later. If her mother's boasting fails to broadcast her new liaison widely enough, Robert Winter will certainly ensure no one in the village is left ignorant.

Cry Havoc and Let Loose Phoebe and Lily

If Eleanor had expected the departure of the production company to lessen her workload, she was to be sorely disappointed. Larkford's normal event business resumes, and many of the alterations requested by the film company need to be returned to their ordinary state, and yet more work, postponed due to the filming, must now be undertaken.

It is with relief that she and Jacob head home from the final meeting of the day, at the end of the working week. Ptolemy is due tomorrow, and she is looking forward to seeing him again. She has been kept abreast of news from the film company by a stream of messages, not only from Ptolemy, but also from Frankie, Claire and Mia, less so from Chloe. She does not know whether they are aware of her relationship with Ptolemy; she has not announced it for fear of bragging, but neither she nor Ptolemy hid their movements the last week of filming. She has every reason to believe he would openly acknowledge her as his girlfriend if asked, or if propositioned, but to ask her friends to confirm it would be to invite attention and maybe disappointment.

If Eleanor had understood what this day would portend, however, she would have gone back to bed and refused to get out. The first indication anything is amiss is when Jacob slows and pulls the big car over onto the soft verge to let an ambulance pass. They are not far outside the village, and they are easily able to keep pace with it. They follow the flashing lights as they progress along the country lane, enter the village, and then slow to turn into the Estate.

Eleanor's alarm is mirrored by Jacob's as he breaks the speed limit to close the gap between the two vehicles. She fears her father has collapsed with a heart attack like his father before him; she can practically see him sprawled on the floor, his staff panicking. That fear is supplanted by a different anxiety when the ambulance continues past the Hall and takes the narrow West Drive. It now seems more likely one of their employees has had an accident. Gruesome images flash through her mind, agriculture being the most dangerous occupation in Britain. Jacob's apprehension, she knows, is for his father, especially as their cottage lies at the end of the West Drive, although what the hard-working gardener would be doing home at this time is a mystery.

The hoggin laid by the film company allows the vehicle much faster progress than would have been possible on the old, pot-holed road. Without instruction from Eleanor, Jacob follows the ambulance down the track. It skids to a halt, its wheels slipping on the unmade surface. With more control, Jacob brings the car to a stop behind it, and the two of them jump out in time to see two women descend from the ambulance, one older, one younger, both shrouded in the dark green uniform of a paramedic. They turn to stare across the water.

Eleanor hurries up, breathing a little fast. "Can I help you at all?" Then she adds in response to their frowns, "I'm Eleanor Mortimer. I'm the owner of the Estate." At moments like these, accuracy is unwarranted.

The younger defers to the older, who says, "We've been called to an incident. The caller gave co-ordinates, but they seem to be coming from over there." She points towards the island at the centre of the lake.

"There's a boat," Eleanor says, also pointing. "We keep it tied to the jetty just round here."

Jacob is already moving, but the paramedics are headed back to the ambulance.

"Just a minute," the older one calls. When she re-appears, she is carrying a massive day-glow backpack and the other one has an orange spinal board. "Control have lost contact with the person who called it in," she says.

Jacob intercepts them. His phone is out, but he pulls it away from his ear to talk to them. "No boat," he says shortly. "They must have taken it over."

"Do you have another?" the grey-haired paramedic asks.

Eleanor shrugs. She is about to pull out her phone to call someone, but Jacob is ahead of her. "Dad says they used to have one, but the engine is seized." His next words are directed at Eleanor. "They haven't got around to replacing it, seeing as it won't be needed until you dredge the lake next."

The afternoon sun is gleaming on the smooth water, tiny puffs of cloud reflected on its surface, the deep blue of the summer sky reflected in the lake. The leaves on the magnificent trees are still, but the merest breath of wind rustles the reeds on the edge of the lake. A bird calls completing the idyllic scene. It is alien to think that someone, somewhere is in danger.

Jacob looks at the lake and then turns back to the paramedics. "Someone will have to swim over to fetch it."

"Can't swim," the young one says.

"I can," says the older one. She looks down at her rounded waist, and then meets Jacob's eyes with a challenge. "But I'll never make it across."

Thinking this is fast turning into a debacle, Eleanor says, "I'll go."

"Not happening, Eleanor." Jacob shakes his head. "If you have a seizure halfway there, you'll drown." His hands have already moved to his waist as he unbuckles his belt. He drops his trousers and hears the quick intake of breath from the younger paramedic as she catches sight of his prosthetic. It is precisely why he always wears trousers. He knows other men from the rehabilitation centre who wore shorts from day one; a way of forcing the world to acknowledge their injury. But Jacob lives in a village with his life under a microscope and it is one thing for people to know, another for them to see. Some stop seeing the person and see only the disability.

The older paramedic steps forwards. "You shouldn't do this, sir. We will notify the Coastguard. They will attend."

"How long will that take?"

She shrugs.

"By the time they get here, I could probably have swum there and back ten times." He chucks Eleanor his phone. "Dad is on his way," he says. His shirt follows his trousers, and Eleanor has just time to accept the bundle that is thrust at her before he is striding to the jetty.

At the very end, he detaches his false leg and lays it safely on the wooden boards, with its liner and sock, before he slides into the water. He takes two breaststrokes till he is clear of the duckweed and then he switches to crawl. Strong, steady strokes power him through the water, heading for the matching quay on the island.

In only a few minutes, it's hard to distinguish the swimmer, his head dark against the water. An all-terrain vehicle roars up, and Robert Winter and one of the young groundsmen spring off.

"Where is he?" he demands of Eleanor, all of his normal deference forgotten. Eleanor points, but Robert's eyes are far older than hers and if she can hardly see Jacob, she doubts the father can. "In the water," she adds helpfully.

They wait in silence until Eleanor sees a flash of white. "He's there," she announces to his father, in case the older man missed it. She also sees a figure run down the island's jetty and stop at the end before retreating again. Then it's back to waiting as the little rowing boat starts its slow progress back across the lake. Robert and the young lad, Oliver, are waiting to pull the boat in and haul Jacob out of it. Robert changes place with his son and beckons the paramedics forwards.

"I'm not sure we're allowed to do this without life vests," protests the elder.

"I don't think you have much choice," growls Robert. "Get in."

Eleanor is grateful for once someone else is taking the role of bad cop, so she adds some encouragement. "Robert knows what he's doing. You'll be safe with him," she says although she has no idea of the truth of the statement. Robert works for her father, not her.

"Lily is on the other side," Jacob cuts in. "Phoebe stayed with the casualty. He fell through the roof. I think he's in quite a bad way."

His words appear to spur the young paramedic into action. She moves to the end of the pier and hands her spinal board over to Robert Winter before clambering inexpertly on board. The older one follows, carrying the bulky rucksack, reluctance clear in every shuffled step. The boat dips low in the water as she lands. Oliver pushes the boat out and Robert Winter takes an oar into each of his large, capable hands and begins a firm, regular stroke – dip, pull, lift. Despite having twenty-five years on his son, he powers the over-full boat to the other side as speedily as his son rowed it back, empty.

Satisfied Jacob is fine, merely exhausted, Eleanor uses her phone to call first Lily and then Phoebe, but both calls go straight to voicemail. She is not surprised that Phoebe doesn't answer, for her sister often forgets to charge her phone, usually relying on Lily to be more organised. Frustrated, she concentrates her attention on the crossing. The fluorescent bag is a much easier marker to track as the little boat surges its way across.

Clutching Jacob's clothes to herself as if they form a comfort blanket, she is vaguely aware of the two men beside her muttering, but her eyes remain fixed on the rescuers as she follows their progress. Despite her reassurances to the paramedic, the boat is so low in the water that the danger of sinking is not zero, an occurrence that could turn an emergency into a disaster. Suddenly, Eleanor feels Jacob's clothes being tugged out of her hands.

"Miss," Oliver says as he yanks at the bundle once more. So intently has she been watching the far shore, she has missed the lad's repeated requests. Lily, for it must be her, runs down the island jetty once more and catches the mooring rope thrown to her. Slowly, the rescue party climb out of the boat onto the quay, and then the bright backpack is moving along the pier and into the trees.

Jacob, his prosthetic re-attached, strips off his wet undershorts, revealing one buttock flecked with small scars, the same as his amputated leg. Eleanor might wonder at his lack of modesty in front of her, if they weren't both aware she has seen it all before, when his skin was still smooth and unmarked, when both his legs were intact. He uses his shirt to dry his body and then pulls on his trousers, tugging them carefully over the obstacle of his false foot. He hands Oliver his keys and the lad takes off at a sprint.

"You did well," Eleanor says, the words inadequate. She wants to embrace Jacob, but that would be inappropriate, especially shirtless as he is. She contents herself with putting a hand on his shoulder. "Thank you."

Jacob nods. But the drama is far from over, and they both turn to watch for movement on the island. Oliver finally returns with a white T-shirt and towels for Jacob. Jacob dries his hair, slips on the tee, and hangs his shirt and towel out in the sun on the posts supporting the jetty. Then Eleanor, Jacob, and Oliver sit at the end of the quay to wait.

A half hour later and Eleanor's patience is strained enough for her to murmur, "What the hell are they doing over there?" Although she has been sitting quietly, her mind is anything but. Who is injured? Why are they on the island? And, with a sense of dread that makes her stomach clench, how are Lily and Phoebe involved?

While she is generally scathing about the twins and their irresponsible ways, she does love her siblings. The twins were Lady Larkford's babies, her last children, and she was inclined to spoil them. As a result, the twins have always run a little wild, unchecked, and Eleanor has long feared they will end up in trouble of some sort. Neither of them has the sort of character that would allow them to cope. Phoebe, the younger of the two, is the stronger in spirit, but she is wilful, focussed only on her needs and unwilling or unable to consider the wider world. Lily, while rather more sensible, is quieter and tends to defer to Phoebe, avoiding confrontation by letting her twin have her way.

Eleanor's worries are interrupted by Oliver, who pipes up with the pertinent question, "How are they going to get him back across the water?" But it is not too much later when he has the answer, in the distinctive whump of a helicopter.

The machine approaches fast, flies past the island, and circles around before hovering above the folly, its roof just visible among the trees. A dark figure on a line descends from the helicopter, inching down towards the tree canopy. The figure descends below the tree line and is lost from their view. The island is heavily wooded, but the folly itself stands in a clearing on a slight rise. Every year a maintenance crew will cross to the island and cut back the vegetation, clearing it from inside and out of the folly, but otherwise it is left to Mother Nature. The clearance visit is late this year, postponed because of the demands of the film production on the small resource that is the ground-keeping team.

The helicopter hovers, almost unmoving in the air, and then the watchers see a figure in a harness clipped to a long, red parcel emerge above the treetops. They swing under the machine, the cable winching them slowly higher as they spin in the downdraught. When they reach the helicopter, it starts to move forwards, heading for the hospital. Two minutes, and they are gone, disappearing behind the trees on the horizon.

Still Eleanor, Jacob, and Oliver sit and wait. It isn't long before they see activity on the dock the other side. First one figure, then the next, until five people are crowded together. Two stay on the jetty, but three of them start the journey back. Progress is slower. After all, time is no longer of the essence, but to those waiting, the journey feels excruciating.

This time, Jacob and Oliver are ready to pull the boat in and to help the paramedics clamber onto the wooden dock. Robert Winter follows them, his place taken at the oars by Oliver. He plainly doesn't have the skill at rowing that the Winter men possess, but he is young and has the upper-body strength of one who labours outdoors for most of the year. By halfway across, he has developed a rhythm which, if not elegant, is at least effective. The girls are ready for him, and he is making his return journey within minutes.

The paramedics are still talking to the Winters, and Eleanor wonders why they haven't repaired to their ambulance and started on their way until she catches a flash of fluorescence and remembers the big bag. Wise of Robert Winter to insist on it travelling with the slightly built Mortimer girls.

As soon as the bag is returned to the paramedics, they lay it on the floor to check its contents. Finding nothing damaged or missing, the elder one starts back towards their vehicle. Eleanor is trying to get to her sisters but finds her way blocked by Jacob.

"Do you mind if I head off home, now?" he says with a twitch of his head in the direction of his parents' house. "Oliver's going to drive you back. Dad's going to stay with the ATV and see the boat is taken out of the water so no one can get onto the island. The folly isn't safe."

"Oh! Yes, of course. You probably have things to do ..." She waves her hand vaguely. "We'll be fine. Thank you for everything this afternoon. And thank your dad for me, too."

She goes to wait by the car, texting her father an update. She is certain he will be getting a full report from Robert Winter as well. She glances up to see Jacob and the paramedics move off together. They stop at the ambulance, and the younger one reaches into the vehicle, coming out with a piece of paper. She passes it to Jacob, her movements sinuous, like she is being coy. He glances down, then grins at her. He nods, says a word or two, and salutes an adieu. Then he is striding away as the paramedics back their ambulance up to turn it around and head back to base.

Eleanor is a little flabbergasted at what she has just witnessed. It seems there is no occasion which is unfit for flirting these days. If she is not mistaken, the young paramedic has just given Jacob her number.

She is still staring at the ambulance when Oliver comes up, having finished conferring with his boss. He beeps the doors unlocked, and Eleanor opens the rear door for Lily to climb in. As her sister walks past her, something about her seems off. She catches hold of Lily's arm and wheels her around. She sees the dilated pupils, hears the self-conscious sniff, and the realisation crashes over her that there is a reason why Oliver is driving. Jacob must have known.

She is not about to scream at her sisters in front of the staff, but just wait until they get home. She is definitely going to get answers to some questions, starting with just who, precisely, has been injured.

Trouble at the Hall

Lord Larkford, in all his paternal fury, is waiting for his errant daughters on their return. Lily, seemingly contrite, retreats into the furthest corner of the sofa in the mistaken belief its cushions can hide her from his wrath. Phoebe, however, chooses defiance.

"How were we to know?" she demands.

"Do you never listen to a word that's said in this family?" her father thunders. "How many times, Eleanor, have we discussed the folly? You girls know it isn't safe!"

"Well, it's not locked up. If it's not safe, it should be."

"It's on an island! How much more inaccessible do you want to get? There are 'No Entry' signs all over it. Have you two forgotten how to read?"

For the first time, Phoebe is silent but her father is on a roll. "And what were you two doing there anyway?"

Phoebe chews her lip and Eleanor can see the lie form as clear as day. "He asked to see it."

"Who asked to see it?"

"Jamie Smythe."

There it is, finally. The name of the injured. Eleanor's first instinct when she had met Jamie Smythe was that he was trouble. Then she had found him by turns charming, philandering, and criminal. Now she is back to trouble. Jamie had tried for Anna initially, then, unless Eleanor was misled by her own vanity, he had transferred his attentions towards her. Was there a Mortimer daughter he had not tried for? Perhaps she should check with

Jasmine, although – kudos to Jasmine – that would be a hard hill for him to climb.

"Jamie Smythe?" Lord Larkford echoes. "That pretty boy actor? I thought all the film crew had left?"

"He had the day off, so he thought he'd come and see me. He likes me." Phoebe is almost petulant about it. "And he's a celebrity." Eleanor is sickened by the note of pride in Phoebe's voice. It's not like getting screwed by Jamie Smythe is difficult – you just have to stand still long enough, and he'll get around to it.

"He's an idiot, more like!" her father contradicts. "But a lucky one. Robert tells me the paramedics think he's broken his hip. Could've easily been his neck or his back. What were any of you thinking?" But the last words are spoken with something more akin to despair than anger. At last, he subsides. "Go on. Go to your rooms. You're both grounded."

Lily legs it for the door but Phoebe isn't finished.

"We're adults," she fires back. "You can't ground us."

"You either follow my rules or you support yourselves. Which is it to be?" The threat hangs in the air but neither of the girls want to face a future without funds.

"I hate you," Phoebe shrieks. "That's not fair." But she follows Lily out of the room. Eleanor catches them in the corridor. "Which of you has the drugs?"

Lily looks startled but Phoebe glares. "Neither of us, Miss Prissy Pants."

"I'm serious," Eleanor states flatly. "Do you want me to ask again, in front of Daddy?"

Lily pipes up, "She's telling the truth."

"Yes, Silly there threw it in the lake." Phoebe has long tormented her sister by mangling her name as an insult. "And Miss Butterfingers managed to drop her phone in at the same time."

"What would you have done if the cops had turned up?" Lily protests.

"We called an ambulance, not the police, dipshit."

Eleanor has had enough. "Enough! I can't stop what you do at university, but if I catch you bringing anything home again, you've had it. I won't think twice about dobbing you into Father." Then she turns on her heel and heads for the sanctuary of her own room before the twins can resume their squabble – or unite against her.

Far from being calmed by the imminent arrival of Ptolemy, the next morning Eleanor is jittery. A strained breakfast where Lord Larkford's ire at his two youngest seems to have translated into a general irritation with his entire family further unsettles her. She is used to her father being a rock. She leaves his grumpiness to be assuaged by his wife, who cannot escape it and is thus making a valiant attempt to mitigate his temper with small smiles and gentle caresses. Eleanor, though, takes the first opportunity to abandon the room, almost knocking over Mrs Hill in her haste to get away. The housekeeper manages to save the tray she is carrying, and as Eleanor looks down at it, her mouth firms into a line of displeasure.

"Miss Lily isn't feeling so well this morning," the housekeeper explains, needing little empathy to sense the condemnation in Eleanor's stare.

"I'll take that." Eleanor lifts the tray out of the housekeeper's hands and sweeps up the stair. She taps on the door of Lily's room, giving her sister but a second's notice before she pushes the door wide and storms in.

"Out!" she commands. "Get out of bed. You made this mess; you face it! *You* don't get to hide."

Lily has always been more afraid of Eleanor's disapproval than even Anna's sharp tongue, and though she scurries to obey, she still protests, "Phoebe's going to the hospital later. I don't see there's anything I can do."

But Eleanor ignores her remark and instead asks a question that has been troubling her since the events of the previous day. "Why didn't you row the boat back to wait for the paramedics?"

Lily's reaction is one of surprise. It had obviously never occurred to her. "I didn't think about it," she murmurs, her head low. Then she continues, as if this explains everything, "I don't know how to row."

Eleanor sighs in frustration. Therein lies the vast gulf between the two of them, not just age but attitude. She has never rowed in her life, but she would have tried. How difficult can it be to put an oar in the water and pull? With only one leg, Jacob must have struggled to brace himself, but he hadn't hesitated. She was sure the young groundskeeper, Oliver, was as much a rowing novice as Lily and it had not stopped him. She considers each of her siblings in turn. Anna wouldn't have balked and even Jasmine, though she might have grumbled a fair bit, would have put her back into it.

Sometimes she worries neither of the twins is canny enough to be a survivor in life. They will depend on their men to an unhealthy amount and – God knows – there are enough men out there unable to resist the lure of a needy woman. A fair few of those will be looking to exploit that vulnerability and Eleanor doesn't want the twins to end up like Aunty Mary, controlled, isolated, broken.

She translates her worries into testiness. "Get dressed," she orders peremptorily as she puts down the tray on the dresser, then leaves for her own room.

When the sound of a car outside finally signals Ptolemy's arrival, Eleanor clatters down the smooth stone stairs at a frankly hazardous pace and is at the front door to greet him before he has extracted his bags from the boot.

Seeing her standing on the porch waiting for him, her navy tea dress plastered against her body by the wind, is enough to lift his heart. His face is wreathed in smiles, even as hers is frowning. Her presence here to welcome him is enough; it says she is impatient to see him and he is desperate enough to relish any sign of affection on her part. Every time she looks at him with warmth, every time she laughs at his wit, every time she shares a small confidence, his hope he will own her heart grows. He cannot help it – he has tried to be cautious, but he is by nature a man of deep feelings and this passion, for having been so long denied, is springing out in wisps and tendrils despite his attempts to contain it.

He feels encouraged, and as soon as he is close enough, he drops his bags to wrap her in his arms, pulling her close and placing his lips firmly on hers. Eleanor closes her eyes at his kiss. She is waiting to be transported, for his touch to burn away all the niggles of the morning, but despite the fact it is a good kiss, fervent and amorous, she is still very much standing on the porch. It is not Ptolemy at fault; it is her. In any one family, a single person can set everyone's mood and today, it seems, her father has set the tone – irritableness.

Ptolemy keeps hold of her hand as he picks up his bag and follows her through the hall to his assigned room. He looks around it and says, "Nice," before turning his attention back to her and pulling her closer with the words, "I've missed you."

Eleanor desperately wants to reciprocate, because she has missed him. She has missed this feeling of closeness to another, the comfort of being touched. But when she goes to open her mouth, the words that come out are wrong.

"We've got time for a walk before lunch, if you want," she says.

Ptolemy, who couldn't care what they do so long as they do it together, nods his agreement. She leads him towards the West Drive; another little thing nibbling at her good humour is the need to check the little rowboat has been removed. She is quite confident Robert Winter and his crew will have done their jobs but it never hurts to make sure. She has always hated the saying, but it's true: assume makes an ass of you and me.

It rained overnight, and the weather is fresh and blustery, little marshmallow clouds blossoming, hiding the sun from time to time. It is not unpleasant, if a little chill from the wind, and Eleanor is glad to be snuggled into his side, his arm around her waist. Except the entire population of two villages seems to be on the same path to gawp at them. The first couple they meet are Annabelle and her mother. The maid is clearly on her way in for her shift and Eleanor knows Mrs Green is a stalwart of the church cleaning rota, so she dares to hope they will be able to get away with nothing more than a greeting, but this is dashed when Mrs Green halts.

"Eleanor, my dear," Mrs Green has never subscribed to the Estate worker's practice of calling her Miss Mortimer, and why should she? Age has given her a reputation for a sensibleness that is sadly lacking in her daughter. "How are you all? We saw the helicopter."

"We're all well, Mrs Green," she replies. She knows better than to believe the older woman is ignorant of any of the particulars of the accident. The Greens and the Winters are old friends, their son Matthew and Jacob having grown up inseparable. The woman nods and transfers her curious eyes to Ptolemy, noting the way his arm has slid up to leave a proprietary hand on Eleanor's shoulder. With a sinking heart, Eleanor realises unless she says something, the four of them will stand in embarrassed silence until she does cave.

"Let me introduce my friend, Ptolemy Hyde," she hurries to add.

"Oh, I've heard of you. An actor, aren't you? How exciting," Mrs Green responds with a pleasant smile and a gentle handshake. "My, you've caught a handsome one here, Eleanor." And then with a look of devilment in her eye, having achieved what she wanted, she adds, "I'd best leave you to reel him in."

Grateful Annabelle had been too star-struck to speak, Eleanor moves off, dragging Ptolemy with her but they have not gone another hundred metres before they are stopped again. By the tenth such meeting, Eleanor's nerves are on edge, her teeth are grinding together. Each acquaintance has been torn between prurient curiosity about Ptolemy and their excitement at discussing the rescue, and each has been loath to let the young couple escape.

The last person they meet just as the path runs beside the lake is Jacob, and Eleanor presumes he is headed to the pub for a lunchtime pint and a good gossip with his mates.

"Nora," he says and with a courteous dip of his head, "Mr Hyde."

That is all it takes. Something inside Eleanor snaps. She is already angry with Jacob for trying to cover up the twins' drug-taking. The frustrations of the morning boil over with this one perceived insult.

"That's rich!" she snaps. "It seems you *can* show respect! But only if it's an upper-class, white man with a posh voice. How very Army!"

Jacob is stunned and Ptolemy aghast at her rudeness, but she doesn't care. It's no bad thing if Ptolemy realises she isn't perfect, and it's about time Jacob realises there is a limit to his constant needling.

When he gets his voice back, Jacob's words are perfectly frosty. "We have upper-class, white women with posh voices in the Army, too, Ma'am."

Eleanor's heart sinks as sanity returns. She knows instantly she has been childish and that Jacob, of all men after yesterday, doesn't deserve her criticism. When he continues in the same frigid tone, she cringes. "I'm sorry to have disturbed you. I only stopped to ask if there was any news on Jamie Smythe. Excuse my impertinence."

Jacob deliberately tugs his forelock, and before Eleanor can respond, he is gone. She is faced with the choice of running after him like a desperate groupie or leaving it be. Wisely, she stays where she is.

"What's up with Jamie Smythe?" Ptolemy too has recovered his wits, seizing on a name he recognises but hoped never to hear linked with Eleanor.

"He came to visit the twins yesterday, but he had an accident and had to be airlifted to hospital." Eleanor's explanation is succinct but flat, betraying none of the drama of the preceding day. "We think they operated last night. Phoebe's going to the hospital later."

She leaves out any mention of the drugs; Ptolemy knows Jamie better than she does and he can probably guess the reason the three hapless adventurers went looking for the most inaccessible spot on the estate.

"Has anyone told the film company?" he asks.

Eleanor shrugs. "It wasn't really top of our minds. We left it to the paramedics and the hospital to notify his family."

While Ptolemy calls the Producer and the Director to give them the bad news, Eleanor wanders over to the jetty and is relieved to find no boat, only a couple of anglers from the neighbouring village. She retreats before they notice her presence and returns to wait for Ptolemy to finish.

No matter how many times she passes this way, she is always struck by the beauty of the lake. The rush of the water over the weir as it runs back into the river drowns out any reminders of the modern century, and you are left instead with the song of the white-collared reed bunting, the rustle of the breeze teasing the willows on the riverbank behind, and the occasional harsh call of the mallards chivvying their brood. This is one of her special places, a place that calms her, where she can feel her connection to the earth.

Not today. Ptolemy drops his phone in his pocket, glances around quickly to locate her and says, "We'd better get back. I don't want to be late for lunch with your parents."

Halfway along the journey back, he breaks his silence to ask, "Are you okay?"

"Not really," Eleanor exhales loudly. She moves apart from him and tries to kick a hole in the hoggin with the toe of her shoe but all she does is scuff the leather. "I'm angry at Lily and Phoebe for being so stupid. But it's not just that. I hate everybody gawking at us. And I've just lost it with Jacob, who was genuinely a hero yesterday … and now I'm spoiling our time together when I haven't seen you all week. I guess I'm crabbier than usual because I didn't sleep well last night. I've just got this sense of disaster. Like worse is to come."

Ptolemy's answer is to wrap her in his arms and hold her for several minutes. When he finally pulls back, he tips her face up to his and says, "After lunch, why don't you have a nap? I've got some stuff to read through in preparation for next week's filming, so I can do that while you sleep. Then you'll be good for dinner and the theatre tonight." He drops a light kiss on the tip of her nose and Eleanor begins to understand what a prize Ptolemy Hyde could be.

Lunch is a distinctly subdued meal with Lady Larkford and Ptolemy carrying the conversation. Lily joins them, not daring to hide in her room for another meal and having few other options to satisfy the appetite of the young, but she contributes nothing. Lord Larkford is reticent to a degree that leads Eleanor to suspect he may not approve of her boyfriend, and she makes a mental note to tackle him on it after Ptolemy has gone.

By the time she is lying in her bed that night, she has already forgotten her intent, her mind preoccupied with the disastrous end to what would have otherwise been a very pleasant evening. Dinner had been good and they had chatted agreeably about the friends they had in common. They had laughed together at the play, and Eleanor had been lulled by the ease of the evening to let her guard down and step into Ptolemy's room for a goodnight kiss. As the embrace had deepened, Ptolemy had felt confident enough to slide his hand under her skirt, his palm warm as it slid up her thigh. Her body had reacted, anticipation flooding her middle and a hunger long denied exploding. Her mind, though, had started shrieking, *No! Too fast! Too fast,* and Eleanor had panicked. She had pushed Ptolemy away like a startled virgin and fled without a word.

Her phone is alive with texts she is too embarrassed to return, and she lies in the darkness glad Ptolemy does not know exactly which room is hers, trusting he will be too circumspect to risk knocking on a stranger's door. The day has been full of frustrations from start to finish. If the evening has shown anything, it is Ptolemy that is further down the path to commitment than she is. Alone in the darkness, she can own the truth: though her toes are on the path, she still has no idea if she wants to walk it.

Bad to Worse

Ptolemy, it turns out, is not put off by her resistance. He is confident enough of his charms to be sure she did not bolt because she found the idea of intimacy with him repulsive. In the brief glimpse he had of her face before she ran, he had seen her pupils dilated with lust as much as her eyes had been wide with fear. Much like a skittish animal, Eleanor has to come to him of her own accord. He had let her go. He does not blame himself for what happened. What man could have Eleanor in his arms and not want to take it further? Nor could he blame her. After all, last night was enough to confirm she wanted him but also that want scares her. His thoughts turn to another villain and, not for the first time, wishes, much as Eleanor herself, that she had never met Sebastien.

And so time falls into a pattern. Weekdays, Ptolemy and Eleanor are apart but weekends they are together. He does not attempt to take things further again. She knows his hopes; he is convinced she will make the approach when she is ready. In the meantime, they spend their time together deepening their understanding of each other. The wait might frustrate but the reward is the promise of forever.

Eleanor, having apologised to Jacob for her rudeness, finds they have a sort of détente, not as warm as before but decidedly better than constantly being addressed as "Ma'am". Today, she is uncharacteristically chivvying Jacob to break the speed limit. Ptolemy has a day free of filming and is due on the Friday, a whole day earlier than usual. When Eleanor had told her mother Ptolemy was coming that day, she'd thought the Baroness might combust with joy. Lady Larkford, with the merest hint of guile, enquired if he would still require a separate room, and the disappointment was clear on her face when the answer was affirmative. Eleanor is conflicted enough about Ptolemy without the additional confusion of lust.

Eleanor has cancelled her meetings, for they have planned to have afternoon tea in the summer sunshine. She does not want to be late, for she is bringing the cakes from her favourite patisserie, but Jacob is sticking precisely to the signs, not even allowing the needle to drift one or two miles an hour higher. He has already reminded her twice; it is his licence at risk. She dare not push a third time. She is relieved when they turn into the Estate, only five minutes late, but Jacob proceeds to crawl along the drive, virtually coming to a stop at each junction, before inching forwards.

Ptolemy's car is already parked outside the Hall, and Eleanor, feeling guilty at keeping him waiting, exits hers with barely a shouted farewell to her driver as she flings her present of churros towards him. She finds Ptolemy on the terrace, ensconced on a lounger, a cup of tea already poured beside him. She bends down to place a kiss of greeting on his sunglasses, knowing it will irritate, hoping it will distract from her lack of punctuality.

"Eleanor!" he protests with a soft smile. He reaches out and snaps the tip off a nearby shrub and throws it at her. "Grow up!"

She arranges the cakes she bought on the bottom of the tea stand and brings it over to the little table between the two loungers before returning to pour her own cup. She brings plates and napkins. Gone are the days when the Mortimers could afford to have a servant hovering with no other duties than to make ensure their every comfort was provided.

They have not got past the opening discussion of the traffic conditions before their little feast is interrupted by her father's bellow, "Eleanor!"

In answer to her return call, Lord Larkford erupts onto the terrace, puce in the face and waving some sheets of paper. Eleanor is reminded of the sudden death of her grandfather and has no wish to see history repeat itself.

"That snivelling little weasel! That conniving bastard," the Baron splutters. "Not content with trying to seduce my daughters, now he tries this! I should have shot him that first night!"

Eleanor's first glance is at Ptolemy, but when he shakes his head, she turns back to her father. "Who are you talking about? And what have they done?"

"That cockroach – Jamie Smythe! Look here." Lord Larkford shoves the papers under her nose but retracts them before she can read the first line. He taps them. "The bastard is suing us!"

"He can't, can he?" she asks.

"Oh, Eleanor, you know better than that. If a thief falls down an uncovered hole on our building site while robbing the place, we're negligent. The folly is on the island, so we never bothered to fence it."

Eleanor hands her father her own cup of tea and pushes him into her chair. "Precisely," she says.

"But we left the boat there."

"But it's for carp fishing!"

"It's still a boat. We fail the first test for negligence: was it foreseeable? Could a reasonable man believe someone might use it to row across to the island? Yes!"

Eleanor finally understands what has been worrying her father. He has been tetchier than usual. But he had also allowed Phoebe to visit the hospital while she was grounded. He must have been half-anticipating this.

A thought occurs to her. "Does Phoebe know?" she asks. She wishes she could be certain her sister would have given some warning if she had a suspicion of Jamie's plans, but the girl could be contrary at the best of times and her ability to carry a grudge might have trumped her loyalty to her family.

"I've no idea." Lord Larkford reaches for a macaron and swallows it in two bites. He picks up another.

Ptolemy pipes up from his lounger, "How much is he asking for?"

"A million."

"What?" Eleanor gasps.

"He'll never get that," Ptolemy reassures her.

"I know."

"You have insurance?" Ptolemy asks.

"Yes, of course," Eleanor says.

"That's not the point," Lord Larkford interjects, helping himself to the smoked salmon sandwiches. "These things don't go away quickly. And the banks will be wary about lending any more money with a potential court case hanging over us. This jeopardises everything."

As usual, her father's anger has abated as quickly as it came. He seems more despondent now than anything else. A mille-feuille disappears, followed by a raspberry religieuse. After a few more words of encouragement on Eleanor's side, Lord Larkford abandons the cake platter and wanders off to call the solicitors.

Eleanor looks down at the devastation her father has wrought on the afternoon tea. She supposes the bargain well-made – a few cakes exchanged for better humour – but she was rather hungry, having only had a light lunch. Ptolemy quietly slides half the remaining cakes and sandwiches onto her plate before taking his own.

"You know he's expected back on set in a couple of weeks?" he comments.

"Who? Jamie?"

"Yes. They've moved around the filming schedule to accommodate his injury. Wickham doesn't appear in the Hunsford, Netherfield, or Pemberley scenes at all. They're going to use a body double for some scenes, where they can get away with shooting from the back. He's only got a few village scenes left."

"I'm sorry if this is going to cause you trouble."

"What are you sorry for? If anyone has caused this, I'll lay bets it's Jamie himself." Ptolemy reaches a hand to hold hers.

"You aren't far from the truth. They were on the island to hide their drug use. You know Jamie."

"I do know Jamie," he says with meaning. He looks at her. "Sorry, Eleanor. I've just remembered, I've got to make a call. Do you mind?"

At the shake of her head, Ptolemy gets up and retreats indoors, out of earshot. Eleanor is a little surprised, but she supposes it is some private business with his agent or similar and tries not to be hurt by the lack of trust. She sits alone in the sunshine, eating the last beautiful cake that now tastes like ash.

The entire weekend is odd. Ptolemy is distracted and leaves earlier than expected, her father is withdrawn. Phoebe had been strangely disingenuous when asked if she had prior knowledge of Jamie's lawsuit, and Eleanor can only assume Phoebe had been aware of it. Her opinion of her sister sinks yet lower and that, in itself, is distressing. Lily keeps to her room as much as possible, avoiding everyone in the family. Even Anna cannot help. Their last call had been interrupted by an emergency at the hospital and Anna has not called back since.

By the time Eleanor and her father head into Bridgetown to meet with a litigation expert, her spirits are truly depressed. Jacob has asked for a day's leave, so Lord Larkford is driving, an experience Eleanor is always happy to forgo. Still, remembering her intent from some time ago, she takes the opportunity to ask, "You do like Ptolemy, don't you, Daddy?"

"What's brought this about?" her father takes his eyes off the road to inspect her, which is somewhat unnerving given the contortions of the lane they are travelling.

"You seem a little reserved when Tolly is around, that's all."

"He's perfectly amiable and I'm sure he will make a very good sort of son-in-law."

"Daddy! Be serious!"

Lord Larkford hesitates before saying, "I can see he's a handsome young man. And clever, I'll give you that. A bit full of himself but time will knock that back. There's nothing about *him* that concerns me.

"Then what's the problem."

Her father is silent again for a moment. "Eleanor, charismatic people are often overwhelming. Just make sure you love the man, not the lifestyle."

"Oh," says Eleanor. Is that what she is doing? But they have now reached the outskirts of Bridgetown, and she would rather her father concentrate on his driving than her questions.

When Eleanor visits Cobb, Cobb and Hoyland, she usually parks in the public carpark and walks to their offices. Lord Larkford, however, swings into the staff carpark behind the old mansion which houses the law firm, ignoring the warnings of clamping in effect. They gather up their belongings and head inside.

There are few more chilling words in this life than when a balding, greying solicitor looks over his half-moon glasses and says, "I'm afraid I've got bad news."

Lord Larkford, a man who has always appreciated directness, says, "Go ahead."

"The insurance company are denying liability. Mr Smythe is alleging your daughters, Phoebe and Lily …" Here, Mr Barley-Williams, stalwart of Cobb, Cobb and Hoyland's litigation department, peers at the father and daughter and waits for confirmation.

"I'm well aware of what my daughters are called," the Baron says with some asperity. "Go on."

"Your daughters took him to the island and led him up the folly. As such, it was a deliberate act and not negligence. Mr Smythe did not discover the boat and, driven by curiosity, crossed to the island and visited the folly. He was taken, by people who were resident on the Estate and beneficiaries of the trust – not employees, you understand. He was taken there by people who could be expected to know how dangerous it was." The solicitor clears his voice. "In brief, short of the girls pushing him off the roof, the injury to Mr Smythe could not have been any more deliberate. They consider this sufficient grounds to deny liability."

"Can they do this?" Eleanor asks.

"Well, this is law," Mr Barley-Williams says, a little pompously. "There is always an argument, and in this case, it is certainly worth arguing. But in general terms, not talking about specifics here, insurance contracts are written by the insurer and their legal departments are well-versed in what comprises their liability. I'm not saying we won't win; I'm just setting expectations."

"So, what is the worst we are looking at?" Lord Larkford's voice remains calm despite the disastrous news.

"With no insurance?" At the Baron's nod, the solicitor continues. "Mr Smythe's legal costs, his loss of earnings, but he is young and will mend quickly. Also, he is an actor, so he's probably paid peanuts – this is the UK after all, not America. A bit for the injury – mercifully the courts are far less fanciful about these amounts than the claimant thinks. The problematic area is future debilitation. This is what most of the debate is about. Will this injury cause him further trouble when he is old, and if so, what sum should we pay him now? No one will want this to go to court; both sides will be looking to settle. It becomes a negotiation to get them to accept as little as possible. In this, time is our ally. The longer we can draw it out, the more desperate the claimant becomes, the more likely he will settle for less."

"But the longer it takes, the longer we will struggle to raise financing for future projects. And some of those are urgently required," Lord Larkford contends.

An hour later, and Mr Barley-Williams limps off to get some papers copied, leaving Eleanor and her father alone in the boardroom. Lord Larkford is preoccupied reading through a document, so Eleanor stands and crosses to the window, for want of any other amusement. The grand Georgian building fronts on to the High Street, and the boardroom, being situated at the front, affords every opportunity to watch the people of Bridgetown hurrying about their business. Mama Cortada's café lies opposite, the sign picked out in gaudy colours of yellow and pink, much like Mama herself. When she first came to Bridgetown towing her love of fresh, dark roasts in her wake, the townsfolk had spluttered into their cups of instant granules when they saw the cost. But the quality of the coffee was matched by the quality of the food, and soon Mama had built up a faithful band of coffee aficionados. Even now, with two other coffee chains in the town, Mama's business is thriving. Locals willingly support her café, leaving the tourists to sustain the nationals.

Throughout the summer months, Mama places half a dozen gleaming metal tables on the pavement. Eleanor inspects each in turn and draws in a sharp breath when she recognises Jacob at the end table. He is not alone. In the seat opposite him is a slender woman with long brown hair. Their heads are together, their hands linked on the table. Eleanor's breath explodes out of her in a little exhalation of surprise, misting the uneven surface of the two-hundred-year-old, handblown glass pane. She wipes the condensation away. There is no mistaking the intimacy. Even as she watches, Jacob kisses his companion's forehead, rises to his feet and, as the woman joins him, he puts his arm around her shoulders, and together they head off down the street.

"Oh!" Eleanor whispers to the pane, "it's like that, is it?"

She thinks back to the night she watched Jacob sitting on the wall and the woman who joined him. She thinks about the time she spent trying to work out who it was. Now she has her answer, for she recognised the girl as she flicked her hair back and rose to her feet. Annabelle. But that thought is rapidly followed by another. *Annabelle?* For she is astonished – out of all the film stars and the production crew and the women of beauty or intelligence in the area, Jacob's choice is the young, timid housemaid.

She is called back into the room by the return of Mr Barley-Williams and his lugubrious throat-clearing. Jacob and Annabelle are forgotten as she and her father focus once more on the more pressing predicament of Jamie Smythe.

That night when Ptolemy calls, Eleanor shares the bad news with him. He does his best to convince her it will all turn out all right, but Eleanor has her own ability to reason, and looks dispassionately at the evidence to find little that is positive. Of course, in the long-term this will just be one more incident in the history of the Estate, but coming on the heels of the pandemic and the hit it delivered to their income stream, it is disheartening. Eleanor wishes she had never heard of the production company or had turned them down flat. It is not just the money but the way it has torn her family apart. Her mother is the only one still talking to Phoebe; even Lily seems to have realised the duplicity of Phoebe's behaviour and abandoned her twin.

At the end of the call, in an eerie echo of the solicitor, Ptolemy says, "I'm afraid I've got some bad news." Eleanor is not sure she can take much more without weeping inconsolably. After all his protestations of undying love, is Ptolemy about to dump her? His kisses have been just as frequent and just as fervent, but he has made no other attempt to take it further since the night she fled his room. Perhaps he has tired of her sexual reticence.

Ptolemy must sense the ominous tone of her silence because he hurries to say, "It's just I won't be able to see you this weekend; something's come up. But I will be with you the following one. And I'll be thinking of you every moment we are apart."

Relieved, she ends the call with the usual round of endearments and expressions of affection. She lies on her bed and stares up at the ceiling rose, tracing the ornate acanthus leaf pattern while her mind considers her life. Men always seemed to disappoint – Sebastien, Jamie, Harry. Even Jacob, whose partner of choice is little more than a child. In Ptolemy, might she finally find one who doesn't?

Everything is Settled

It is nearly a fortnight before Eleanor sees Ptolemy again, and when she does, it is something of a surprise. Late on a Friday afternoon, she is returning to her office when she stumbles across him coming out of her father's office. It is odd enough to rouse her suspicions. What business could Ptolemy have with Lord Larkford?

The fantastical idea briefly flits across her mind that he may be asking her father's permission to propose, but Ptolemy must surely be aware Eleanor would never accept a man who thought it appropriate to approach her father before her – as if she is some possession to be handed between men. Besides which, despite his declaration of long-held love, he must also know it is far too soon. They have only been together a few weeks and have been on but a handful of dates.

Ptolemy's explanation is decidedly mundane. "I came to see you, but you were out, so your father invited me in to wait." He takes her hand in his. "I wanted to surprise you, but I now realise maybe I should have called first."

She smiles up at him to let him know she appreciates the gesture, while trying to mentally tally up the adjustments to her diary. "Give me a minute," she says and nips in to see Suzy before heading outside to catch Jacob.

She is surprised to find Jacob is not alone. Jeanette Mulwood is talking to him, with her shirt unbuttoned low and far more cleavage on display than normal. It is a windy day, making it chillier than expected for the time of year and Eleanor fancies the older woman is risking catching a cold. Then she feels mean. She remembers her conversation with Jacob when she teased him about Jeanette. Now she pities the older woman. A man who likes nervous girls twelve years younger than him is never going to go for an intelligent woman more than twelve years older. In the light of his attachment to Annabelle, Jacob's mild flirtation with the older woman looks markedly less charitable and rather more inconsiderate of both parties.

Jeanette is startled by Eleanor's arrival. She looks a little guilty as she holds out an envelope. "I was passing so I just thought I'd drop these off," she explains. Eleanor takes the paperwork and turns to Jacob. "I'm taking the afternoon off so you may as well knock off early today."

Eleanor turns to go but catches Jeanette's offer, "If you're free, do you want to go and get a drink?" She leaves Jacob to extract himself from that one, and heads back to Ptolemy.

Her boyfriend is in a remarkably good mood. He spins her into his arms when she returns and gives her a proper greeting, one that demonstrates every inch of his affection. The same note of happiness colours the whole weekend. Eleanor knows filming is nearing the end on *Pride and Prejudice,* and she can only presume Ptolemy is demob-happy because he offers no other explanation for his good mood.

When he leaves on Sunday, he pulls her close and whispers, "All will be well, you'll see. Everything will be all right, I promise."

It is a weird goodbye to make, but Eleanor puts it out of her mind and goes back to her family. Ptolemy's words turn out to be prophetic. Her father comes into her office on Monday afternoon and sits himself down. This is unusual. She is normally summoned to him.

"I've just had a very interesting phone call with Mr Barley-Williams," he starts.

"The solicitor?"

"Do we know another Barley-Williams?" her father asks, and Eleanor feels foolish. "Yes, the solicitor. Jamie Smythe is dropping his suit." Lord Larkford claps his hands together and rubs them vigorously. "That's good news, is it not? That lawyer is worth every penny we paid him."

"How? Why?" Eleanor is puzzled. It does not seem possible Jamie would walk away from the chance of money. It is possible Phoebe got him to change his mind, but unlikely. Jamie seems to prefer women who let him do the thinking.

"Barley-Williams was a bit vague on the reasoning, but I'm sure we'll get the full details in time." With that, her father gets up and returns to his office, leaving Eleanor a little disconcerted. She cannot think of how this can have come about. Mr Barley-Williams had set their expectations most definitely; they were going to have to pay Jamie off.

She pulls out her phone to text Ptolemy. Other than her family, there is no one else who might appreciate the news more. Lord Larkford, when he had recovered enough composure after receiving the news they were being sued, had ordered the family to keep quiet about the affair. He did not want details leaking out for fear it might undermine people's confidence in their business. Ptolemy, of course, had been witness to the Baron's initial indignation, so had escaped her father's gag order. Any expectation Ptolemy would reply with a host of emojis and shared delight are dashed when nothing is forthcoming. She can see her message has been delivered, but not viewed. Logically, she knows Ptolemy is probably on set, but she is disappointed. They started this adventure together; it would be nice to finish it so.

By the time she next sees Ptolemy on the following weekend, much of that original joy is gone and Ptolemy himself is subdued. As soon as they are alone in the drawing room, he says, "I need to talk to you."

Six words which never presage anything good. *I need to talk to you – your grandfather is dead. I need to talk to you – they've found out what is wrong, it's treatable but not curable,* or *I need to talk to you – there's someone else*. Eleanor has heard all these or a version of them before. She knows to steel herself for the worst.

"Since my name has been linked with the role of Mr Darcy, there has been a lot of interest from the big filmmakers and my agent has been sent some promising scripts. She has been in talks for some time with a couple of production companies based in California," he says.

"Hollywood?" Eleanor interrupts.

Ptolemy nods. "This week she was approached by another company. They have already started filming but have just fired their leading man. The long and the short is, I've been offered the part, but I have to leave next week, as soon as I finish filming *Pride and Prejudice*."

"Oh." Eleanor understands perfectly. He has come to say goodbye.

"I wanted to see you before I go." Ptolemy takes one of her hands, holding it gently, and Eleanor is conscious of the warmth and strength of his surrounding her own. "Eleanor," he says, his words sounding strained. "You know how I feel about you. You know how long I have wanted you."

He pauses and Eleanor is flustered. He is all seriousness and gravity, and she can't help but feel the portent of his words. Has he come to say goodbye or to propose? After only a few dates, surely a proposal is out of the question? But there is something about his stance that indicates a man on the brink of dropping to one knee.

"I am not an impulsive man," he begins again, and Eleanor has to acknowledge the truth of his statement. "I think I have proved my constancy and the enduring nature of my regard for you."

Uncertain as to whether she is being called upon to speak, to affirm or to deny the statement, Eleanor merely nods and smiles.

"We have not been together long and I had hoped we would have more time to grow closer," he continues. "But …"

Ah! thinks Eleanor, *here it comes*. In her own mind, she has already settled the issue; it is to be goodbye. She is surprised at how disappointed she is, how much she will miss his company, his conversation, and his affection. She is trying to compose herself, to show herself not affected at all when the blow falls.

"I do not know when I will be free to come back."

His hand on hers has tightened and her fingers are in danger of being crushed, but Eleanor does not extract them.

As calmly as she can, and suffusing her voice with as much warmth as she can muster, she replies, "I am very pleased for you, Tolly. I have no doubt you will be a great success. You have so much talent. Although I will miss you, I will look forward to seeing all your films."

Eleanor is congratulating herself on managing to articulate all the words without a hint of anything other than sincere regard for him. Ptolemy briefly closes his eyes, and Eleanor wonders how much it is costing him to say this farewell, to have to choose between a burgeoning new career and a long-desired relationship.

But he has not finished. "I know we have only been on a few dates, but we have known each other for a very long time, and so I want to ask you to take some time to consider if you would come with me?"

"Oh! Tolly!" Eleanor murmurs.

She is being offered a choice. She can see it before her, visualise the future. The immediate alarm of leaving Larkford and everything she ever thought the purpose of her life, to cross the ocean and live far from her family, is allayed by everything she would gain in return.

She would have the adoration of a man who is everything she wanted. She remembers those words spoken jokingly with Anna: a man of sense and education. She knows his regard for her is not a thing of a moment. These few weeks they have had together have taught her more of his character, and she is sure he would be steadfast and constant despite temptation. He would love her and she would never want for anything. Her beloved Larkford might not be her home, but it would never want for repair because, no matter what Ptolemy's future potential in Hollywood, he is already rich by the world's standards. And, Eleanor allows one wry thought: for once, she would please her mother. Lady Larkford would achieve her dearest wish of a conjugal relationship with her old friend Tissy.

Only a few moments pass, but in that time Eleanor considers all the ramifications as she inspects their entwined hands. Then she lifts her eyes to his; there is only one answer she can give.

The Consequence of Choice

Ptolemy has gone to start packing for his relocation to the States, and Eleanor, who has had enough excitement for one day, is wary of her family. She leaves the house, slipping quietly out of the French doors at the rear of the old building and heads towards the bridge over the lake. Her intent is to sit on the stone railings and watch the water carrying her doubts away, down through the country, away to the sea and beyond. Her footsteps crunch in the golden gravel of the path and alert a figure, sitting on the low wall surrounding the formal gardens, to her approach. A head turns and she recognises Jacob, sitting hunched over his phone. He slides it back into his pocket and stands.

It is too late to avoid him. To not greet him would be seen as a snub, so she arranges her features in a welcoming smile and says, "It's a lovely day to be sitting in the sunshine." Recalling the last time she saw him sitting on this wall, she adds, "Are you waiting for your girlfriend?"

Perhaps it is the tightness in her voice, or maybe it is the evidence of his eyes studying her, but Jacob ignores her question to ask his own, concern threaded through his words. "Is something wrong?"

Eleanor drops onto the lichen-encrusted wall and breathes out a large sigh. She debates whether she wants to have this conversation, especially with Jacob. But sooner or later, everyone will have to be told.

"Tolly came to see me," she begins. "He's leaving for America."

"That's hardly a surprise. He's a good actor and this series is going to make him an international star." Jacob's voice is guarded as he continues, as though uncertain what is the right thing to say, "Is that making you sad?"

"He asked me to go with him," Eleanor says. Her hands are folded in her lap, her thumb sliding up and down her forefinger.

Jacob remembers the gesture from her childhood – she would do it when she was upset at being teased but was trying hard not to show it.

"Oh!" It is a soft sound and drawn out. "I guess I need to find a new job."

"Why?"

"Aren't you going with him? I know you like him."

And there is the rub. Eleanor is silent as she thinks back to the conversation just passed between herself and Ptolemy.

"I do," she says.

He had looked at her with his entire heart in his eyes begging her, asking her to leave Larkford, abandon all she had dedicated her life to, to wrench herself away from her family. And in return, there would be fame and money. There would be a lot of money, so much money that the home she loved would never want for anything again. The lake could be dredged and the roofs mended and the drives repaired. Except, Eleanor had realised, all of this was immaterial. The decision to leave Larkford and go with him could only be based on one question: did she love him? Everything else – money, houses, countries, family – becomes naught in the face of love.

She loved being with him, being in his arms, surrounded by his love. She loved the way he treated her and the thoughtfulness he showed. But her father's words had crept into her mind – love the man, not the lifestyle. And when she thought of the man, she felt fondness, respect, admiration … but not deep, abiding love.

He had risked everything and asked her to come with him.

With a lifetime of regret infused into two words, she told Ptolemy, "I can't."

He closed his eyes momentarily, and when he opened them again, hope still lived. "I can turn them down and stay here. You need only say the word and I will do it."

He was offering to give up the future he wanted, for her. It was everything Eleanor had tried to avoid. By holding herself back, she had tried to stop Ptolemy from gambling with his heart, but she had plainly failed. If she could have manufactured love for him, she would have – but love has always been flighty, passing over appropriate candidates, often landing on the most inconvenient people instead. Eleanor remembers the look on Ptolemy's face as she disengaged her hands from his and said with the kindest words she could muster, "You are one of the finest men I know. I admire you deeply and I respect you greatly, but I do not love you as you deserve."

All hope left his face, his shoulders sagging as he fought to control his grief.

"Do you think you could come to love me?" The words, spoken on a whisper, were a plea.

Mute for the moment, confronted by his pain, Eleanor knew she could not give him any expectation because he would hold onto it. He needed to leave Larkford, with her firmly in the past. She had shaken her head and watched as the small action crushed a wonderful man. He sat down heavily with his head in his hands.

Eleanor saw how his shoulders shook but she dared not approach nor lay a comforting hand for fear it would be misinterpreted. After some moments, the words came to Ptolemy, and he raised his head and let them out, even while dreading the answer. "Is there someone else?"

Eleanor owed him honesty, but she had no words, only a nod.

"So why did you date me? Why be so cruel?" His anguish was unmistakable.

Eleanor had been unable to meet his eyes for she was ashamed of her motivation, a motivation she only understood in this moment when she had been faced with this choice. "He loves someone else. I was hoping *you* could make me forget him."

And Ptolemy, who well knew that feeling of love unreturned, had understood, even if he could not forgive.

They stayed that way, one sitting, one standing, for some minutes until, no longer able to bear the guilt of his presence – she was not proud to break such a man – Eleanor had uttered the words of a hostess guiding her guest to farewell: "I wish you all the best, Tolly and I hope you find someone who is a better person than me, someone who will make your heart sing again."

Ptolemy had taken the hint, giving an odd little formal nod before going.

"Eleanor?" Jacob is sitting beside her now, looking at her in concern for her long silence.

She follows the paths back in her mind until she recovers his question, and then she says, "I do like him but I don't love him."

"You're not going with him?"

"He asked; I said no." Eleanor gazes around. "My home is here. Sometimes I may chafe at the responsibility for this place, but I do love it. I love the house, the land, and I love this community – this merry band of brothers and sisters who live on this Estate. I like to think I protect them, keep them safe and happy, sheltered, employed, able to make something of their lives. Of course, the truth is they would all manage quite happily without me."

"I wouldn't be happy without you."

Eleanor is quiet. The tension between them stretches. Then Jacob moves closer, dipping his head.

"Don't!" The word comes out of her sharper than she intended, and he freezes.

Then he retreats, and when he speaks, his words are laced with bitterness. "I understand, Ma'am. I'm a crippled servant with no prospects. I am no one and have nothing to offer you."

Given the rollercoaster of emotions she has just endured, the crushing guilt she feels for having destroyed Ptolemy, Eleanor is almost incandescent at the implied allegation but retains just enough control of herself to answer with sense. "I am going to be charitable and put those words down to disappointed hopes. I will forgive you before you realise how insulting you have just been." But then her equanimity disappears and she almost spits the words out. "You know what I think of you! You could have lost both legs and one arm to boot, and you'd still be more of a man than any other. I don't give a fig about an accident of birth, one that puts me in one class and you in another. That's all in your head; a product of your precious Army. I see *you*." She jabs him in the arm with her finger. "As far as I'm concerned, an intelligent man who thinks clearly will never be lacking in prospects. None of that stuff matters – not money, not class, not whether you have one, two or three legs. That's not why I stopped you."

"Then why did you?"

Eleanor wonders if he is being deliberately dense and her exasperation is evident as she cries, "Because you are not free to be with me! And I'm not the kind of person who kisses a man who already has a girlfriend." She leaves unsaid, *Even if you are the type of man who would.*

"Girlfriend? Girlfriend? Who told you I had a girlfriend?" Jacob sounds genuinely perplexed, and that does nothing for Eleanor's temper.

"No one told me! I saw it with my own eyes. I'm not stupid, you know." At this point Eleanor could happily strike him, so she keeps her fists tight in her lap. "You and Annabelle canoodling together on the wall at night, right outside my bedroom! Did you think I wouldn't see? Then, the day you were off, in the café in Bridgetown, holding hands as you kissed her before you walked down the street with your arms around each other. I watched you!" Eleanor is a woman in disarray. She no longer cares if her speech makes her sound like a stalker.

"Oh!" Jacob says, for once at a loss for words, unable to combat accusations he knows to be true.

"Just go!" Eleanor has had enough. Without waiting to see what Jacob does, she gets up from the wall, brushes down her skirt and swishes off towards her original destination.

Eleanor does not linger long on the bridge. The slow drift of water failing to have its mesmeric, calming effect, she returns home by a circuitous route to avoid any lingering presumptive lovers. She also wishes to avoid her family. She will have to tell them about Ptolemy eventually, but for now, she sneaks up the servants' stairway to hide in her room.

Finding she has little appetite, Eleanor has elected to forgo dinner and the interrogation that would entail, in favour of lying on her bed. But her agitation will not abate. She replays the scenes with Ptolemy in her head and cringes with guilt. Then she thinks about Jacob and she surges with anger. From one to the other, she can find no balance, no quiet. She sits with her harp and plays her favourite passage from Handel's *Passacaglia* for all of five minutes before returning it upright and flouncing into the armchair. She would like to cry but feels that if she begins, she may never stop.

She thinks of things she should have said and chastises herself for words she did speak. She keeps seeing Ptolemy's face the moment she gave him her refusal and she hopes never to see that look of desolation again in her life.

She picks up every item on the dresser and replaces it in the exact same spot. Finally, she moves to the armchair and sits in front of the window. She cannot look out at the view without thinking of Jacob with his arm around another woman. Try as she might, she cannot see the thoughtful, rational man he has proved to be so many times over the weeks of their reacquaintance admiring the young, unformed but decidedly silly, girl. But then neither would she have believed he would attempt to seduce her while he was enmeshed with another woman – it goes against everything she knows of him.

Finally, she calls Anna.

"Hiya, babe!" Her sister's cheerful tone almost makes her disconnect.

"Hi." It is strange how much family can tell with just one word.

"What's the matter?"

Eleanor gives a big sigh. "Tolly came to see me today. He's going to Hollywood."

"And that's making you sad?"

"Sort of." Another breath. "He asked me to go with him, but I turned him down."

"I can't say I'm surprised." Anna has always been more confident of her older sister's charms than Eleanor herself.

"At which bit?"

"Both. Did you tell Mummy?"

"Not yet. I'm not sure I want to tell her he asked me to go."

"Good. Don't tell her. You'll never hear the end of it otherwise. So, it's not Mother getting you down?"

"It was like killing a puppy. It was the worst thing I've ever done." And Eleanor truly believes her words. "He's such a fine man, Anna, intelligent and interesting and thoughtful."

"But you don't love him?"

"No. And yet he loves me. I shouldn't have gone out with him and given him hope. I feel like a traitor because I encouraged him. I should never have done it … But it gets worse." She picks at a loose thread in the throw on the arm of the chair. "Jacob tried to kiss me."

"Jacob? Who's Jacob?"

"Jacob Winter."

"The gardener's son? Why on earth would he do that?" The incredulity in Anna's voice is so strong, even Eleanor begins to doubt the accuracy of her memory. Maybe the dip of his head, the slight narrowing of the space between their bodies, the focus on the lips had all been in her imagination. Anna may have a point – why on earth would Jacob want her?

"Maybe he thought I liked him."

Anna laughs, loud and long, as if there is nothing funnier, and Eleanor's courage falters.

Anna cuts off chuckling, and she says, "I'm being called, I'm going to have to go, but I'm off tomorrow. Do you want me to come home?"

Eleanor appreciates what Anna is offering. A six-hour round trip after a full week of ward rounds and operating theatres, all to give her a hug. She closes her eyes and blows out her breath before answering. While there is almost nothing in the world she wants as much as a sisterly consolation, she knows it is too much to accept.

"No," she sighs. "Don't worry, I'll get over it soon enough. After all, it's not as if it's *my* heart broken." In a childish gesture to implore God for protection, Eleanor crosses her fingers.

She lets her sister go back to her full-on busy life in the city with its daily drama of birth and death, while she watches as the sun sinks towards the horizon, its rays streaking the low-lying strands of clouds red and orange against the darkening blue of the sky. Eleanor contemplates the glorious sun about to set with no other feeling than that this day cannot end soon enough.

She is about to rise to draw the curtain, when there is a tap on the door and a small voice calls a hesitant, "Miss?"

"What is it, Annabelle?"

"Miss, please may I talk to you?"

Eleanor cannot think of many people she would less like to speak to at this moment than Jacob's girlfriend, but she cannot bring herself to be rude. She crosses to the door, unclicks the lock, and opens the leaf a crack.

"What is it?" she says with more than a little asperity, but when she sees the girl's downcast eyes, her slumped shoulders and the nervous way her hands are clutching at her uniform dress, Eleanor relents.

"Come in," she says rather more charitably, opening the door wider and guiding Annabelle to her recently vacated armchair. "Sit."

Annabelle obeys, but having gained entrance, she seems reluctant to speak, instead appearing fascinated with picking at the polish on her nails.

"I saw Jake earlier," she finally says in a small voice.

"Did you?" Eleanor's words are short but laced with disapproval of Jacob, although Annabelle misunderstands, bursting into tears.

Eleanor is not a natural at giving comfort. While she cares for people, it is always in a sort of brisk, practical fashion. She has no words for the heartbroken, especially those she barely knows. Moreover, she suspects what Jacob might have done – cutting Annabelle loose in the hope of freeing himself up – and her increasing anger at this notion is making it difficult to adopt the requisite sympathetic tone. She casts around the room looking for something, anything which might help, and eventually settles on a box of tissues and a glass of water.

Annabelle takes both, clutching the glass with one, white-knuckled hand while the other dabs at her snotty nose. After a few minutes, the sobbing has abated enough that Eleanor can discern some words.

"He doesn't know I'm here." Another sob. "I wanted to explain."

"Explain what?" Eleanor is truly baffled.

"Please don't fire me," Annabelle sniffles. "I like it here."

Eleanor tries to sound kind and reassuring, "No one is going to sack you, Annabelle." Eleanor knows her promise is meaningless if the girl has done something that would come under the definition of gross misconduct, but she needs first to find out why Annabelle thinks she might be sacked. "You're fine – your job is safe. Now tell me what's happened."

Eleanor kneels in front of Annabelle, proffering tissues, but being careful not to touch her or do anything which could be misconstrued. She is aware she is Annabelle's employer, not her friend.

It takes a few more frustrating minutes before the wretched girl can squeeze out the next intelligible phrase. "Jake was only helping me."

Trying hard to be encouraging, when all she wants to do is be demanding, Eleanor asks, "What do you mean? What was Jacob helping you with?"

The reply comes out on a wail, "An abortion."

Annabelle, having finally got the word out, collapses back into tears and Eleanor rocks back onto her heels and thinks she would quite like to join Annabelle in her howling grief. Eleanor appreciates a termination is a difficult decision; not all women have the same chances in life, and a teenage pregnancy is a life sentence in poverty. She respects Annabelle's right to make her own choice and doesn't condemn the girl. Jacob, however, is another matter.

"Annabelle," she asks after a little while, "this is important. Did Jacob force you to get the termination?"

"Oh no! No! Nothing like that. I told him I wanted an abortion and he helped me. He took me and stayed with me after. I couldn't tell my parents. They'd be devastated to find out I'd killed their grandchild!" The tearful girl turns big, frightened eyes to Eleanor and pleads, "Promise me you won't tell my mother? Please?"

"I won't tell her."

Eleanor's good opinion of Jacob is falling fast, but she takes comfort that at least he did not force Annabelle into this course of action. Although she cannot see what either of them hope to gain by telling Eleanor they had aborted a teenage girl's pregnancy.

"Annabelle, why are you telling me all this? None of it is any of my business."

"Because Jake told me you wouldn't believe him. I thought if I explained. He helped me when I had nowhere else to go. I owe it to him."

"Rubbish!" Eleanor couldn't be any more scathing. "You owe him nothing. He got you pregnant – the least he could do was to help."

"Oh no!"

Eleanor was beginning to tire of the exclamation.

"Jake wasn't the father."

"He wasn't?"

"God! No!" Annabelle's tone demonstrates her genuine revulsion. "That would be like having sex with my brother!"

"So, who was?" Eleanor is aware she is only asking out of prurient curiosity, not concern, but Annabelle doesn't seem able to distinguish, and having begun the confidence, seems unable to draw limits to it.

The answer, unfortunately, brings on another wave of wailing. "Jamie."

Eleanor casts about her memory for all the local Jamies. "Jamie Carter?" she ventures. Even though she cannot visualise the sweet, young girl before her with the portly, grumpy milkman, history is littered with stranger bedfellows.

"Oh no!" This time disgust paints Annabelle's interjection. "Jamie Smythe."

"Jamie Smythe?"

Annabelle must hear the doubt in Eleanor's voice because she launches into an explanation.

"It was after that awful party. I was clearing up in the bar and he was sitting there drinking. He asked me if I wanted to go back to his trailer and I did. I wanted to, so much. He's so handsome and when would I ever get another chance to sleep with a film star?"

Eleanor remembers the night and understands; Jamie had struck out twice, first with Anna and then with her. She sighs at the recollection.

"When we got there, he told me I was beautiful. Nobody's ever told me that before."

And Eleanor closes her eyes at the naivety. Did no one ever tell this girl that men lie? That they lie the most when trying to get a woman into bed. Internally, Eleanor rages at all the misguided parents who believe in keeping their children innocent, when all it does is make them more vulnerable.

"He had some vodka in his trailer and we did some shots. Then he gave me this pill. I've never taken drugs before, but he made it seem like everyone took them and I didn't want to look stupid. So I took it. I don't remember much about the night, but when I woke up the following morning, I threw up all over his trailer and he was angry. So, I left.

"Two weeks later, I didn't get my period. I was so afraid ... I'm never late. I did a test, and when it came back positive, I cried. I tried to talk to Jamie but I couldn't get near him, so I asked Jake for help. He's always been like an older brother to me. When I was a child, he looked after me more than Matthew did."

Annabelle pauses and then her voice breaks as she says, "I knew I didn't want to keep it – I'm only eighteen. If I had a child now, I'd be almost forty before I got to live my life again."

"I don't blame you. It must have been a shock." Eleanor keeps her voice soft.

"I've been good all my life," she cries. "The one time I try to have fun, I end up pregnant. It's not fair."

"Annabelle," Eleanor says as gently as she can, "you had unprotected sex. You also need to get tested."

Annabelle's confession appears to have been cathartic. Her tears have dried up and her voice is firmer as she says, nodding vigorously, "Jake said that, too. He said he'd take me, but it's too early yet. He asked me if I wanted to talk to the Police, but Jamie didn't force me to do anything ..."

"Just to be clear," Eleanor summarises, "what you are telling me is, Jacob is not, and never has been, your boyfriend?"

Annabelle shakes her head. "You won't tell anyone, will you? About the abortion."

"I won't tell anyone. It will be a secret." She ventures a hand on Annabelle's own. "Thank you for telling me. It was very brave."

The girl blushes. "It was really easy, actually," she confides. "I was less than ten weeks gone, so they just gave me a pill. Then it was like having a heavy period. I was so glad I didn't wait too long. That was Jake really – he said if I was sure I wanted an abortion, it was best to be quick." Having taken so long to start talking, it now seems as if Annabelle won't stop.

"Yes, I'm glad it all went well." Eleanor says. "I'm very grateful you came to see me, but you probably want to get off home now. It's getting dark."

She waits for a moment after Annabelle leaves, re-ordering all her thoughts. She thinks back over her interactions with the girl in the last few weeks and wishes she had been kinder. Eleanor now has a better understanding of the lesson *be kind to others, for you do not know their story*. Poor Annabelle had been used by Jamie and practically thrown away without a thought. She was lucky to have had Jacob to help her and support her. It seemed to be his defining character trait.

Thoughts of Jacob make her squirm. Despite her accusations, he had not had a girlfriend. He was free. All the time she spent with Ptolemy, she could have been with him. He'd had to watch her, running around with Ptolemy, feeling the way she felt watching him with Annabelle. It had scrambled her own orderly mind, created a whirlpool of emotion, altered her normally calm temperament to mercurial.

Except did Jacob feel the way she felt? He had attempted one kiss which she had roundly rejected. Had that sunk his regard for her? But then, why did he talk to Annabelle? Was it only to warn the young maid before she came face-to-face with Eleanor in the morning? And why had Annabelle felt compelled to tell her Jacob was unattached, especially as it involved such a personal disclosure? Could it be because he was, and always had been, hers?

With that thought, she finds she cannot wait a moment longer. She straps on her trainers because she is going to need to run. She takes the back stairs because they are marginally quicker, and almost mows down her mother.

"There you are, Eleanor. Where on earth have you been all day? You've missed dinner."

"Not now!" she cries as she crosses the Great Hall, but then a thought occurs to her and she doubles back to her mother.

"Tolly and I have split up because he's leaving for a job in America," she blurts out before she dashes back across the room, pushes the heavy oak door open, and bursts into the twilight. She cares not a whit for the beauty of the coming night, the softly glowing echo of the last ray of sun on the clouds is her beacon, signposting her destination at the end of the West Drive.

When Eleanor runs, she does it at a controlled pace, keeping her heartrate in the optimal fat-burning zone. This is not that – it is a mad dash at full speed. She is grateful for the smooth surface of the hoggin dumped on the pot-holed tarmac by the film company, which keeps her from breaking an ankle in her frantic sprint in the growing darkness. She hurtles past the cattle in their pasture, huddled together for the night. She streaks through the coppice and around the head of the long lake until she finally catches sight of the flint cottage with the red door.

The head gardener's home is a testament to his trade. On one side of the path to the front door are beans in neat rows, scrambling skywards up their bamboo canes, their flowers long replaced by swelling pods. On the other side is a traditional cottage garden border, showy dahlias, big-headed sunflowers and tall spikes of hollyhocks, looking like effigies in the gloom.

By the time she gets to the gate, Eleanor's headlong pelt is over. It's a mile almost, door to door, and she can no longer breathe. Sweaty and red-faced, she tries to open her chest, drawing big gulps into her lungs but she is close to vomiting. She cannot have a seizure now. She leans heavily against the capping brick on the garden wall, gasping, trying to stop the blood pounding. But still, she won't be stayed.

She staggers up the path and bangs on the door, the knocker cold in her damp palms. The heavy metal sounds urgent and ominous as she crashes it down again and again. When Jacob opens the door, he does not find his Eleanor, the woman who lures him with her dignity and self-possession. He finds a madwoman with her hair awry, face like a beetroot and perspiration staining her fine silk dress. Eleanor, though, does not hesitate; she is ready for this. She pulls him forwards by the simple expedient of grabbing his shirt front. Off balance, he takes one step, two. She reaches behind him and slams the door shut.

"Do it again!" she commands. She has him pinned against the front door, her face tilted up to his, expectant, but Jacob merely looks bewildered. "For God's sake! Kiss me!"

The doubt disappears from his face as comprehension dawns.

For one dreadful moment Eleanor thinks he will refuse, thinks she's missed her chance. Then he dips his head, the lightest of touches on her lips, then another and another, until finally his hands come up to press her mouth to his. Her lips part and their tongues touch and the world disappears.

The kiss does not last long because Eleanor needs to draw breath. But she stays motionless under the honeysuckle-draped porch, their foreheads touching, both of them panting, breaths mingling.

Jacob's hands slide down her back, pulling her body tight against his, until their hips, their chests, their legs touch.

Hardly daring to form the word, he whispers, "Mine?"

"Yours," she says.

Odds and Ends

As the first flush of ardent love recedes, both Eleanor and Jacob realise the most likely reaction to news of their relationship will not be uncontained joy but, most probably, disapproval. Their love will be dissected by those around them, commoners and nobles alike. And they can anticipate the harassment they will both receive on an announcement of their liaison, Jacob likely more so than Eleanor. Unwilling to risk their fledgling affair, they come to a tacit understanding – silence is the wiser course for now.

When Eleanor walks into breakfast the following morning, her father puts his paper down.

"I understand from your mother that you and Ptolemy are no longer dating?" he says, much as a lawyer laying out facts of a case.

"That's correct," she says as she pours herself tea. "He's been offered a role in America and it starts right away."

She sits down at the table and pulls the horn off her croissant to eat it, expecting her father to go back to his reading, but he stays looking at her.

"Over a week ago, Ptolemy came to see me, but he asked me not to say anything about it and I respected his wishes at the time. But now the two of you are finished and he is gone, I feel you should know."

Eleanor remembers the day she bumped into Ptolemy coming out of her father's office. "What did he want?" she asks.

"He came to give me a file. The Hydes are bankers, and as such they often require the services of an excellent firm of private investigators, human nature being fallible and bank employees not always being completely without faults."

Lord Larkford clears his throat before continuing. "Ptolemy had a suspicion Jamie Smythe supplemented his acting income with dealing drugs. He also supposed that while Jamie was recuperating, he might step up his dealing to bring in extra income. He had an investigator look into it. They really were very good – I've kept their details in case we ever need such a thing, although God forbid our employees' larceny ever goes further than the occasional bag of fertiliser or book of stamps. Anyway, they're used to providing evidence in court, so everything is videoed, logged and backed up with extensive notes.

"It was quite a package of evidence eventually. Enough to send our little cockroach away for a holiday courtesy of the King for a little while at least. It certainly got his attention and he understood suing the Estate might not be in his best interests. You never know what our defence might have to use in court."

"You blackmailed him!" Eleanor is horrified.

"Now, now. Blackmail is such an awful word. I like to think we reformed him. We merely suggested that a good barrister could make the case he was luring two naïve young girls to the folly for a drug deal. We also indicated he might want to cease his illicit career and concentrate on his acting going forward. He was entirely in agreement."

"And Tolly told you not to tell me? Why?"

"Oh, my sweetheart. You know the answer to that."

Eleanor did know the answer. He wanted her heart given freely, not out of a sense of obligation. She was glad now that she hadn't known he had saved the Estate when he asked her to go with him. She doesn't believe, in the end, it would have changed her answer, but it would have made it even harder to deny him – and that had been difficult enough.

"Thank you for telling me," she says, leaving a world of thoughts unsaid. Her father must know a man who goes to such lengths to help his girlfriend's family would not willingly have left her. He must deduce the ending of their relationship had been her decision, and his silence on the subject can only be taken for support of her actions and belief in his daughter. So much love expressed merely by unfolding a newspaper and quietly bringing an end to the affair.

Unfortunately for Jacob and Eleanor, being unacknowledged lovers is much harder than either of them expects. It is at once exciting and frustrating, in equal measures. While she believed him in love with another, Eleanor had calmly sat beside Jacob for hours in the past with no visible discontent. Now, it becomes impossible to be close to him without longing to touch. That both live at home with parents, never previously a handicap, now is an obstacle of the most challenging kind. Eleanor and Jacob become quite crafty in constructing opportunities to escape to indulge their passion.

Eleanor innocently mentions to her mother one morning that she is gaining weight and might step up her running schedule, especially while the long days allow her to exercise late in the evening after work. Her mother merely nods, blithely accepting Eleanor's solution to her own preoccupation – a woman's battle against a thickening waist – despite no evidence of such in her daughter's figure. Jacob's parents are rather more surprised when he comes downstairs carrying his old fishing kit and announces his intention to while away some hours lakeside, but they feel it is one more step on his road to recovery and therefore something to be encouraged.

Independently, the unprofessed lovers make their way to a little, secluded copse on the south side of the lake, an area less trafficked, devoid as it is of any buildings. There, Jacob sets up his fishing rod as camouflage, spreads a rug on the ground and proceeds to gain a more intimate knowledge of the dips and curves of Eleanor's body. His kisses are fervent and his fingers leave a trail of fiery lust as they move across her skin, and Eleanor knows she has never felt such longing before, such a yearning to be with him.

In between the moments of obsession, they talk. Eleanor's mind soon turns towards those questions every person wants answered.

"When did you know you liked me?" she asks, his head in her lap as she tickles his torso lightly with a stalk of Yorkshire fog. She pushes his shirt further apart and traces the line of his rib cage, watching his skin pebble at the light, tenuous touch.

"From the first day I drove you. When you insisted on no cap and sitting in the front. I knew then you still had spirit and I was in danger of falling for you, but I didn't think I stood a chance. You?"

"The day of the festival. I was sitting on your lap, remember. Even though you tried to keep space between us, every so often I would brush against you, and it was obvious you wanted me." Eleanor moves the grass stalk to tease his nose. "Not all of those brushes were accidental," she confesses. "That night, although I tried not to think of it at the time , all I could imagine was what might have been, if I'd have been brave enough to press myself against you."

She sighs. "Then the next night, I saw you with Annabelle." She subsides but the bitterness she felt that night at her disappointed hopes bleeds through her words and Jacob reaches up and pulls her down. It is some time before either of them can speak again but when they break apart, Eleanor begins again. "Why me? Why not Anna or Lily? I'm not half as pretty."

Jacob outlines her lips with his fingertips. "It's the way you look at me, the way you smile at me. Your smile is more beautiful than anyone else's."

"*What heavenly smiles! O Lady mine, Through my very heart they shine*," Eleanor quotes, her hands raised high dropping to her heart theatrically.

His eyes light up with a playful spark and he teases, "Of course, I haven't seen Anna since she was a child." But when the light goes out of Eleanor's eyes, he relents. He realises, she doubts her worth in a way he never could. "None of your sisters have your warmth and your strength and your compassion, Nora. What is beauty, if it is cold?" He tips her head up until she is looking directly into his eyes, "Never doubt that I want you. If I had a choice of all the women in the world, I would pick you. Every time."

And Eleanor thinks her heart will explode.

It is not long though before snatched hours and stolen kisses become insufficient. And while Jacob sometimes fantasises about pushing Eleanor against a tree and taking her there and then, he wants their first time together to be exquisite in every way. In an era of social media, it is impossible to manufacture a social engagement which can't be checked, and Eleanor's father is well-acquainted with all her business dealings.

Eventually, it is Eleanor's friends who provide the opportunity, although the occasion is far from a happy one. Eleanor had been mildly concerned by radio-silence from her old schoolfriend, Maria. It had happened from time to time, usually coinciding with a drinking binge, but never for so long. Eleanor's worrying had almost reached the point of inspiring action when she is contacted by Adelaide. Maria had taken the step of entering a treatment programme for her alcoholism at a private clinic, deep in the countryside, and had progressed enough to be permitted visitors. Assuming Eleanor to be mired in depression over her break-up with Ptolemy, Adelaide had intended to visit on her own but a crisis at work had led to her being sent to Hong Kong and she rang to ask Eleanor to take her place.

Eleanor is delighted. Her pleasure is not only from the enjoyment of visiting Maria, but the treatment centre is far enough away to warrant an overnight stay, and Jacob will have to drive her. For the first time, they will have the chance to spend the night together, to wake up in each other's arms, to openly be a couple.

They leave early on the Friday afternoon in case of traffic, but the journey down is easy. Their hands are clasped at the check-in, barely able to look at each other. No sooner has the door swung shut behind them than Jacob swings Eleanor into his embrace and they fall on the bed laughing. Eleanor has never been so desperate to strip a lover of his clothes as she is to see Jacob naked, and it translates into a boldness which sparks a reciprocal bloom of lust in her lover.

When Jacob slides inside her, Eleanor has a sense the world has changed, and when he moves, slowly, sensuously, drawing both of them to a heady climax, she is swamped by the depth of love she feels. When they lie together in the aftermath, their limbs still entwined and their bodies embraced, neither of them wishes to break the connection. They stay on the bed, mouths hungrily kissing and fingers exploring until Eleanor feels him stirring to fullness again. This time she takes charge, astride his hips, rocking herself to frenzy.

They order room service, neither wanting to admit any other to this bubble they've created. Eleanor fetches the tray, and they sit on the bed to devour fish and chips and chocolate tart, using food as a plaything. When they finally fall asleep, nestled into each other, they are exhausted.

In the morning, when Eleanor wakes, Jacob is already sitting up in bed beside her. He has been watching her breathe, playing with a strand of her hair, struggling to believe a man like him could have a woman like her. But when Eleanor looks up into his eyes, a slow smile flowing from her lips across her entire face, her desire for him is almost tangible.

That doubt of being worthy returns later. The news is playing on the television and a segment on entertainment features Ptolemy Hyde, who has reportedly replaced a well-known actor in a long-awaited adaptation of a best-selling book.

"Do you regret choosing me over Ptolemy Hyde?" Jacob asks.

Eleanor is a clever woman; she knows he sees the choice, in his mind, as between obscurity versus wealth and fame. It goes to the very heart of how he sees himself and how he will think of himself in the future. For what person can hold to a place in the world if even their partner does not respect them? Her next words can end their affair forever. She picks them carefully.

She stares straight at him. "Well, he's rich and handsome and talented. I guess he's perfect, isn't he?" She watches him blanch. "But love isn't about perfection. You tease me all the time because you know my flaws but you love me all the same. You are provoking and stubborn and occasionally bitter, but I still want you. Love is about the imperfections, knowing they exist and not caring."

She pauses, closes the gap between them, and reaches her hand to his cheek. "So, no." The word is clear and emphatic. "But there never was a choice. By the time I started to date Tolly, you had already sneaked into my heart and taken up residence. That morning I woke up beside you at Ellingham Hall, all I wanted to do was to pull you down on top of me. The feeling was so strong, it frightened me. Quite apart from the fact you were my father's employee and that would have been a clear case of sexual harassment, I also thought you had someone. I knew then I had to do something to distract myself from you, so I took Tolly up on his offer.

"It really wasn't fair on him. It might be the meanest thing I've ever done. I can see how people might look at him and see that he is famous and intelligent and charismatic. But life has always been easy for him, and people like him assume life is just as easy for everyone else. He will never be the man for me because he can't comprehend what it is to live the life you have to live, not the life you want.

"You have a compassion for others who struggle that men like Tolly never recognise. Money, looks, charm – these are empty things which mislead only people with little understanding. I love your compassion, your sense and your good humour. I love you." Eleanor looks at the man she has chosen and takes his hand, willing him to realise how certain she is. Then she lightens the mood with her next words.

"Besides," she says flippantly, "whoever marries me is going to have to change his surname. The Mortimers have been at Larkford Hall for centuries. Ptolemy Mortimer would have been a bit too much of a mouthful, don't you think?"

Eleanor thinks she has been very sly in introducing the topic of a future together, but she is unaware Jacob was there before her. *His* only hesitation is in how to ask and when. But her words are enough to allay his niggling feelings of insufficiency. Indeed, he is so inflated with confidence they are decidedly late in leaving their room.

Eleanor is pleased to see Maria looking much better than she has for a couple of years. They sit out in the late summer sun and chat about innocuous things. When Jacob goes to fetch everyone coffee, Maria asks, "So you're back with Jake, then?"

Eleanor is startled for a moment, and then remembers Maria met Jacob at the festival and must have assumed they were dating. To her friends, she must seem fickle – Jacob, Ptolemy, Jacob. Eleanor shrugs away the complicated events that have led to this moment.

"Yes," she says simply. "I realised he's the one for me."

"I can see that," Maria replies and they turn to other subjects.

When Bertie unexpectedly joins them, Eleanor is pleased to see both her friends making an effort to include Jacob in their conversation and enquiring as to his opinion on the lighter issues of the day. Politics, religion, and personal problems are sacrificed in favour of anecdotes, gossip about friends, and holiday wish-lists.

Jacob finds it remarkable that people with access to wealth still have things they've never done and places they've never been. The day passes pleasantly, but soon it is time to make the return journey to Larkford, and Eleanor and Jacob must each go back to their own homes, dining with their separate families and sleeping in their distant beds.

One night is not enough. The feelings they have revelled in refuse to be contained again and keep bubbling out. They have sex in the car, going to and from meetings, pulled up on the side of country roads, risking exposure in all senses of the word. They have sex in the woods and in the office, after everyone else has gone home. They take more and more chances, until it is clear to both of them – they will be caught and maybe the time has come to face the world.

Eleanor goes first. She starts with Anna, but the call does not go quite the way she is hoping.

"The gardener's son?"

"He's a war hero. Why not start with that?" Eleanor corrects her sister with no little asperity.

"I'm sorry, babe. But you were the one who said you wanted a man of sense and education and then you turn down Tolly Hyde and choose Jake Winter instead. How the mighty are fallen!" Anna's laughter echoes down the phone.

"He is sensible and he has seen the world – more than you or I will ever know!" Eleanor defends her beloved robustly.

"Are you sure he's not just sensible of your fortune?"

"I don't have a fortune, remember. It's mostly controlled by trusts." Eleanor is starting to bristle. "Look, are you, or are you not, going to support me in this?"

"Eleanor, I haven't seen the man in years. How am I supposed to know if he is a gold-digger or pure gold?"

"Come home. I'll arrange for you to meet him."

Anna can tell this is important to her sister. She sighs, then says, "Okay. I'll come for a day trip to Bridgetown. You can introduce me."

While awaiting the meeting with Anna, support comes from an unexpected quarter, in a text exchange with her middle sister, Jasmine.

I'm dating Jacob. It's serious.

Jacob?

Jacob Winter.

Do you mean Jake? How on earth did you manage to snare him? You better treat him well. He's about the only decent heterosexual man left on this earth.

While the lack of sisterly esteem is not overly gratifying, the comment is enough for Eleanor to conclude Jasmine approves and at least one member of her family would welcome Jacob. The specified day for the meeting with Anna arrives, and the hopeful lovers are at the station to meet her off the train. They walk up the hill towards the town centre and the little coffee shop, Mama Cortada's, where Eleanor had spied on Jacob and Annabelle, weeks before. The autumn air is chill, and they opt to sit inside at a table and chair set.

As soon as Jacob returns with drinks, Anna fixes him with a steely stare and says, "So, Jacob, are you sleeping with my sister?"

If she expects him to be taken aback, she is disappointed. Jacob grins and says, "Only as often as she lets me."

"You realise she hasn't got any money. She has to beg for every penny she spends from a trust?"

"That's okay. I've got my compensation award. We'll manage."

Eleanor watches Jacob throughout this bantering exchange for any sign he is bewitched by Anna. He would not be the first of her lovers to reset his sights on meeting the younger Miss Mortimer. But Jacob's hand has crept under the table and now rests on Eleanor's thigh. At a slight pressure, she looks up and sees Jacob gazing down at her. "I don't want her money or her land or her status or her family. I just want her."

"You may come to regret that." Anna gives a bitter laugh. "This is your chance to escape. Save yourself and run away now because, unfortunately, our Eleanor comes with the money and the land and the status and the family. And all of it is trouble."

Jacob is still looking at Eleanor, not Anna. "With or without, I'm hers."

"That's enough of the nauseating love-fest, thank you." Anna reaches for a muffin. "Okay, Eleanor. He's passed. Now what do we talk about for the next two hours?"

When the time comes for Anna to depart, she hugs her sister. "He is sensible," she says. "As sensible as you are. And this is the maddest thing you two will ever do. I wish you both luck. God knows, you will need it. Can you imagine the village gossip? And Granny dearest, she'll have a heart attack!"

At breakfast the next morning, Eleanor tackles her father, having decided he is likely to take it better than her mother and may even help her with Lady Larkford.

Summoning all her courage, she says, "I've been seeing someone, and I'd like to bring him to dinner this evening."

Her father drops his newspaper enough to peer over the top of it. "Jacob? It's about time you two came clean." At his daughter's flabbergasted expression, Lord Larkford laughs long and says, "You must think I'm a half-wit. I'm not in my dotage yet." Then he raises his paper and goes back to perusing yesterday's stock market performance.

When Eleanor's wits have recovered, she moves to make her father an asset. "Oh!" she says, as innocent as an angel, "could you let Mummy know for me?"

This time, her father does not even bother to lower his paper. "Oh no, darling daughter, that is all on you. If your love is so insubstantial as to be frightened away by a little opposition, it is best you find out now." He turns a page, and she knows that is the end of the conversation – she will get no help with her mother from her father.

Eleanor postpones heading out to the office to wait for her mother but it is another hour until Lady Larkford wanders into the breakfast room. When she does, Eleanor opens with the same statement she used on her father. The effect is profoundly different.

"Oh, Eleanor!" her mother exclaims. "You're back with Tolly! I'm so pleased. How long has he been in England?" And then, more worryingly, "I wonder if Tissy knows? I must call her."

"Stop!" Eleanor nearly shouts. "It's not Tolly I've been seeing. It's Jacob!"

"Jacob? Do I know him?"

"Jacob Winter."

"The gardener's son?"

Eleanor is beginning to be heartily fed up with that description. Jacob is a man in his own right. At thirty years of age, he deserves to be known for his own exploits rather than his father's. She keeps her words short because she doesn't trust her tongue. "Yes. Him."

"Oh, darling. I know you must be getting a bit desperate since Tolly left for America, but someone will come along. You don't have to date the staff. If you were to let me talk to a few of my friends, I'm sure we could find you a nice, young man."

"I have found a nice, young man." Eleanor continues quickly before her mother can utter another word. "Jacob is my boyfriend. He will be coming for dinner and you will be nice to him."

Lady Larkford sniffs. "I would never be rude to a guest," she says. "You know me better than that."

Eleanor leaves the room quickly before the entente evaporates and one of them says something that will upset the other.

Jacob does not fare much better with his parents. To be fair, they are genuinely concerned for his welfare.

"Those Mortimer girls go through men like babies through nappies," is his mother's expostulation, although, when he defends Eleanor, his mother is forced to admit she is steadier than her sisters.

While his father cannot bring himself to criticise the noble family, he is obviously unhappy. "Are you sure you know what you are doing, lad? That girl is right clever, been to Oxford and all that. You – well, you barely made it through school. There's no happiness where there's no respect."

Jacob shakes his head at their lack of confidence in him. Both of them are adamant in their belief Eleanor will chew him up and spit him out when she is done with him. "Like a fat cat with a poor mouse!" his mother warns.

At least, Jacob rationalises, they are so entrenched in the idea that his relationship with Eleanor cannot last, they have not yet contemplated the awful possibility that Lord Larkford, their landlord and his father's boss, could well be Jacob's father-in-law. Jacob is happy to give them time. After all, he has not yet ascertained Eleanor's feelings on the subject, though he is certain of his own.

Although Eleanor had considered it, to Jacob the change in the way people treat him is unexpected. When he walks into the pub, people fall silent. The easy-going rapport he has had with most of the villagers since he could talk evaporates. Congratulations come from an unexpected quarter – Jonas Brown takes him aside to wish him and Eleanor well, but any illusion of comradeship disappears when Jonas asks him to put in a good word with Lord Larkford. Even Matthew calls him from some remote corner of the world where he has been deployed to ask him if he has lost his mind. Informed of the gossip through the keen perception of Annabelle, the call starts badly and ends worse with his friend accusing him of getting above himself.

Jacob can only hope the passage of time, the quiet temper of daily life will take the notoriety out of their relationship. That people hold him in so little merit and place so little faith in Eleanor's judgement is, to his mind, shocking. For, like Eleanor, he now sees the two of them well-matched.

Making their relationship public is sufficient in Eleanor's mind for Jacob to spend his nights in her bed, although he is less comfortable with the idea. Jacob is careful to come late and leave early, avoiding most of the family. While he has dined *en famille* occasionally – a strained affair with forced bonhomie from Eleanor and scarcely a word of civility from Lady Larkford – he has never dared to appear at breakfast.

He is sneaking out of the Hall one morning when he runs into Eleanor's father on his way to breakfast.

Lord Larkford is, at first, surprised but then, recovering, he nods and gestures to the door of the breakfast room, ushering Jacob before him. When they are both seated, he begins.

"It is some months now since Eleanor's last seizure and the doctor feels she should be safe enough to drive again."

Ah, thinks Jacob. *This is it.*

"I'm afraid your work as her driver will no longer be necessary."

Jacob waits patiently. He is wary of the Baron but not afraid. There is nothing the man could say or do that would dissuade him from his feelings towards Eleanor.

"I will be frank – the way the two of you have been going on is quite unsatisfactory. And if I have to listen to another polemic from my wife on the subject, I will surely have to be committed."

"I'm sorry you feel that way."

"You cannot continue to drive my daughter, and you cannot continue to sneak in and out of this house. That is not the behaviour of a man." Lord Larkford taps his folded newspaper in emphasis.

Jacob is mutinously silent.

"I have watched my daughter and she is quite besotted with you. She is not a stupid woman, but this fancy of hers is interfering with her ability to think straight or she would see it, too." Eleanor's father pauses to fix Jacob with a pointed stare, which is just as well because he is a primed grenade. "I propose you come to work on my team. You can learn the Estate business under me, although you will always defer to Eleanor, and until your father retires, the Head Gardener will continue to report directly to me."

Jacob's mouth drops open. He had thought he was being fired, not promoted.

"You can thank me later," Lord Larkford says briskly and then continues. "The tenants of Glebe Cottage have given their notice. I intend to have it refurbished, and then you and Eleanor can make it your home. Perhaps if you are not under my wife's feet, she will be more relaxed about things." The Baron pauses to take a sip of his coffee. "Its rooms are smaller than anything Eleanor has ever lived in, so you will have to take that on board, but I think it will do the two of you very well. My parents, of course, moved into the old South Wing when I married Sarah, but no one wants to repeat that experience, and obviously, the twins are still at home for a large portion of the year. Yes, I think Glebe Cottage is the answer."

Without waiting for a reply, Eleanor's father opens his paper and silence descends. When Eleanor appears ten minutes later, she finds both of her menfolk apparently engaged in breakfasting in the most convivial manner, in total silence.

It is one thing to be Eleanor's boyfriend, Jacob reasons, but another entirely to live with her in front of the entire village. He wants no one to misunderstand. Accordingly, one day, close to the Winter Solstice, when the cold is so deep you can practically feel the frost in the air, he takes Eleanor up to the bridge over the lake. As the sun is setting, he drops to one knee and asks her to stay with him forever. The ring he offers her is not big and showy, but the diamond, like Eleanor herself, is perfect. When she takes it from him and slides it onto her finger, she cannot imagine any greater happiness exists than this moment. She considers how well Jacob knows her, to make this most intimate of moments private and in a place she loves.

Given that she and Jacob have been in a relationship for months, when Eleanor announces the news of her engagement at dinner, she does not anticipate any problem. She is completely unprepared to hear a flat "No".

She turns to her mother. "What do you mean, 'no'?"

"Just no."

"I don't think you get a say."

"Don't take that tone with me. I'm your mother. I've only got your best interests in mind. Unequal marriages don't work. They almost always end in divorce."

"Why do you think we're unequal?" There is no disguising the challenge.

"Don't be coy! Even he knows you are far smarter than him. And richer. And … just better." Lady Larkford had been no captain of the school debate team, whereas her daughter was.

"Let's talk about qualities then," Eleanor begins. "He's braver than I am. And mentally tougher. And far more experienced in the world. He's much better with people. And you can ask Daddy, he's a natural born manager! In fact, now that you mention it, we may be unequal. He may be out of my league. Which is why I intend to marry him."

With a glare at her husband, Lady Larkford says, "Peregrine?"

If the use of his full name was not warning enough, the way she snapped her lips together should have been sufficient indication that they were on course for marital discord if he did not support her stance.

Lord Larkford looks down at his plate. "Jacob has been invaluable in the office. I would hate to lose him."

Eleanor's mother stands and throws her napkin on the table. "This is your fault," she tells her husband. "You said give them time. You said it would burn itself out. I should have stopped this at the start. Mark my words, Eleanor. This will end in heartbreak." Then she sweeps out of the room, shrouded in anger.

There is one more unpleasant task intruding into the general contentment of Eleanor's life. She has never bothered to inform the Dowager Baroness exactly whom she is dating. Although rumours must have reached her grandmother's ears, the Lady Jessica probably discounted them as the wildest fabrications. Eleanor's acceptance of Jacob's offer of marriage changes things, and it becomes necessary for her to inform her grandmother of her engagement sooner rather than later. After her mother's reaction, Eleanor undertakes the visit by herself, expecting her grandmother's response to be even more dreadful. It is worse.

"A servant!" Lady Jessica cries in horror.

"A war hero," Eleanor corrects.

"Rubbish!" the Dowager Baroness counters. "He got his leg blown off. That's not heroism, that's incompetence."

Eleanor never tells anyone what was said during the visit, but suffice to say the exchange was so bitter with such acrimonious slurs uttered by both sides, it ends with each party feeling thoroughly outraged. Eleanor, that her own family can be so prejudiced; her grandmother, that one of her blood has been raised in such a lax and spoiled way as to have no regard for heritage, duty, and rank.

Although an invitation to the wedding is issued to the Dowager Baroness, she is notably absent when the day comes.

Family and friends gather in the little church on the Estate, cramming into its small interior. Matthew Green, repentant of his earlier resistance and home on leave, stands as best man to his childhood friend. Eleanor's sisters together with Serena form a wall of bridesmaids, but in a move which shows Eleanor is no slave to tradition, Charlie Fairfax stands with them. Eleanor was particularly surprised but inordinately pleased when Jasmine accepted the role. One or two of the younger bridesmaids spend the service eyeing up the manly soldiers in dress uniform on the groom's side. As the Reverend Parrish unites Eleanor and Jacob in the bonds of holy matrimony, the bride's mother sobs into her handkerchief and the groom's father gulps deep, calming breaths.

The newlyweds emerge to a path lined with villagers, showering them with confetti. Eleanor spots Kylie nestled under her husband's arm, Julia Fairweather cooing desperately to gain the couple's attention, and even Jonas Brown is present, wearing a smile for once. The eldest Mulwood boy stands by his brother, with his arm around the cricket-playing Lola, although his mother is missing. Carl Taylor, who was present in the church with his entire family, stands outside waving madly.

As for Lord Larkford, throughout the day Eleanor notices her father has a rather wolfish expression on his face, the same one he wears after he challenges her to a game of chess and wins.

Dear Reader

I very much hope you enjoyed this book. It was a delight to write, though rather less wonderful to edit and publish but I got here in the end.

As an independent author, I don't have the power of a massive marketing engine behind me and I live or starve by reviews and ratings (okay – that might be a slight exaggeration. My long-suffering husband would not let me starve and, if truth be told, food is one of his love languages). If you can though, please leave a review on Amazon or Goodreads (if you do both, know that I will love you forever). If you can only manage a rating, that too is valuable.

Keep an eye on my website for news of my latest books www.hazelhatman.com.

Acknowledgements

The first people owed thanks on the road to producing this book are the Breezettes Book Club (Maggie R, Carol, Bex, Fiona and Janine) who provided honesty, beta reads, tea and support throughout. Not to be forgotten is ex-Breezette Maggie S for continuing practical help whenever I need it.

Next on the list is the invaluable Eleanor Leese who curbed some of my baser instincts with her editorial assessment. Then the amazing Claire Strombeck, who took brass and polished it into gold.

Having been thrown out of art class at the tender age of twelve for my extraordinary lack of talent, I am ever grateful for the gifted Lisa Firth and her truly eye-catching cover.

And finally, I need to express my eternal appreciation for my magnificent and long-suffering husband who has always had my back.

Printed in Great Britain
by Amazon

19557803R00139